Man Behind the Wheel

Steve Rzasa

Man Behind the Wheel by Steve Rzasa
www.steverzasa.com

Cover illustration and design: Kirk DouPonce

International Standard Book Number: 9781530125524

Createspace

Other Writings by Steve Rzasa

www.steverzasa.com

Novels

Science Fiction

The Word Reclaimed: The Face of the Deep 1.0
The Word Unleashed: The Face of the Deep 2.0
Broken Sight: The Face of the Deep 2.5
The Word Endangered: The Face of the Deep 3.0
Quantum Mortis: A Man Disrupted
Quantum Mortis: Gravity Kills
For Us Humans
Empire's Rift: A Takamo Universe Novel
Man Behind the Wheel
Multiverse
Severed Signals

Steampunk

Crosswind: The First Sark Brothers Tale
Sandstorm: The Second Sark Brothers Tale

Fantasy

The Bloodheart
The Lightningfall
Just Dumb Enough (contributor)

Acknowledgments

Driving is fun. We in America view it as a God-given right. Problem is, the Constitution is mum, unlike its statements on guns and speech.

The idea of a future in which the law could take that ability away from most citizens is not one I like, because I would be one of the first people to protest. Would I miss long, boring drives? Not if my infallible robot chaffeur gave me more time to write and visit with family.

This novel's for my dad, John Rzasa, who's been a car guy since before he was a father. I'd never have known about the importance of Steve McQueen as a driver both on screen and in the real world were it not for him, and my fascination with automotive technology is due entirely to his influence.

Special thanks to proofer Howard Ohr, advance reader Mark Bentley, cover artist Kirk DouPonce, and editor Elizabeth Miller.

As always, I could not have done this without my boys and my wife.

A driverless future is approaching much faster than we realize. Until then, keep your hands on the wheel and your eyes on the road.

Chapter One

Roman Jasko's car was driving when the illegal motorist call came in.

He sat sideways in the primary seat of his 2066 Cope Motors Halcyon and paid no attention to the traffic on either side of the highway. Why should he? The Halcyon had a next to zero chance of getting into an accident.

"Hit me."

Rome flicked the holographic deck hovering between himself and his information technician. A card glowed bright blue, lining up with the one facedown card and its face-up companion. "Twelve."

Aldrich Burns made a face like he'd licked a tire. He rubbed at his beard. "Okay. Hit me."

"You sure, Aldo?"

"Do it."

Another card. "Eight."

"Damn!" Aldo flipped the face down card.

Rome grinned. That brought his total to twenty-seven. "Dealer wins."

"Dealer cheats."

"Not my fault you hit too often. Forty for me."

Aldo muttered dark curses under his breath, but swiped his palm across the center console. "Financial. Aldrich Burns."

[Confirmed.] The voice was female, with a lilting Irish accent.

"Transfer forty dollars from Checking to Roman Jasko."

Spatters of liquid hit the windshield. Rome looked up. Dark clouds rolled in from the north, scudding over the South Dakota plains. A forest of wind turbines loomed to the northwest, beyond a set of hills topped with swaying brown grass. The tall, curved blades twisted like white whisks, a manic collection of kitchen implements brought to life.

[Confirmation, sir?]

"Roman Jasko, confirming."

[Standby… Transfer complete. Would either of you care to see your balances?]

Aldo's emphatic "No" simultaneously overran Rome's "Yes."

[I did not understand that response.]

"Transaction complete, Marcy," Aldo said. "Thanks."

[You are welcome.] Whenever she paused, Rome expected the comp to hum. Never did. [Sir, Condor Three Three is transmitting data.]

"Gabriela? Here's hoping she's got something. It's dead out here," Rome said.

There were few vehicles on the Ninety with them. Six Class Two shipping freighters trundled along in the right lane, bumper to bumper, separated by mere feet, each one dragging a pair of huge containers. A flock of Family Travel Cars in the left lane, a hundred yards back, all identical bug-shaped domes with large windows darkened for privacy. Still, Rome could see the shadows of a family of three playing a holographic matching game on a center table in one Famtrac, and a pair of couples eating and laughing in another as the vehicles sped along.

One—a sleek black and blue Mustang with oversized wheels—passed them. Its windows were tinted gold. All Rome saw was the reflection of his Halcyon—a sloped nose, seamless chassis of white and gray, no different than the six other Halcyons that appeared on his scanners. Each one was computer-crafted with the most efficient combination of aerodynamics and safety. "Got a Thumper."

Aldo ran the registration code printed on the rear. "Let's see who our lucky winner is."

"Definitely polarized windows." They rounded a curve, and a flash of light made Rome squint. "Too polarized. Write 'em up."

"Roger that."

Polarized windshields weren't a problem for people—after all, there wasn't a single flesh and blood human driving any of these vehicles—but the intermittent flashes of light reflected off mirrored windshields could interfere with distance scanners.

Rome pulled up the inter-car traffic. Yeah, already had two safety complaints from the Famtracs behind them.

"Got it. Tony Riordan, twenty-five, Minneapolis," Aldo said. "Two priors for illegal modification of an autonomous vehicle."

"Third's a charm. Stamp him and send it up."

"Right." Aldo frowned. "Why do you guys call it a Thumper?"

"Thumper. Like the horny rabbit."

"The what?"

"Classic cartoon. Thumper, the rabbit. Every time he saw a hot lady rabbit, he started thumping his foot on the ground."

"Thanks for spelling that out. What's that got to do with our shiny pal?"

"Why'd you suppose the windshields are tinted that way? Privacy."

Aldo sniggered. "At four in the afternoon?"

"Nature waits for no man."

Their link flashed red. Data transmission complete. Rome tapped the panel. It lit up with the face of Gabriela Soares—skin like bronze, coal black hair tied tight in a ponytail. A headset looped over her right ear and down across her cheek was festooned with flickering lights.

"Pursuit One Twelve, this is Condor Three Three." Her voice was a pleasant alto.

"Three Three, this is Pursuit. How's the weather up there, Gabriela?"

"Sunny, Rome. It's 10,000 feet. Thermals are bumpy—nothing the stabilizers can't handle. You've got a thunderstorm headed your way."

Sunny, like her personality. "I see it." They crested a rise. In the distance, all traffic slowed going into and out of the storm. Forty-three vehicles, per the scanner's count. "But you didn't call to chat about the weather."

"Nope. Unregistered driver."

Rome straightened in his seat. "Got coordinates?"

"Sending. It's your quadrant, traveling east on the Ninety, speed eighty-eight miles per hour. No registration code. Car is not responding to pings for ID."

"Big surprise. Probably doesn't have anything for your comp to ping. Aldo, catch up."

"I'm workin' on it." Aldo dragged the data from Gabriela's transmission into his display. A holographic map of their patrol quadrant lit up. It was a long rectangle of glowing green. Numbers trickled along the leading edge. Aldo reached into the holo, grasping for the ribbon of light bisecting the quadrant and bearing the tag "Interstate Ninety Free Travel Zone." Tiny pips moved back and forth along its length. One of those white lights pulsed with red circles. "Got him. We'll pass in three and a half minutes. There's a turnaround coming up."

"Thanks." Rome pressed his right hand against the dash. His heartbeat thumped against the plastic. This was the moment he waited for, day after day, following hours of monotonous patrol. "Marcy, confirm authorization to drive."

A ghostly copy of Rome's U.S. Department of Transportation driver's certification appeared under the surface of the dash as if it were an object trapped beneath an icy lake.

[Certification confirmed. You are authorized to conduct pursuit.]

"Log the time and heading. Prep occupants."

Rome's seat closed tight around his body, holding on with the grip of a giant hand. An extra pair of restraint straps crisscrossed his chest. Aldo's seat underwent the same transformation, sliding him back a foot.

The dash in front of Rome split, reminding him of the shutter on the antique camera his dad owned. A steering column extruded, white as a pearl from an oyster shell, with twin black handles that popped out from either side. Rome settled his hands on them, feeling the foam conform to the contours of his fingers.

Below the dash, a panel drew back, letting his feet alight on three pedals—acceleration, brake, and clutch. Finally, the gearshift popped up from the center console.

"Happy now?" Aldo chewed on a grain bar. The smell of oats, sugar, and something Rome took to be figs filled the car.

"That obvious?"

"You're grinning like an idiot."

"Marcy, keep traffic clear of us." He pressed down on the accelerator. The Halcyon's engine rose in volume, the vibration subtly increased throughout the cabin. "Watch your crumbs, Aldo. Didn't you just eat?"

"Yeah. That was a half hour ago."

Rome shook his head and switched lanes. A second hologram appeared above the dash—the Halcyon, in four-inch miniature. The rear left segment of its bumper glowed red, both a visual warning and a signal sent out to all other cars within safety radius.

Immediately, the two Famtracs ahead of them accelerated and moved in front of the freighter caravan. The two Famtracs behind them slowed, increasing the safety distance to its maximum.

Speed and tach dials appeared on the dash. Rome nursed the engine until they travelled at ninety miles per hour.

"Your pull-off's coming up."

"Where's the target?"

A gold bracket flashed in the windshield. Rome watched the speck race over another hill, heading their direction in the eastbound lanes. The target vehicle swerved. A freighter comp's quick thinking got the other traveler out of the way in time to avoid a collision. Two rows of eight cars were forced to deviate from their perfectly paced intervals as the target car raced toward them. They parted like a pulled zipper. The target roared down the middle.

"Can you hear that?"

Aldo nodded. He swiped through a series of displays. "Scans confirm it. He's running combustion."

"Somebody's got money to burn." Rome slowed prudently for the turn-off. "Hang on."

The target rushed by. Rome got one good look before it vanished in a blur—black and red, dark windshields, and, yes, exhaust pipes. Its engine was a throaty growl he heard even through the sound-dampened walls of the cabin. The rest of traffic was so quiet they were no more than a steady background rush of air. The target might as well be a howitzer.

Rome spun the car, drifting across the paved curve of the turn-off. The back wheels caught on the dirt—and for a moment—they slipped. Rome grit his teeth. If the adaptor was one second off…

But it wasn't. The tiny Halcyon's image showed the change. The normally even treads of the car's street wheels thickened, became knobby, and took the appearance of an off-road military transport's tires. They churned dirt. The Halcyon leapt forward.

Aldo yelped. The remainder of his bar hit the floor, scattering crumbs across the thick black mat.

"Your turn to clean when we get back." Rome shifted into third gear and punched the accelerator.

"That's what the bots are for!"

"Quit whining. Get me whatever specs on this ride you can find."

The Halcyon's front left and right rear bumpers flashed red while the opposite corners lit up blue, turning the car into a mobile emergency beacon. They were superfluous, Rome knew. All important warnings were transmitted from Marcy's CPU to the computers that operated all cars within a five-mile radius. But, he supposed it was comforting to the passengers in those same cars to have a sign that someone would deal with the hazardous driver.

He tried not to think of the target car smashed into a gaggle of

Famtracs, or wrapped around the center of a freighter. Bodies bloodied and mangled inside twisted frames—the memory sickened him. Only someone who was completely selfish would risk the well-being of fellow travelers for the chance behind the wheel.

The irony of the situation didn't escape him.

Rome passed a freighter, earning a warning from the truck's on-board comp that he exceeded safe driving speeds. Fortunately, the obnoxious flashing red alert disappeared from his displays once Marcy relayed the USDOT certification and his pursuit status.

The modified car was a mile ahead.

Aldo brought up an image among his holos. "Camaro. That's the base chassis, anyway. No transponder, no registration number. If there's a comp aboard it's a bonehead… don't even think it has a distance warning sensor array."

"He drives like he doesn't need one." Rome swept between a pair of Famtracs and a black BMW. All three scattered like mice, shifting lanes and reducing speed to get out of the way.

Rain spattered the windshield. Air-pushers on either side of the car activated. They blew across the windshield before raindrops could cloud his view of the road, making sure nothing obstructed the glass.

Lightning struck the plains to the south with a great crooked finger of gleaming white that left an afterimage streaked across Rome's vision. The accompanying boom shook the windows. With it, came the smell of dry grass suddenly turned wet.

"He's not slowing," Aldo said. "And there's a traffic buildup two miles ahead. Thirty vehicles. Looks like they're all slowed for the storm."

"That isn't going to do us any good."

The Camaro braked hard, slewing side to side. Rome tightened his grip on the steering handles.

"C'mon, get out of the way," Aldo muttered.

The herd of cars split apart, letting the Camaro through. Rome accelerated as fast as he dared. With this much water streaming across the road, hydroplaning was a very real danger.

Spray shot up from the Halcyon's sides.

"Got in," Aldo announced. "The entertainment system."

"Nice work. Marcy, open a call."

[Signal connected.]

"Illegal driver," Rome said. "This is Pursuit One Twelve, operating by authority of the U.S. Department of Transportation on contract to the Ninety Free Travel Zone. You are operating an unregistered motor vehicle on a public roadway. Pull over to the side and relinquish control of your car."

He glanced at Aldo, who gave him a thumbs-up. The driver of the Camaro received Rome's call as a disembodied voice from the speakers of his entertainment system. Nine times out of ten, the drivers pulled over and submitted to the fines, the records stamp, and inevitable court summons.

The Camaro drove on and sideswiped a Famtrac.

"Get into that car!" Rome shouted.

"I'm on it, I'm on it!" Aldo pulled the Famtrac's registration number and overrode the security protocols. One benefit to being an authorized pursuit unit was having legal access to any car's onboard control systems, which was handy in emergencies. Unless the driver had erected blocks—which was where Aldo's skill as an information technician came in.

The Famtrac skidding sideways across two lanes of traffic was a perfect example. The vehicle's comp couldn't compensate properly as it steered diagonally toward a freighter in the right lane.

"That thing's hauling furniture," Aldo said. "Nobody aboard."

Rome scowled. "Block it!"

Aldo routed a new set of commands to the Famtrac, veering it sharply away from the freighter. Rome drove the Halcyon within two car lengths of the Famtrac. They rounded a sharp curve, complete with guardrails on one side and a steep drop-off on the other.

Then, Rome understood what the Famtrac's comp was doing—it would smash the vehicle into the freighter to avoid all the other passenger cars around it, thus minimizing casualties to the three occupants of the single Famtrac. No one cared much if a truckload of furniture was lost. No one, save the manufacturer, that is.

Rome wasn't about to sacrifice three people's lives to cut down potential casualties. He didn't do that math. Instead, he sped to the left side of the Famtrac and nudged the skidding vehicle's left front bumper. The Halcyon shuddered, its tires squealing. Rome steered into the other car, opposing its turn, and hoped it gave the Famtrac's comp enough time to figure out an alternative.

Aldo yelped as the carbon-fiber chassis collided again. "It's accepted the new command! Lay off on the slamming us around!"

"Not until it's actually corrected."

Finally, the Famtrac regained its footing, straightening out in its lane. A warning flitted across Rome's displays. He shook his head. Add that to the other two.

"Every one of those cuts a few hundred bucks off the bounty, you know." Aldo ducked down and grabbed for his grain bar.

"You'd rather we had a pile-up?"

"No, of course not. I'm just saying, the comps know what they're doing. When was the last time there was even a major wreck along the Ninety?"

Rome didn't argue. He returned his attention to the Camaro, which zipped around a pair of freighters hugging the right delineator. "Marcy, what's it look like up ahead?"

[There is a sharp turn within four point five miles.]

Aldo's map shifted, zoomed in on a curve that did indeed look like a doozy.

[Recommended point of removal.]

Rome smiled. The techs, Aldo included, told him Marcy and the automated driving systems for all cars were a very rudimentary artificial intelligence—smart, capable, but not self-aware. There were times, though, he swore Marcy knew how to tell a joke.

The Halcyon gained on the Camaro, coming within a handful of car lengths.

"I've been replaying your message," Aldo said. "Constantly. Talk about constant headache."

"Hearing my voice? Yeah, I'll bet it is. You can vouch for that."

Aldo grinned.

"What about his navigation systems?"

"Ah, you're an optimist, aren't you? He's got the basics. Nothing I can interfere with from here. But…" Aldo's lips moved, mouthing something to himself as he swiped in new commands into his interface. "Ha! Yes! Nav screen's down. So's his displays."

"So, he's got no indicator of how fast or where he's going. You think he cares?"

The Camaro's speed dropped.

Aldo nodded. "That's a yes."

"Last chance," Rome muttered. "Pull over, pal."

It accelerated again, spraying up water like twin fountains.

Rome shook his head. "Oh, well. It was a nice car anyway. Ready on the grapples."

"Ready."

The Camaro could not speed up fast enough to elude him. Rome closed their separation to a car length. The Camaro's driver was either too scared to switch lanes or was watching the approaching curve.

"Go!" Rome snapped.

Aldo triggered the grapples. A muffled thunk sounded from under their feet as two projectiles slammed into the backside of the Camaro. They were black and gray nodules, each the size of Rome's fist. Red lights flashed in a circle at their center.

"Good attach," Aldo said. "All yours."

Rome eased on the brakes.

The Camaro's tires skidded as the grapples slowly but steadily drew the vehicle backward. On the miniature holo, powerful electromagnets mounted to the undercarriage of the Halcyon and pulsed as they siphoned power from the car's core.

"He's losing speed," Aldo said. "Got him down to sixty-five."

Rome had his own grappling match with the steering column. They entered the curve and the Halcyon drifted right toward the guardrail and the drop-off beyond. The Camaro suddenly jerked left, dragging the Halcyon with it, but Rome urged the engine into a better gear. It was a question of whether the Camaro had enough horsepower in that black market combustion engine to outmatch Rome's power core.

Suddenly, the Camaro's speed plummeted.

Rome slammed on his brakes.

Aldo must have realized what had happened because he gripped the door and the center console.

The Camaro's back end shot toward the Halcyon, as if someone had held apart a rubber band and let one side go. One second from impact, the Halcyon's front exploded with a human-sized inflatable bag. The Camaro bashed the Halcyon. They twisted into a spin. Rome steered into it as the driver's side of both cars dragged along the guardrail, sending up a spray of sparks that hissed steam in the rain. They slid backward, slowing down.

"The drop-off flattens out in a quarter mile!" Aldo yelled. "We've got traffic incoming!"

Rome threw the Halcyon into reverse and gunned the engine. The maneuver pulled both vehicles clean off the highway.

[Off-road alert], Marcy reported. [Compensating.]

The seats prodded Rome and Aldo upright. Both ends of their car squeezed in as the wheels dropped down half a foot. The tread on all four tires grew back to the thickness that had saved them from their initial spinout. The Halcyon's conversion left it fully capable to handle dirt driving.

Once he regained control, Rome killed the magnetic grapples. The Camaro, its left side scraped with black streaks, bounced along the rough terrain until it slumped into a drainage ditch. It tipped back, its front right wheel reaching for air as if the car had its hands up.

The front collision bag deflated faster than a popped balloon and was sucked back into the car.

"Suspect is off-road." Rome popped the seal on his restraints. "Pursuit specialist is exiting vehicle for apprehension."

[Logged and noted. Visual and sensory surveillance continuing.]

Everything he did and said would be recorded—even their vital stats, along with the suspect's.

"Got the spazzer?"

Aldo pulled a short, stubby weapon from its mount behind his seat. It was flat, gray, and hummed with the intensity of angry wasps. "Check and check."

"Watch yourself."

The canopy doors opened. A cool breeze brought the strong scent of rain, wet grass, and mud in, cleansing the car of its body odor. Rome saw his breath in white wisps. He slipped into his jacket—dark brown—and let it adjust to the exterior temperature.

[Vitals within norms. Heartbeat and blood pressure slightly elevated.]

Marcy's voice sounded tinny in his ear. Rome pulled his Hunsaker 10mm from his shoulder holster. As soon as it touched his palm, the implanted sensor in his wrist vibrated.

[Weapon active. Warning: Lethal force enabled.]

"Noted." He could do without the disclaimer, but that, too, was recorded. Rome made sure his badge was plainly visible on his belt as he and Aldo approached the Camaro, shoes squelching in the mud. Rain slicked Rome's hair. He could stand there forever as it soaked his face. "Pursuit Specialist!" he hollered. "Get out of the vehicle! Hands where we can see them!"

The canopy cracked open. A pair of hands did exactly as ordered. Above the hiss of traffic on the Ninety, a distant thrum grew louder.

"Get out of the car! Get on your knees!"

Whoever he was expecting, it wasn't the girl. She was tall and gangly. Half of her head was shaved to green stubble, while the rest was chartreuse and hung over her right eye. Her face was olive-toned, and she was Asian—Filipino, by Rome's guess. Broad nose, wide eyes. The sneer on her lips was accentuated by purple gloss. Couldn't be any older than 17.

She knelt in the mud, bare knees sinking into the muck. The girl wore a ripped jacket with no sleeves and black shorts.

"You guys are in some serious scat," she muttered. "My Dad's got all the balance to pay the fees."

"Whatever." Aldo holstered his spazzer. He yanked the girl's hands behind her back and clamped them together with magcuffs. "You're detained for operating an unregistered motor vehicle and intentionally causing a collision. Your record has been stamped. You are by law afforded the chance to dispute said stamping before the court."

"You can't do that! It's my car!"

"Not anymore." Rome leaned through the canopy into the Camaro. Perfume washed over him in waves. It was sickly sweet. "Your unregistered vehicle is hereby confiscated by the U.S. Department of Transportation, to be remanded for scrap to the State of South Dakota. Pursuant to Code Three of the Interstate Ninety Free Travel Zone, you will be charged for any and all damages incurred to property and person on this date."

"Not fair! Not right!" She didn't resist but kept mouthing off as Aldo walked her back to the Halcyon. "I can have a car if I want to! No one says I can't."

"Please. You know the law. Can't have a private vehicle without express permission from the FTZ, Miss..." Aldo glanced at his wrist. The implanted screen cast a lit square on his face. "Ruiz, Alexis Mae, age 17."

The thrum increased overhead. Rome glanced up, squinting through the rain. A broad-bellied aircraft with four wide wings and evenly spaced turbofans broke the cloud cover. There was a giant white bird with blue lines streaked on both sides.

"Pursuit One Twelve, this is Condor Three Three." Gabriela's voice carried the familiar mix of exasperation and amusement. "Just once, I'd like to pick you up without seeing your car in a ditch."

"Just once, I'd like you to not be a killjoy." Rome checked the interior closely. There—an activation stud, linked to a personal computer. He secured both in his jacket pocket. "Got you an unreg driver and modded car for transport."

"Make that two cars for transport. FTZ has a priority case for you."

"Oh yeah?"

"We're to drop the suspect and her ride off at Rapid City and head for Seattle."

Seattle? FTZ West was headquartered there. Rome could count on one hand the number of times in ten years he'd been summoned there—make that on two fingers. "What's the word?"

"Zilch. Communiqué is 'Eyes Only' for you and Aldo. As in, hard copy."

Rome stopped halfway back to the Halcyon.

Whatever it was, it must be bad for his bosses to send him an actual letter.

Chapter Two

Condor 33 might have a narrow fuselage profile when viewed from the outside, but to Rome, it felt as roomy and comfortable as a hotel suite. It was a Xian-Talbert lifter, CL-200 series, with variable adjustment wings and a top speed of 550 miles per hour. Twin pulse jets provided forward propulsion—big gaping units that bulged from the tail. The turbofans were used primarily to hover and maneuver sharply at ground level. With a body 100 feet long, there was more than enough space for the plane to stash the impounded Camaro, plus the Halcyon, and still have tie-downs available for two more vehicles if necessary. An automated winch dragged the damaged Camaro up through the open left side hatch, securing it in one of the four bays.

Rome stood to the side of the Condor's forward landing struts, watching as the Halcyon parked itself under Marcy's guidance.

"Haven't been to Seattle in a long time, have we?" Aldo chomped down the last bit of his grain bar. He licked his fingers.

"Two years."

"Anniversary of my contract? Oh, right," Aldo grinned. "That was a crazy party at the vodka bar."

"You've got crumbs in your beard again."

Aldo turned beet red and brushed furiously at them.

The kid was good at his job, but cocky. He needed to be dropped a couple levels every so often.

"Hey boys." Gabriela stood at the open hatch inside the Condor, just ahead of where Marcy parked the Halcyon. "You going to stand there admiring the prairie grass all day or are we going to lift?"

She was a head shorter than Rome, with a curvy body that fit well inside her pale blue flight jumpsuit. It was emblazoned with the FTZ logo on the right shoulder and the American flag on the left.

"Soon as my partner cleans up his mess." Rome checked his implant. "Marcy's got the car powered down and locked in place."

"At least I can grow a beard." Aldo stroked his chin "Unlike some people who are sixteen years my senior."

Gabriela shook her head. "Come along, Aldrich. I saved you the best seat."

Ruiz sat nearby, hands bound, swearing in fluent Tagalog. Aldo pulled her to her feet. "You got a nice one for her, too?"

"Only the finest incarceration cabin. Even has its own toilet so she doesn't piss all over my plane."

The plane's interior was organized around a central corridor. Aldo shoved Ruiz into one of two empty cabins—no windows, just a bench, toilet, and a few lights. He placed his palm on a scanner mounted by the door's frame and the hatch slid shut. He waved cheerily at the scanner.

"First time offender?" Gabriela led them to the cockpit.

There was a single seat surrounded by various screens and controls. Rome didn't recognize one third of them. The wrap-around canopy offered a breathtaking view of the South Dakota plains. Rome and Aldo strapped themselves into two of the three seats behind her.

"Yeah, she's a first-timer," Rome answered.

"Offender and offensive," Aldo muttered.

"That doesn't even make sense."

"Sure it does. Did you see her hair?"

Gabriela rolled her eyes. "Not everyone values their locks as deeply as you, Aldrich."

Rome tried to hold in a laugh but snorted instead. Aldo glared at him. Though he didn't have a riposte to Gabriela's comment, he did smooth a portion of his well-combed, thick, auburn hair.

Gabriela ran a check on the hatches. Once they were all sealed, she eased the Condor into the air. It bobbed on turbofans, reminding Rome of boating in the Chesapeake Bay and fishing with Grandfather. The smell of Old Bay Spice and burning campfire filled his memories.

Aldo held onto the arms of his seat, letting the straps wrap around him like a spider's web with a mind of its own. He looked far paler than his usual white and freckled self. "Hokay. Hurk. That bar might've been a bad idea."

"How is it you survive Rome's driving but can't keep your food down when you fly with me?"

Aldo didn't answer. He was busy holding his hand to his mouth and squeezing his eyes shut.

Gabriela guided the Condor up through the clouds. Her hands rested atop a pair of guide panels that extended from her primary console. Sunlight blasted into the cockpit, making Rome's eyes water. The cockpit's canopy darkened to filter out the brightness. The Condor banked sharply left and boosted on its jets, accelerating to its cruising speed in a matter of minutes.

"Got a bit before we drop by Rapid City, then a couple hours to Seattle." Gabriela brought up a file on her displays. Ruiz's face moped at them. "What's her deal?"

"She's got nothing in her citizen's record besides disciplinarian actions at school—petty theft and altercations," Rome said. "Implant to her home comp verified as much."

Gabriela's console chimed. Scans of the Camaro must be complete. "Not a lot to go on with the chassis and the shell, but some of the electronics are promising. I've got two serial numbers somebody neglected to laser off. That should give us a lead as to the mod shop."

"Run the data up to FTZ Security and they can issue the warrants."

"She's a minor. Did you notify the parents?"

Aldo scowled. "What, do we look like student drivers to you? Marcy pinged their home comp the second I magcuffed her. I have no doubt 'daddy dearest' is hollering until he's red in the face at some reception screen at whatever Grand Rapids PD precinct he's in."

"Odds are, he'll pay the fines, spare her any correctional time, hopefully drop her into a decent community service program. But the stamp stays on her record. Any chance she had of training for a legit driver's certification from DOT is gone." Rome shrugged. "She wasn't dangerous. Just stupid."

"Well, she was a Driver. That makes her dangerous."

Aldo winced. "Um… incoming signal, Gabby. So's your buddy right here." He jerked a thumb at Rome.

"That's different." Gabriela turned away from the scanning station. Her cheeks darkened and her tone grew strident. "Rome's well-trained at operating a car. Few people have the talent he does, and fewer still are authorized to use it."

Rome raised his eyebrows and smiled. He couldn't deny the boost to the ego, even if it was just Gabriela. "Hear that, Aldo? Talent."

"Yeah. That's exactly the word I thought of when you had us ass-backward on the Ninety with another car magged to our bumper," Aldo said. "Oh, wait. It wasn't."

"You two are incorrigible." Gabriela rolled her eyes.

"Even better," Rome said.

"Look, Rome, you know as well as I do most people would just be road hazards behind the wheel—even if their cars were built with steering wheels, which they're not, thankfully."

"Hang on," Rome said. "A person's way different than a deer running across your lane or a sheet of black ice. People react."

"Badly. That's why the comps are better. You can't deny the decline in accidents. They've plummeted in forty years."

"I get that." Rome ticked off numbers on his fingers. "No drunk drivers. No elderly going the wrong way up an on ramp. No rookie teenagers who feel the need to do twice the speed limit."

"See?" Gabriela enlarged the radar.

There was nothing within a couple miles of their position as far as Rome saw.

"Sure. It's a lot safer when individual choice is removed from the equation."

Gabriela sighed. "Now you're just being contrary."

"You know, Rome, I think she's just scared." Aldo's holographic screen floated inches above his wrist implant. Just a bunch of junk scrolled by—people talking about themselves, critics complaining about this entertainment or the next—filler for the brain to keep it from focusing on anything worthwhile. "Independent contractors like us aren't controllable. Yet she wings around in a plane thousands of feet up in the air with nothing under her, slinging along at ten times our speed."

"Nothing… that isn't how flight works!" Gabriela said. "And you know full well those same cars that go ten times slower than my Condor were far more dangerous than air travel!"

"We know. It's just too much fun to argue with you, Gabby." Aldo winked at her.

"You know what's more fun?" Rome gestured at the hatch. "Cleaning those crumbs out of my car."

"Our car."

"I stand corrected. Now go get vacuuming."

Aldo mumbled the full length of the cockpit.

Condor 33 leveled out atop the circular landing pad at the FTZ complex on the north side of Rapid City. A single, angular building six stories tall poked up amidst the four, flat-sided, and sloped storage and maintenance structures. It was all glass with a huge wind turbine built in the middle. The shorter buildings were sheathed with solar panels, giving them the appearance of iridescent purple beetles.

Rome remote unloaded the Camaro. The poor thing was battered, though none of its windshields had fractured, and—as far as he could tell—there were no missing pieces.

The air here was bone dry. Pines were healthy enough and Rome thought he caught a whiff their sap. Grass struggled to turn green amidst an endless sea of brown. What had the weather report said en route? How many consecutive weeks without rain? That thunderstorm farther east must have been a fluke.

Aldo turned over the young Miss Ruiz to a man and a woman from the Pennington County Sheriff's Office.

"Got your transmission," the female deputy said. "Anything else off data we need to know?"

Ruiz spit on the ground. Aldo scowled, and scuffed his shoe against his pant leg.

"Off data? She's a pain," Rome said. "Rest of the data's collected from our comp—vids, scans, and all."

"Right. We'll drop you a signal when the prelim hearing comes up. County attorney will want both your testimonies."

"We know the drill. Enjoy."

"Thanks, Driver." The deputy and her partner each took one of Ruiz's elbows and led her across the tarmac.

Rome watched her go. Stupid kid.

"You think Daddy's really going to delete this mess?" Aldo asked

"Who knows? Not our problem." A pair of beeps caught Rome's attention. Both his and Aldo's implants flashed green.

"Ah. Favorite color." Aldo tapped his. "Bingo."

Rome did likewise. Got to hand it to the FTZ—once your target was turned over to local LEOs, the bounty was in your account within seconds. Minus federal taxes, of course.

"Ten percent." Aldo moaned. "Man. That's America for you."

"Don't knock it. Roads, parks, and guns. That's all we're paying for."

"Yeah, well, still…"

Another light flashed on Rome's implant—yellow, double pulse. Incoming signal.

The whine of the Condor's engines increased. Aldo glanced up. "Better get back aboard before Gabby leaves us stranded in West Nowhere."

"Give me two. Got a call."

"Okay. I'll tell her. But you know how she gets."

"No kidding. But she's more likely to take off without you than without me."

Aldo gave him the finger and sprinted for the hatch.

Rome tapped the screen. A girl's face appeared—all smiles with black, curly hair cascading over her ears. She must have registered his face on her end because her smile—impossible as it seemed—got bigger. Eyes like blue sky sparkled.

"Daddy!"

"Hey, Viv."

"I signaled 'cause Mommy said to remind you the concert's Friday."

Her voice was warm in his earpiece as if she stood right there. He imagined soft, tiny fingers wrapped in his hand. "Yeah, I remember. Early Level Band."

"You're coming?"

"Wouldn't miss it."

"Okay." She blew him a kiss. "Love you, Daddy!"

He put two fingers to his lips, kissed them, and then pressed them to the tiny screen. "Love you too, Pumpkin."

Her face ducked out of view. The woman who replaced her was slender with blonde hair and hazel eyes. No smile, though a hint of one hid in the curve of her lips. "Hey, Rome."

"Hey, Kelsey."

"You are coming." Less of a question, more of a command.

"So far as I know I've still got the time off logged."

"Double check, please. I don't want you to miss Vivian's concert."

"I don't want to either."

He felt awkward during the pause as Kelsey looked off camera. Wasn't any easier on his end. "Where's Jake?"

"Out. One of his friends. The car tracer shows them downtown. Who knows where they walked after that."

"Tag turned off again?"

"He's eighteen. Legally he can switch it on and off any time. We—I don't have the PIN."

Rome nodded. "Funny how the kids always experiment with shutting down their tags. Pursuit can switch 'em back on whenever we want."

"I don't want our son's every movement tracked, like everyone else's," Kelsey said stiffly.

"Really. Is yours on right now?"

"That's none of your business, or anyone else's," she sighed. "Sorry."

"Yeah. Me too. Wasn't aiming for a fight."

"We always seem to find one." Kelsey smiled, but it looked hesitant. "I'll tell Jake you're coming."

"Thanks." Rome scratched the back of his neck. "He didn't answer my last signal."

"I'm not surprised. He's hardly ever around. Maybe—when you're in town—we could all go out for dinner."

"That'd be nice." He wished he could stay longer. Things used to be different—tense, but not awkward. He liked tense better. But that's why they called it divorce. "Got to go. My ride's waiting."

"Okay. Be careful."

She always said that. Even five years out. "Thanks. I will. Take care of yourself."

Kelsey's face vanished.

Rome stared at the tarmac, shadowed by the hovering Condor. Wind blew his jacket and his hair around. For a moment, there was just the rush of the air… the roar of the jets. In the distance, cars and trucks rushed back and forth along the Ninety.

Orderly.

Safe.

Not a single person in control.

His palms itched. Rome climbed aboard the Condor and patted the side of the Halcyon as he walked through the bay.

The Cascades were a jagged row of dark emeralds capped with snow, turning pale blue in the fading light. As the Condor crossed the mountain range, Seattle's crown of lights exploded through the gloom. The first things to greet westward visitors were the soldierly ranks of agricultural towers that sprouted from the foothills on the edge of Bellevue and Issaqah. They sparkled like columns of gems, verdant sprinkled with rainbow colors the closer they flew.

Beyond that, the sprawl of dimly lit city streets was barely visible. Only intersections and housing complexes were well lit. The faintest glow of car indicators turned the streets a soft gold.

Gabriela locked the Condor into auto-approach, monitoring for gusts. The FTZ West complex was a compound of nine identical domes stretched along the south seafront, not far from the old Sea-Tac airport and at the dead end of the old 405. The Ninety had long ago subsumed that road into its own network. Headquarters was two, twelve-story offices joined by a garden skyway topped with solar sheeting. Gabriela took manual control for the final seconds of flight and settled the craft into an open dome. Its top split open like eyelids.

"Better get the Halcyon over to the garage," Aldo said as they disembarked on to the tarmac.

Rome breathed deep. The air was muggy—saturated with moisture. A far cry from the dusty, rain-desperate plains they'd left.

"Negative on that, boys," Gabriela called to them from the open hatch. "Director wants you in his office without pause. According to him, you're queued up for departure in an hour."

Aldo made a face. "What? How's that enough time to—"

Rome clapped his shoulder. "Have the garage send a tech team over to retrieve the car, Gabriela. Relay the same time frame. Tell them we need the basic repairs."

"Roger that. Good luck."

Security was tight in the lobby of FTZ West headquarters. The walls and floor were polished stone—white and gray, respectively. A guard-bot waited beside the white arch of a body scanner. It was as tall as Rome, and a bit on the pudgy side. Its oblong barrel torso made him think it'd be out of shape, were it a human.

[Identity.] The voice was stern and echoed like a grating gear throughout the empty lobby.

"Wow. The new Pike series aren't much for public relations," Aldo said.

"Don't have to be." Rome extended his left arm, wrist bent down, hand in a fist. "Pursuit Specialist Roman Franklin Jasko."

The Pike had a single circular port on its "face," near the top of its pointed head. It flashed red, casting a light on Rome's implant.

[Confirmed. Clearance accepted.]

"Information and Support Specialist Aldrich Harold Burns." Aldo's forced formality was almost as funny as his ramrod stiff posture.

[Confirmed. Clearance accepted.] The guardbot rolled aside.

Rome and Aldo walked through the scanner, which pulsed with a soft, golden glow. Nothing to object to, apparently, for they were admitted without further scrutiny.

One elevator ride to the top floor deposited them outside the opulent office of Director Marcus Cho. The walls were entirely glass—transparent ones fronted the corridor while the polarized ones looked across the bay and Seattle. Here, another Pike guard-bot let them pass without interrogation.

Two men flanked the doors to Cho's office. They were of larger build than the robots. One had dark brown skin while the other was of Chinese descent,

"Security check." The black guy held up his arm. His implant glowed.

"We did this downstairs," Aldo muttered. "Think we picked up contraband between the lobby and the penthouse?"

The black guard's face was immobile. He scanned both their implants. Something blinked red on his screen. "Firearm? Turn it over."

"Licensed to as an independent contractor for FTZ," Rome said. "Resolve Interception. We have a federal waiver."

"Don't care. FTZ house rules." The black guard held out his hand.

"Which part of 'federal' are you not understanding?"

"You wanna argue? Send your Senator a signal. Hand it over."

Rome waited a full five seconds, then pulled the Hunsaker from its holster. He ejected the magazine, and racked the slide. "Don't lose it."

"Like I could do anything with it." The guard handed it to his counterpart. "Tagged to you. Store it."

"Yes, sir."

The black guard opened the door and led them through a small waiting room, furnished with four chairs and a small silver table. Off to the right, a woman with white hair styled in a long braid sat at a desk of black stone and blue glass. Her glowing nameplate said simply, "Mrs. Liu." Six holo displays cast a rainbow glow on her face, turning her pale gray suit and skirt into something approximating stained glass. She didn't look up.

"Driver Jasko and his tech, for the director," the guard said.

"They're expected. Pass." She arched a single, razor-thin eyebrow their direction.

Rome met her stern gaze and winked.

"Drivers," she muttered.

Aldo snorted into his hand.

A double door slid open on the other side of the office. The guard left them there.

"Ah, good! Thanks, Garrick. Fellas, come in… pull up a chair."

Marcus Cho had an easy smile, and his posture—though relaxed—was that of a man who knew he was in charge and wanted everyone else to be cognizant of the fact. A silver-gray jacket hung over a black leather chair. His slacks and shirt were charcoal and his tie was a solid, bold blue. Cho had white hair and brown eyes as dark as Rome's.

"Driver Jasko, a pleasure to meet you in person. And Mr. Burns, likewise."

Cho's grip was sturdy, not something Rome expected from a desk-rider who looked as pale as one who didn't see much sunlight.

Though—this being Seattle—Rome doubted anyone got enough Vitamin D outside their daily supplements.

"Glad to put flesh with the faces. Please."

Rome and Aldo sat in chairs facing Cho's desk. Rome realized the seats were a few inches shorter than the director's. Yes, the glass desk with its onyx top and the chair were centered on a dais—one Rome had missed when they first entered. Besides the bit of commanding furniture, the office also contained a loveseat and sofa in the far corner, nearest the windows that revealed a breathtaking spread of the harbors. Pottery adorned the end tables and shelves.

"The Ninety Free Travel Zone is in the black," Cho said without preamble. "I want it to stay that way. Our profitability is based on our safety record. People need to feel they're as protected in their cars as they are in their homes."

"Wasn't aware there was anything troubling that record, Director."

"What do you and your partner experience out there, Rome? What's the primary disturbance?"

Rome and Aldo shared a glance. Aldo's eyebrows were raised—it was his "Is this guy freaking kidding?" stare.

"Come now, I'm not asking for you to sugarcoat anything." Cho spread his hands in a slow sweep. Holographic reports sprang up from his desk like plants in time lapse—white and yellow sprays of words, charts, and images. "These are reports from all seventy-seven of the pursuit contractors running across the United American States. I pay special attention to the ten operating on the Ninety. Regardless, I want to hear it straight from you."

"Unregistered drivers," Rome said. "No question. They cause the most accidents—more than 80 percent of them. The rest can be chalked up to severe weather. You know, car users who override their automaton systems when they really feel like they have to be somewhere."

Aldo snorted. "Only the people rich enough to afford cars modified for the overrides. So, we wind up sending in a Condor to pull Moneybags out of a ditch."

Cho chuckled. "Understandable. Some people are loath to give up their independence when it comes to driving, or even owning a car. But I suppose you can commiserate, Driver."

Rome shifted in his seat. Something about the way the guy scrutinized him—with a gaze as deep as any Pike guard-bot—made him uneasy. "Anything else?"

"That's what I ask of you. Besides unregistered drivers…?" Cho paused.

"Theft," Aldo said. "You wouldn't believe it unless you'd seen it, Director. Guys who'll roll up on a Famtrac doing eighty, with these specialized rigs they latch right onto the sides—"

"Remoras."

Aldo stopped, mouth open, hand in mid-gesture. "Uh, yeah. That's it."

"I've seen the specifications from the reports you filed back in August of last year. Two of them, weren't there? Operating between Boston and Niagara Falls."

"Ballsy." Rome's head crowded with memories of the month-long operation. "Night raids. Like the train robbers of two hundred years ago, only faster. Took us a while to figure out where their base of operations was."

"A little more than that. You posed in a modified Famtrac to catch them."

Rome shrugged and smiled.

"Yeah, that was slick," Aldo grinned.

"See, I knew I'd selected the right men." Cho's expression became stonily serious. "There is a grave new threat running the Western stretch of the Ninety. A new gang of thieves is targeting travelers."

"Haven't seen any bulletins to that effect, Director," Rome said.

"That's because we've kept them quiet. Do a deep search on the Net and you'll find the commentary. People are worried because of the frequency, and the audacity."

"What are we talking about?"

Cho brushed his hand through the data displays. Most disappeared, except for one stream cascading down the right side of his desk. "Eleven robberies in the past two weeks."

Aldo whistled.

"That's… quick work." Rome kept his profanity stuffed back in his head.

"Too quick. These people are fast… and brutal." Cho moved his hand again. One image from the stream expanded to the size of his chest.

Rome recognized the implant immediately. "That's a Garelli. Has to be worth upward of twenty grand."

"Is that… skin?" Aldo's face paled.

"Yes. The thieves gouged the implants out of the hands of one couple who was targeted just five days ago. The attack happened in Montana. Authorities recovered one implant nearby, in Wyoming."

"Ow…"

"Certainly is. They took jewelry, too, and the silver and gold coins the couple were carrying. Those, apparently, are long gone."

That piqued Rome's interest. "So, this wasn't just a data hit. They knew the couple carried currency."

Cho nodded. "That was the case in all the other thefts, too. Not random. We know that much."

"Any hints to ID? We can start with DNA left behind and—"

"There is none."

Rome laughed. "Sorry, you said none? Not possible."

"I mean what I say. The only DNA present was from the couple, and the last tech to work on their car."

Aldo cleared his throat. "Okay, that's wrong. Has to be. What about Bact?"

"No bacteriological profiles, either." Cho ticked off on his fingers. "Nor is there facial recognition or voiceprint."

Aldo shook his head. "You can't have a complete failure of every known evidence gathering method. We need data."

"This, gentlemen, is all we have."

A video played at the center of Cho's desk—a highway, with cars spread apart by wide, precise margins. A black Lexus cruised into the frame.

"And… here."

The vehicle that rolled alongside the Lexus was a cross between a Famtrac, a freighter, and an off-road Search-and-Rescue rover. Its broad body filled the whole lane. A bulge on its top gave it a hunchback appearance. It was colored a mottled gray.

Somehow, it seemed familiar to Rome. "Where's the feed from?"

"Patrol drone."

The vehicle matched speed with the Lexus. The top sprang apart and a docking collar—like the kind used at shipping warehouses—slapped over the roof and the passenger side door. It was loose until whoever was at the controls triggered the solidification process. The two cars drove along, linked.

Data sputtered across the bottom of the screen. Cho pointed. "The drone picked up a signal transmitted on military channels. Whatever it was, we figure it prevented the Lexus's automaton from calling for help."

"Or trying to maneuver away." Rome watched the robbery—or rather, the view from the outside. Whoever ran this operation was good. Scary good.

"Right here… when they separate… is when we get our one good look."

Cho accelerated the video. The collar retracted. Rome saw a young, black couple—well dressed—yelling inside their car. Their roof and passenger door were missing. The collar dropped both parts, letting them disappear down the highway. A person hung partway out of the collar—a woman's body wearing a form-fitting black suit. Her face was masked with a reflective visor and a breathing apparatus.

"That's a stealth suit," Aldo murmured in a tone Rome reserved for Sunday services. "Special Forces. Marvelous piece of tech."

"Yes. And then there's this."

The vehicle rippled and faded from view.

Rome blew out a breath.

Great.

Chapter Three

The techs at FTZ West had the Halcyon dent free by the time Cho's briefing finished. Rome gave the car a once-over, making sure nothing was altered from its prior settings.

[All systems restored within parameters,] Marcy reported. [Structural integrity reinforced to specifications.]

"Good to know. I'm still going to eyeball it, if you don't mind."

[Understood, sir.]

There was barely time to sign off on the repairs before Gabriela signaled their hour was up. Rome and Aldo walked the Halcyon back to Condor 33's landing pad, letting Marcy drive. For something as simple as guiding the car from the repair garage back to its berth aboard the Condor, Rome didn't need to waste his time with the override and the manual mode conversion.

"You should see all this stuff." Aldo stared at his implant, eyes wide, as data flickered by. "Man. These guys are professionals. When was the last time we saw someone run an operation like this?"

"Never, in your case." Rome nudged Aldo aside, clearing the path for a tech that rode an equipment cart laden with power cells and electronic components. Too bad humans didn't come with standard issue distance and proximity sensors like their automotive counterparts. "Military grade stealth for both their suits and their vehicle. That isn't good."

"No kidding! Plus side—all their hits follow the same pattern, so we know what kind of vehicle to keep an eye on."

"It'd be far better for us if they'd stick to one geographic region of the Ninety. They're all over the map."

"Did you even read the case notes Cho uploaded?"

"Yeah. I don't consider between the Rockies and the Mississippi to be a narrow enough range. As soon as we're aboard and you can sync Marcy with the Condor's mainframe, I want a listing of every registered auto traveling the Ninety between their hits that's a brand name with a value greater than $50,000."

Aldo rolled his eyes. "That'll narrow it down."

"Cross check with purchases of coins. There won't be nearly as many."

"Yeah, I got it."

Gabriela had the Condor's engines running when they got back. Rome was surprised to see that the forward bay hatch opposite the lifter was open. "You get any notice that we're taking another ride with us?"

"Nope. Why?" Aldo still had his nose tucked into the mini hologram.

Rome shoved his wrist down and pointed.

"Oh… huh… yeah, I got no—Whoa!"

Rome saw another car approach from a different repair bay, accompanied by a driver and info tech. It was a sleek Rishi Panther, metallic blue with multi-form wheels at least two upgrades newer than the Halcyon's. Gold stripes along the running boards flashed with the rare rays of sun that poked through the thick clouds. Unnecessarily flashy, but fast. Rome had no doubt. He figured the car—not the drivers — elicited Aldo's outburst.

Two men of Latino background approached them, wearing identical forest green jackets over brown jumpsuits. Their boots were black leather, shined to a ridiculous reflectivity. One man was tall with olive-toned skin and a bald shaved head. His Van Dyke beard was trimmed to perfection. The other was short, stocky, and mocha colored. He too was bald, though a tattoo of angel wings wrapped from the back of his head out over his ears and a black, elaborate cross marked his forehead.

"Ah, Roman. I wondered who was gonna share our ride." The bearded man stopped a few feet from the base of the landing pad.

"Thad. Didn't expect to see you anywhere there wasn't an open bar."

"Such a kidder. Unlike some of my compatriots—one Driver in particular—I don't have a gearshift permanently inserted in my posterior."

"Cute."

Aldo glanced back and forth between the two. "Okay, I'm getting the vibe you don't like this guy. Am I supposed to like him?"

"Not my call." Rome folded his arms.

"Who's the gringo sitting in your lap these days, Rome?" Thad asked.

"Aldo Burns." Aldo held out his hand. "Piss off. Oh, wait. I meant 'pleased to meet you.'"

Thad sneered and regarded Aldo's outstretched hand with the same expression most people gave a piece of litter stuck to their shoe.

"Thaddeus Mancos, Driver for Del Norte Tactical," Rome snarled. "And his pet troglodyte, Enrique Bassa."

Enrique grunted. Whether it was a greeting or dismissal, Rome couldn't tell.

"Charming. I hope you don't mind us commandeering your ride, Roman." Thad's words oozed.

"Not my business whom FTZ transports on its birds. What's your drop-off?"

"The Ninety."

"Any particular case?"

Thad shrugged, but the sneer never quite left his lips. "Oh, standard patrol. I'm certain there's some lawbreaker we can roll who will bring us substantial bounty. Why, just the other day my superiors at Del

Norte tasked me to investigate rumors of robberies of the strangest nature taking place on the mighty north road. You wouldn't have heard any such talk, would you?"

"Can't say a thing." Rome kept his face placid. Inwardly, he fumed at that idiot Cho and his insistence on operational secrecy. What good was it if Del Norte and the other contractors running down on the southern roads already knew? Of course, he had no idea how detailed their intel was. Better to keep it vague. "We should all load up. Gabriela doesn't like waiting."

"Ah, Gabriela. Such a vision." Thad tossed them a mock salute. "Enjoy the flight."

Aldo glowered as they loaded up the Panther. "Asshole."

"Big time. But good. Make no mistake. And his pal Enrique is, too." Rome leaned in closer. "Make sure every database and link is locked up tight. I mean, tighter than usual. I don't care if whatever you do crosses the gray. Follow?"

"You're the driver, Driver." He whistled. "This guy must be bad news."

"Del Norte doesn't play nicely with independent contractors, if that's your question. Long time back, when I was working for another interception company, the branch that handled southern road contracts fell under the influence of some Arizonan solar tycoons with too much money and too much time on their hands. Stole a bunch of contracts and company secrets, including operational protocols for pursuit cars." Rome gestured at the Panther, nestled inside the Condor's bay. "Del Norte was formed in the aftermath of that mess. They've got eight drivers, spread out across the highways. Thad's their best."

"So, we steer clear."

"Literally and figuratively. Thad won't hesitate to swipe this case out from under us." Rome frowned. "If we're lucky, he won't run us into the nearest guardrail."

❖ ❖ ❖

The Condor swooped low over the rimrock cliffs north of Billings, Montana. The local geology stood out against the silver and red buildings of the city's downtown and adjacent college as bulwarks between civilization and nature. Residences and farming domes were splotches of green against the brown landscape.

Gabriela's navigational system flashed a red warning for high wind and thick dust. The latter rolled across the rimrocks, obscuring most of the city from view.

"I have to let her circle for a few minutes until the wind dies down," she said. "I'll put you boys on the east end of town—there's a landing circle not far off the main road."

Rome leaned on the back of her chair. "I see we've still got our friendly passengers back there. They getting the boot after us?"

"Yes."

"And that would be where?"

Gabriela pursed her lips in a smile as she took over the controls from the automated system. "That would be wherever they've got a contract with the Ninety FTZ to operate. Which is not in your contract, so not your business."

"Thad is bad for my business, which makes his location my business."

"Go sit down and strap in. You know how it works, Rome."

He bowed and quipped "Worth a try" to Aldo, who chewed studiously on a fruit strip that was a hideous orange brilliance.

"Yeah. Funny. I'm busy." Aldo swiped through image after image on his wrist display. "Cho wasn't kidding. There's blank for physical evidence."

"Local LEOs could have missed something. If the big four weren't present they probably stopped looking."

"Well, the data stream from the Lexus's onboard doesn't help matters. We've got video and sensors, but the car could have been trying to scan a block of stone for all the info it picked up through those stealth suits. I mean, the robbers had body heat and they were human, but even that first one's iffy because the suits tamp down on excess thermal discharge."

Rome nodded. He'd skimmed most of the data, though he hadn't delved too deep.

"LZ coming up," Gabriela said. "You sure you don't want to divert to the rimrock plateau? It's a lot clearer and broader up there."

"True. But I don't want everyone and their vids to see where we're going." Rome grasped for an overhead console bar with one hand and held to the back of Gabriela's seat with the other as the Condor shuddered. "This will do. Provided you can see through the dust."

"It's cleared off enough." Her canopy lit up with scan overlays of every building, tree, and light post within a half mile. It made Rome think he was stuck inside an antique video game—those pre-virtual reality ones the local history museums liked to promote.

Gabriela touched them down with no more fuss than a feather falling. By then, Rome and Aldo were already strapped into the Halcyon. Marcy rolled them onto the landing pad and drove onto the nearest street.

[Destination is not input.]

"Five Oh Five East Paintbrush Court," Rome said. "Marcy, make the route circuitous. We're in no hurry."

[Understood.]

Aldo didn't even notice it took them ten minutes longer than it should. The dust lifted, and the sun beat down through the barest tatters of white clouds in an azure sky. Marcy dimmed the glass as the car's internal temperature rose.

"Keep running your analyses, but in the background," Rome ordered Aldo as they drove up a curved gravel road tucked amongst scrubby pines. A half-dozen houses poked their roofs over a nearby hill. "I need you focused on the real world."

"Nothing more real than numbers," Aldo muttered. "It's all numbers in there. And when you ask the CPU to run comparisons, then have me sort through possible matches, I need—wait... what real world are you talking about?"

The Halcyon turned a corner past a sandstone outcropping into an oval parking area. Two cars were tucked into a submerged parking slot at its far end. It was the black Lexus—missing its passenger side door and its roof—and a pearl white BMW. The Lexus was the most forlorn of the pair with red sheathing stretched across the damaged area.

"Both are leased," Aldo said.

"I'd be more shocked if these people were the owners. Granted, it's Montana, so the car ownership rate's about double what it is on either coast."

"No way I'd have the title to my own car. Too much hassle. Way too much money."

"You realize who you're talking to?"

"Um… duh… but it isn't my car."

Sage grass and rocks dominated the area, adding chalky red and pale green to otherwise drab brown. Two water vapor siphon towers stood at attention to the southeast. Each one was twenty feet tall with broad vanes like the rigging of an old sailing ship mixed with a mutated, giant plant of white and silver. A single residence was perched atop the parking slot. It was a half cylinder, two stories tall with a long, broad wing sloping down to the north. The west side of the cylinder was a reflective surface, mirroring the blue skies and distant hills. As soon as Rome got out of the car, three sections of the bottom side of the cylinder blinked into transparency. He spotted a tall, lanky, man with dark mahogany skin walking by a music stand and several couches set atop a marble floor.

"Our victims. Joseph and Deborah Brace." Rome straightened Aldo's collar. "Shine up your badge. Smile. Make eye contact. Answer their questions, and ask direct but polite ones of your own."

Aldo blinked. "What're you, my stepmom?"

"I'm the one getting you paid." Rome led him to the front door, treading carefully on polished sandstone steps. "These two saw our robbers up close. I want to know everything they observed that the comps didn't."

Aldo snorted. He buffed the shine back into his badge with the sleeve of his jacket.

The black man answered the door. Joseph Brace had his hands clasped behind his back. He wore a navy blue jacket, white pants, and white shirt with the collar undone. A slim silver chain with a slanted gold crucifix hung around his neck. "You're the investigator?" His voice was deep and mellow, but there was a hammer behind every syllable.

"Pursuit Specialist Roman Jasko." Rome smiled full wattage and held out his hand. He made sure the badge was plainly visible on his belt, even with a shine from the sun.

"Joe. Joe Brace." Joe ignored the outstretched hand. "A Driver? Hmm. Come in."

Rome and Aldo followed him past a small pond. The re-circulator gurgled from some unseen water trap. Rome guessed they hooked into the hidden cistern from which the vapor towers collected their bounty.

"I'll be plain. I don't trust a man who feels the need to threaten others." Joe stood by the music stand, arms folded.

"I'm sorry, sir, I don't understand. Just have a few questions to ask regarding your theft. No threats." Rome spread his hands wide, making a show of their emptiness.

"Not that. Your driving. No man needs to drive. The want? That's what endangers every person out there in the safe hands of their cars. You got questions? Ask them."

Great. One of those. Gabriela's arguments filled Rome's memories. Last thing he needed was a lecture on the hazards of human directed transport. "Tell me about the people who took your implants."

Joe held up his left arm, fist facing out. There was a slick, translucent patch of flesh that was a shade lighter and free of hair and wrinkles. "They gouged them out with a blade. One of them… a woman… did this."

Rome felt an itch around the edges of his implant. He made sure the device recorded the entire conversation—including imagery of Joe

Brace. "Start from the top."

"We were headed back to Billings from Denver. Deb had a symphony holo running, by this composer guy we'd heard play a few months ago. I told her it was funny, watching those tiny people playing their instruments on our dashboard with their micro conductor waving little arms around." A smile broke the edges of Joe's frown. "I've never been much for classics. Old Jazz and New Pound for me." The smile faded. "The truck showed up. Our car comp, Cliff, he saw it was getting too close to our lane so he tried to move us out of the way. But there was some kind of system failure—like he was stuck at one speed in one lane and nothing was gonna change that. Next thing I know, all our navigation info goes dark. The symphony guys vanished, and the right side of our car, plus the moon roof, gets covered by this..."

"It's a docking collar," Aldo interjected. "They use them with freighters. You know, transfer cargo out of the weather. Those guys were using it on you to make sure they had easy access."

Joe's demeanor hardened. Rome stiffened. He should have left Aldo in the car. "Continue on, Mr. Brace. They locked the collar on your Lexus..."

"They tore it open. Guy dressed up like a ninja shoots us with a neural disruptor, twice." Joe mimicked a gun firing. "My body's numb, so's Deb's. We don't feel a thing when that lady scoops our implants out like she's dishing ice cream. Not until the thing wears off, and the pain sets in."

"Spazzer set on localized stun," Aldo muttered. "That takes some doing. Most models can't be reprogrammed for specific limbs."

"Aldo, shut up," Rome said.

Aldo scowled, but did as told.

"Mr. Brace, what can you tell me about the people themselves?"

"Before or after they helped themselves to our coins? We'd just got them all appraised."

"We hope those can be recovered. But the people involved."

"They didn't speak. I heard murmurs but it was like radio

communications, maybe in their masks." Joe paused. "There was a smell. Funny smell. It stank when they opened that first door."

"What kind of smell?"

"Industrial… lubricants?" Joe's nose wrinkled, as if he smelled it again. "Something else, too. Coconut."

"Coconut."

"Reminded me of a lotion my brother uses. He works on those floating neighborhoods in Florida, New Miami. Always either in the water or the sun."

An odd detail.

"I'd like to look inside your car."

"Cops here already did."

"Still, they might have missed something. They were only looking for the big four, most likely—DNA, bacteria, video, and audio."

Joe glared at him, but shrugged. "Sure. Why not."

"Could I speak with your wife?"

"No. She's not up to it. Had a hard enough time getting used to the idea of re-grown skin as big as this."

"She might remember something you didn't," Aldo said.

"I said, no. We're done."

Aldo made a face. "Look, man—sir—we're trying to get this thing fixed. But if we're gonna catch these ghosts we need more data than what we've got."

"I don't have anything else to give you, and I'm not obliged to answer any more stupid questions from you." Joe prodded him in the chest. "Those coins were in my family for six generations, you follow? Three hundred years! My people worked their way up from nothing to where we are now. First hundred we were slaves and sharecroppers. Next hundred we spent fighting the Klan and the police. This time around? We don't back down from any man. You find these wheelers, you get back what's mine, and you bring 'em here so I can stomp on their balls."

Aldo stared, wondering if he was about to get pounded. Rome gave him a 25 percent chance of laying a few blows on Joe before the bigger man snapped him in half. Rather than wait for it, he inserted himself between the two so he was nose to nose with Joe.

"We'll do our job. Right now, stay out of the habit of hauling your valuables around. We'll see ourselves out." He gave Aldo a shove, before Joe could.

"That guy was fun. By fun, I mean rude." Aldo leaned against the front of the Lexus. His eyes were glued to his data stream.

Rome had the red plastic pulled back. The inside of the car smelled new, fitting with its appearance. The seats were so plush they didn't look like they'd ever been sat in. The wood paneling he took for faux until he caught the scent of actual oak. There was black and gold trim on white surfaces. Even the dash was top model.

"You know, that questioning session would have gone better and lasted longer if you'd kept your trap shut."

"Hey! You wanted me in there. I tried what you were doing."

"Being an insufferable prick is not what I was doing." Rome took out a pocketknife. He used the three-inch blade to slit part of the upholstery under the footrests and pry up the edge. He wore a pair of black gloves. "You can't punch his buttons like you're searching for data. The man's traumatized—even more so because his wife was there and he was unable to protect her."

"What, you've got a brain link to that guy?"

"It's the same way I'd act and feel if it were Kelsey." Nothing under that side. Rome pushed the carpeting back into place, and dug around the wrecked frame.

"She isn't even your wife."

"Used to be. And that's complicated."

"Can't be that complicated."

"How about after you get married and divorced, you get to lecture me on what's complicated and what's not?" Rome snapped. He caught a whiff of something. Tropical. He cut off a chunk of the upholstery. "Joe's recollections were right, though. Smell this."

Aldo took the swatch from him and sniffed, his hands sheathed in identical black gloves. "I got nothing."

"You're holding it out like a dirty sock, Aldo. Press it to your nose."

"Okaaaay…" Aldo sniffed with great exaggeration, sounding as if he would inhale the piece of carpet. "I don't get what… oh. Hey… Coconut?"

"Yes, dumbass. Bag that."

"Sure. What about the lubricant smell?"

"I couldn't catch anything but hopefully Marcy can tell us what's on that carpet."

Something else was stuck in the frame. It was in a deep groove left from where the door ripped out and the collar clamped on. Rome aimed his right wrist. Tiny implanted beacons in his sleeve cast bright circles in the darkest spots. Well now… "Get me a smaller container, too."

"Another one? Hang on." Aldo shuffled through his pockets, doing it all one-handed while trying to read his implant. "Here."

"Thanks." Rome took it. With the care of a surgeon—or what he imagined the robotic equivalents exercised—he slowly prodded the object from the gouge mark with the tip of his knife blade. He held it up. It was barely a half-inch, brown, and crumbled at the edges. When his wrist lights shone on it, the surface glittered.

"Prairie dog turd?"

"Funny guy." Rome climbed out of the car. "Run a scan of the entire interior. Every surface."

Aldo rolled his eyes. "Really? Their automaton Cliff would have done it."

"His systems were screwed up. Whatever results he got were compromised by the robbers' intrusion. Do it again."

"What about the cops' scans?"

"Good idea. Get them requisitioned from their department. Don't forget to check with the leasing company, compare any anomalies with the service and repair record for the Lexus," Rome smiled. His implant buzzed gently against his wrist. Incoming text only. "Then run the scans."

He let Aldo grumble all the way back to the Halcyon for the portable scanning unit. As soon as his partner ducked inside their car, he checked his own implant.

<Rome. Good to hear from you.>

The implant sprayed light onto his sleeve, projecting a keypad. Rome typed out his responses as fast as he could. <Likewise, Freddie. Any good news?>

<Yes and no.>

<Give me both.>

<Good: I poked around for Thad Mancos. Found his contract, and peeked.>

<Bad news?>

<Director Cho's hedging his bets, Rome. Thad's on the same case, with a promised 10 percent bonus if he rounds up the bandit crew before you and Aldo.>

"Wonderful," Rome muttered.

<Wonderful,> he typed.

<I know. Watch your rear view.>

<Same same. Later.>

Rome wiped away the holographic keypad. Aldo trudged back from the Halcyon to the Lexus, carrying a smooth-edged box in one hand. "I checked. Local LEOs didn't do a scan. Marcy's getting Cliff's records downloaded now. She should have a better idea of what they did to him, what data he's got, and whether any of it is reliable."

Rome nodded. "You still got friends in DOD?"

"If by friends you mean a handful of people I trust in three different state National Guards? Then, yes." Aldo let go of the box. It hovered in place three feet off the ground and hummed. Five red lights blinked, one on each end and one on top. The container unfolded into a small aerial drone, complete with ducted fans and sensor posts. "Doubt they have access to stuff that's Special Forces grade."

"But they may have heard something. Get them to work."

Aldo smirked. "Already did on the trip out from Seattle."

The scanner flew through the passenger side of the Lexus. Beams of light played over every surface.

"Oh, and that list? The one of cars versus old coin owners? Got some potential matches."

"Spill."

"There's a gal who rides out from Pierre to Madison every couple months. Next trip is in a few days."

"Good work. We can get there in plenty of time to shadow her, provided there's no dust advisories."

"Gabriela didn't wait around?"

"Couldn't. She's taking Thad to his drop-off."

"Right. The mysterious destination."

"Not so mysterious," Rome said. "He's headed onto the same job."

Aldo tugged at his beard. "Okay then. It's a race."

Chapter Four

The half hour stop on the way to the Wisconsin border increased their travel time to twelve hours. Rome heard nothing from the Pennington County Sheriff's Department at Rapid City, which made him wonder when they'd bother to let him know about Alexis Ruiz's hearing.

"Knowing our luck, they'll signal us right out of sleep at six a.m. and demand a video link." Aldo had his eyes firmly pressed shut.

The sun was just beginning its crawl over the eastern horizon. The Halcyon drove down the steep stretch where the Ninety followed the Mississippi River for a few miles before it crossed sharply over the bridge at French Island. Rome decided that calling it an island these days was a misnomer. The river's level was so low there wasn't a drop of water between French and neighboring Onalaska—just some dried out former marshes.

Traffic swam along the highway under a huge gray arch that spanned from one guardrail to the other. Iridescent solar panels lined the top, shining purple and pink with the dawn. On the underside, sensors dedicated to each lane made note of every vehicle that passed underneath, going both east and west.

The Halcyon's dash pinged softly as they drove under. A notice glowed, informing Rome that the toll for using the Ninety in Wisconsin had been paid. It even showed the percentage breakdown between the state, federal DOT, and FTZ West charges.

"Wake up, Aldo." Rome elbowed him. "Marcy, time to intercept."

[Indicated vehicle is traveling east at a speed of 85 miles per hour. Estimated intercept time based on rates of travel for both cars is sixty-eight minutes.]

Aldo cracked open an eye. "See? I got an hour."

"No, you don't. Get your brain up and running. I don't need you climbing out of a fog when we're driving later."

Aldo groaned. "Okay, all right." He straightened, working a kink out of one shoulder. His seat shifted from a reclined position to upright and relaxed its grip. "Here we go."

The holographic display gave Rome everything he would ever want to know about Eve Sartorian. A full body image of her rotated. It was from a benefit mobile art gala in Minneapolis earlier this spring. She was an inch taller than him and had her blonde hair cut shorter than his. Eyes like ice—a blue so pale they were almost gray. Her jacket and skirt were bright red, though they shifted from a deep vermilion to a soft violet before turning red again as she walked through the crowd of wealthy elites,

"Evelyn Harper Sartorian," Aldo said. "Age 36. Civilly united to Daniel Trong since 2056. Second union. No marriages. He lives in Modesto. Runs the HR department of a farm tower conglomerate at Reno."

"Less on him, more on her."

"Well, she mostly likes spending money. Parents run Solo Source, a power core manufacturer—started it themselves back in '39. Sartorian has a degree in marketing from SUNY—never set foot there, but makes sure they get healthy donations every summer." A list of financial transactions scrolled by Sartorian's smiling image. "Between her trust and her partner, she's loaded."

"So, what's with the coins?"

"Nobody can hack into coins," Aldo said with a smirk. "By my estimate, she's sunk a million and a half into rare and valuable mints. I say 'estimate' because she's one of those people who still makes banknote withdrawals."

Rome frowned. "You can't get cash anywhere. Federal Reserve dropped them way before it was disbanded."

"Not cash. Banknotes. As in, issued by individual banks, backed by precious metals, redeemable across state lines thanks to the Interstate Finance and Commerce Accord. You only use them if you want to buy something completely off record. So, I get the million and a half based on those withdrawals. She could be using them for something other than coins, but considering her purchase records, I doubt it."

"Meaning what?"

Aldo waved a hand, fingers rippling through the holo as if it were water. "I mean, look at all the junk she buys! Perfumes, bags, clothes, paintings, sculptures, enough shoes to put a battalion in heels! My dad always told me stereotypes exist for a reason. Well, she's one of them."

"What's her ride of choice?"

"Ah. That's the good news." Aldo reached into the holo and grabbed a line of text. It expanded outward like an inflated balloon until it showed the full registration of a very sleek, wide car with a silver body and white trim.

Rome thought it looked flatter than most cars on the road, and certainly several feet longer.

"Ain't that gorgeous? A 2050 Rishi Talon. Sure, she's seventeen, but Rishi made some of the best cruisers around. Smart automatons, superb guidance systems, and whisper quiet. Riding in one of those is better than your bed rolling down the road."

"I don't suppose it helps our case that Rishi's been out of business for five years now."

"Actually, it does. Tesla took over the codes and maintenance for all Rishi models when they bought out their remaining stock… not to mention the handful of manufacturing plants." Aldo magnified the car. "Makes the automation easier to crack, for a genius like me."

"With Marcy's help."

"Yeah, sure, I guess she's a decent guide, but this…" Aldo touched his implant. "And especially this..." He tapped the side of his head. "Make the magic happen."

"Please tell me that never works when you're trying to pick up a girl."

"Every time."

"I need holographic evidence."

"You wish."

Aldo spent the next hour working with Marcy on a program that could subvert control of the Rishi Talon away from its comp and over to the Halcyon. However it worked, Rome didn't care. He just wanted to get Sartorian out of harm's way when and if these bandits showed.

He watched the westbound traffic blur by and admired the trees that lined the far side of the Ninety. Most were green, though he saw scattered, rotted trunks with decrepit limbs and leaves that turned yellow at the core. They were tattered. It was a miracle this part of Wisconsin had as many left as it did, considering how fast the Palser Blight spread along the travel lanes across the continent.

Something about Aldo's actions bothered him. Whoever the robbers were, they could seize control of a car's systems. They proved that when they knocked over Joe Brace's automaton Cliff and kept the Lexus right where they wanted it. So why not do what other thieves were known to do? Why not hijack the car right before a destination and steer it off course to waiting thieves?

No. Wealthier travelers had top security systems. Even if it got hacked, the Rishi Talon would still alert local law enforcement, and if Sartorian spent nearly as much on her ride as she did on herself, she'd have it equipped with a stun system to keep intruders out. So maybe that was it. Maybe this crew did their work en route, like a handful of other gangs to minimize those risks.

"Rome."

"Hmm?" He realized he'd been staring out the window for a long enough spell he'd missed Aldo making a face at him.

"Are you gonna answer or do I get to slap your wrist and tell them you'll call back?"

Rome glanced down at his implant. Kelsey had signaled him for the last few minutes. "Right. Thanks."

"No problem, clueless Driver."

Rome keyed the response. "Hey."

"Hey yourself. I wanted you to know before FTZ buzzed in—Jake and his friends were cited for protesting last night."

"Protesting? Protesting what?" Here he thought his son had shut off his tag because he wanted to go drinking.

"Corporate greed. Federal decline," Kelsey's tiny image shrugged. Even at this small resolution he saw dark circles under her eyes and could tell her hair was unkempt—the hallmarks of a mother waiting up late. "His friends are apparently all-in with the New Federalists."

Rome rolled his eyes. "Perfect. Last thing we need is our eighteen-year-old screaming at people about how more of our taxes should go to putting the federal stranglehold back in place. Roads, parks, and the military are enough."

"Some people would rather the central government were stronger."

"Those people aren't the states. I think every capital from Augusta to Juneau is happy enough with the status quo."

Kelsey wrinkled her nose. It simultaneously made Rome want to kiss her and kill the signal because—as cute as it was—it also meant she was getting pissed off.

"You know what? I… never mind. I didn't call to argue. He's going to wind up with this stamp on his record."

"Don't worry about it. He'll get community service. It's legal to protest, as long as it's nonthreatening."

"Well, FTZ decided it was threatening."

Rome made a face. "It was on FTZ property?"

"The toll gate on the Massachusetts border. They painted it… with eagles."

Aldo broke out into a laugh. Rome glared at him. The laugh quickly morphed into a coughing fit, with words like "superb" and "dashed" among the intelligible parts.

"I'll put in a signal to the director at East. See what he can do. They'll have him wipe down maintenance drones for the next month or two."

"You need to talk to him about this. I can't keep tabs on him anymore."

"You don't need to. He's an adult."

"Except he's still living here and we still have to pay for his mistakes!" Kelsey sounded exasperated. Rome figured it was with him or Jake. "I got a fine and a notation on my record because he's listed as a taxable resident at my home."

"Okay, relax. I'll talk to him."

"You always say that, Rome."

"Look, I said I will."

Kelsey shook her head. "Don't let me down… again. And make sure you're in town for the concert—"

"I know, Friday night, seven."

"Vivian will be heartbroken if you don't show."

Just Vivian? Rome didn't say it aloud. Instead he nodded and smiled. "I'll see you all later."

"Right. See you."

The cabin went silent. Rome stared at the frozen image of Kelsey's face.

Aldo cleared his throat. "That right there? Why I'm never getting married or unioned."

The Rishi Talon registered to Sartorian appeared on the tracking display precisely when Marcy calculated it would.

"Keep us at a reasonable distance, Marcy," Rome said. "No more than ten car lengths and no less than six."

[Complying.]

The Halcyon proceeded as an ordinary member of the herd of cars that trekked the Ninety, changing lanes when necessary to form long lines for more efficient travel. Huge freighters rushed by in packs of threes and fours and—in one instance—twelve in a row.

"Okay, we should be all set." Aldo squirmed in his seat. "I've got the program ready to upload. Marcy, how's the link look?"

[Nominal. The Rishi Talon's operating system is compatible with our own. I am anticipating less than 5 percent likelihood it will fail.]

Aldo grinned. "Atta girl. See, Rome?"

Rome's hands itched for the steering column. Rather than grasping for something that wasn't there yet, he drummed out a beat on his legs. "Good deal. You have a backup plan if we hit that 5 percent?"

"Sure I do." Aldo swiped through a series of commands. "Hey... ah... if you want music on, I can crank up the speakers."

"No, I'm good. Got a tune in my head already."

"Rome, if you want to drive, just do it."

"Not a good idea. As soon as I do that we alert every navigation system within a mile that there's a registered Driver in play. You think our bandit pals are going to miss that?"

Aldo winced. "Oh yeah. Right."

"Yeah. We play like we're on a relaxed road trip until they show up."

It only took five minutes before Marcy's proximity sensors chimed. Good thing, too. Rome was running out of beats.

"Here they come," Aldo announced. "Big old black ride. Sorry, I got nothing yet. Marcy, anything?"

[Vehicle is of undetermined origin. Chassis matches a Raytheon Hammershot all-terrain personnel transport, however, it has been the subject of numerous and uncatalogued modifications.]

Rome wondered at the perceived frostiness of her tone. Did a comp like Marcy take it personally when cars were illegally modded? "Passive sensors only, you two. Get me everything you can without tipping them off we're here."

"Roger that." Aldo pulled Marcy's sensor results onto his display. There it was—that same mottled gray, hunchbacked vehicle from the drone video Cho showed them. Aldo wrinkled his nose as if he smelled something particularly foul. "Man. That is one ugly mongrel ride. Like a cockroach mated with a cow."

"No argument there." The sensors showed him armored plating in places he hadn't noticed on the recording. The windows and windshields were colored with the same camouflaged pattern, blending them seamlessly with the armor until Marcy highlighted them in the scan results. "What've we got?"

[The exterior is a reinforced ceramic composite, overlaid with an adaptive camouflage screen. The quality compares with U.S. military databases from the past several years.]

"I don't suppose there's any way to penetrate that screen once they go ghost on us."

[There is no known method.]

"Okay then. Aldo?"

"I'll get cracking. It'll be easier to try to break if we could turn the hi-res scanners on."

"Not until we show ourselves. Marcy, authorize for pursuit but do not—repeat, do not switch modes until I say so."

[Certification confirmed. You are authorized to conduct pursuit. Delaying activation until your signal.]

The suspect vehicle drove up in the left lane, rumbling along with an engine a couple octaves lower than the rest of the traffic. It was certainly more powerful than a Famtrac.

"Sounds like there's a dual core underneath."

Aldo grunted. "Probably. Energy output sure is surpassing most everything else out here."

Cars moved from the left lane into the right with the grace of geese adjusting their formation. Rome checked the rear view images—only a freighter in the left lane a quarter mile back.

Aldo's comment about the energy output struck Rome. "We've got a problem. Marcy, are you picking up any active scanning from the target?"

[None. They are, however, initiating a link between their vehicle and the network governing the safety protocols in this section of road.]

"Going for the Talon," Aldo said. "Wait... why did you ask her that?"

"Because they could scan that our power core is definitely not civilian standard," Rome said. "Run up that program and get inside the Talon."

"You got it." Aldo flicked his fingers across the hologram. "And... done."

"Don't do anything with the car yet. We don't want to let them know we've got it."

The truck slowed down as it approached the Talon. Rome noted the tactical adjustments from the first robbery. They lined up with the prime passenger side this time—what would be the driver's side on the Halcyon. Anyone could see through the darkened glass that Sartorian was the sole occupant.

"Hey... hey! They're establishing the link," Aldo said. "Trying to override her navigation system."

A docking collar slowly arched out from the right side of the truck.

"Marcy, go manual," Rome snapped. "Aldo, block them!"

"On it."

The steering column and pedals appeared, followed by the gearshift. Marcy turned on the lights. Blue and red flashes bounced off the cars around them. Rome switched lanes and raced up behind the truck, both of them topping 100 miles per hour.

"Okay, I've got Sartorian's nav under Marcy's guidance," Aldo said. "We can get her off the road at the next exit. There's one coming up in twenty miles."

Rome glanced at the blinking blue star on the holo of the Ninety. "Marcy, clear the road and open a signal to the truck."

Cars behind them fell back. The remaining traffic slowed ahead. Cars, Famtracs, and freighters drifted over to the road's shoulders.

[There is no acknowledgement of our signal.]

"Go public channel, then."

[Done.]

"Illegal driver, this is Pursuit One Twelve, operating by authority of the U.S. Department of Transportation on behalf of the Ninety Free Travel Zone. You are operating an unregistered motor vehicle on a public roadway. Pull over to the side and relinquish control—"

The modified truck accelerated away.

"Et cetera, et cetera," Rome muttered. He stomped on the accelerator.

"Rome, I don't think I'm gonna be able to knock off his nav system," Aldo said. "Marcy can't find me any way in."

"Not even their entertainment?"

"Doesn't have one." Aldo frowned. "I'll be damned if I can figure out how they're getting any nav."

"They might not have it."

"You think they're old school? No way. They're broadcasting something, because they're knocking at the door of the Talon. Only reason they haven't swiped control from us is that program of mine."

The truck swerved into the right lane. A freighter barreled left, avoiding a collision as the truck rushed to fill the space it vacated. Suddenly the freighter braked, hard… too hard.

Rome punched out of the center lane, shearing dangerously close to a Famtrac. The safety alert from the family vehicle's comp flashed across the dashboard.

"Uh, we got a problem."

"You think? I doubt that freighter tried to butt me off the highway by following standard protocol." Rome raced past the freighter. A Famtrac slipped into the left lane, ahead of the freighter, allowing Rome passage. "They aren't controlling all the other cars at once. Marcy, call it in—we have a breach in the navigational and safety networks on the Ninety prior to Madison. Send the coordinates."

[Contacting Condor Three Three and FTZ Central,] Marcy said.

"I blocked them out of that freighter," Aldo said. "But it's a temporary wall. I can reinforce the network protocols for this vicinity."

"Better get on it." The truck was few hundred yards ahead, plowing its way through traffic. Rome wove a path back and forth, coming within a couple feet of a Famtrac, close enough he saw startled faces in several windows.

An alert flashed in Aldo's displays. He looked incredulous. "What? No, no way."

"Words, Aldo." Rome tightened his grip on the steering handles.

[Malfunctioning car approaching from behind, 100 miles per hour.]

"The Talon! They broke through my program." Aldo's hands furiously swiped through his displays, but instead of green positive results, red lines appeared. "Are you kidding me? That isn't possible!"

"Get ahold of the Talon before they paste Sartorian's guts all over a guardrail," Rome snapped. "Marcy, dial up the EMP."

[Use of the electromagnetic pulse projectiles is prohibited in pursuit when the volume and speed of traffic exceeds—]

"I know the regs! Override, Code Zulu Zero Zulu, confirm authority."

[Confirmed. Charging EMP.]

An angry pitched hum built along the sides of the Halcyon below the doorframes. In the rear view screen, Sartorian's Talon rushed up. Rome cranked the wheel, putting them into the shoulder. Dirt and grass churned up as the right side tires grew their deeper treads. The Halcyon tried to fishtail but Rome fought against the drag.

The Talon shot by. He saw Sartorian. Her expression was one of open-mouthed fear. She slapped her hands soundlessly against the windows.

Two more Famtracs ahead of them braked.

"Screw them!" Aldo yelled. "They're jumping from system to system. I get them locked out of one—"

"Less explaining, more doing!" Rome checked the gauge Marcy ran in the center of the dash. Two-thirds full.

"You'd better get a clear line of fire or you're gonna put a bunch of passengers into the worst pile-up since the early 20s."

"Yeah, I know. Thanks." He didn't have a lot of options. That truck hadn't grabbed Sartorian—which was a bonus—but they were hijacking the signals of every vehicle around them. Not more than two at a time, though. A good shot with the EMP would shut them down and get them off the road. He hoped.

"Got it!" Aldo pumped his fist.

At the last possible second, the Famtracs moved aside, leaving Rome just enough space to squeeze the Halcyon through. The car straddled the center-line.

"There is something else we can do, you know." Aldo sounded as guilty as a student who got busted trying to alter his grades.

Rome nodded. "Not legal in the slightest, not without a judge's express permission."

"Probably will get some of the bounty docked."

"Rather have that than dead passengers. Do it."

Aldo sighed and flicked at a pair of commands in his holograms.

The suspect truck abruptly braked because several freighters broke free from their long line of cohorts and separated across all three lanes. They closed their distance enough so the truck could not squeeze between them. The Talon slowed, too, falling in tandem with the suspect truck.

Their exit was coming up soon. Where was that EMP? "Marcy..."

[Power level at 95 percent.]

"Aldo, keep those two steady. Marcy, clear out as much traffic from around us as you can."

[I have been doing just that. However, several interruptions in the network have made that work difficult.]

"We're good to go," Aldo said. "FYI, got at least ten vehicles coming to the on-ramp at that exit. They try driving into this mess and they're toast."

"Keep 'em out." The target truck grew larger. They were 200 yards away.

Rome flipped the cap off the top of the right handle, revealing a silver button encircled by bright red ring. His thumb poised over it.

[EMP fully charged. Targeting.]

A reticle bracketed the truck. Rome eyeballed it, exhaled a breath he realized he'd been holding…

"Got a power surge!" Aldo said.

The truck rippled and disappeared.

The Talon cranked left, into the line of fire.

Rome's thumb stabbed the button but he simultaneously jerked the steering handles hard left. "Hell!"

Blue-white exploded at the front of the car like lightning. It streaked out in waves. Rome's last-minute maneuver had been enough, though. The EMP burst smacked into the rear of the leftmost freighter. Lights and signals from it died out as bolts stuttered across its surface. The automaton in command had enough foresight to aim for the median in time before the pulse turned its brain off. The freighter drifted off the road and then toppled on its side. No humans aboard to harm, but it dug a long scrape in the grass. The Talon continued down the road, unharmed—a small comfort to Rome as the Halcyon barreled into the median.

There were no trees—mercifully—just a sharp bank. He gritted his teeth and corrected the steering as best he could. It was enough to keep them level. The Halcyon spun out, coming to a jarring halt facing the south.

[I have lost telemetry on Ms. Sartorian's vehicle,] Marcy said. [And the suspect's. The Halcyon is undamaged.]

Aldo gasped, drawing in deep breaths. "Wow."

"Yeah." Rome couldn't let go of the column.

Chapter Five

They found the Talon with Sartorian inside, dumped behind a waste incinerator not far from the first off-ramp into Madison.

She was slumped against the passenger side door, cradling her arm. Rome could smell something burnt and sickly sweet. Sartorian's eyes were bloodshot and her tears had made a mess of her makeup.

"Ma'am? Pursuit Specialist Jasko." Rome leaned in through the open door. At least the thieves hadn't ripped that one off. "I'm here to help."

Sartorian shied away as if she could push herself deeper into the door and disappear from her environment. She held up her hands, covering her face. Rome saw the angry red and black gouge on her left wrist.

They took her implant, too.

"LEOs, Rome." Aldo stood beside the Halcyon. A torrent of information spilled from his implant.

"You'd better strip everything you can from her comp, then." Rome did a quick sweep of the vehicle's interior, ignoring Sartorian's wordless whimpers. He didn't see any coins. He checked the floor. There were the same bits of material as in Joe Brace's car. He bagged one, then reached for Sartorian. "Ma'am? The police are here. Please."

She shook her head. Her gaze was wild with fear. "Get away from me."

So much for trying. Rome scuffed at the shoulder of the road where the thieves had dumped the car. Green grass. Bright green. He could tell it was watered, probably by drip irrigation. He wondered how much that cost the city. Since it sat on a lake that was still mostly full, it probably was not as much as it would have cost Rapid City.

"We've got tracks over here," Aldo said.

"I saw them. Marcy, you got a scan for us?"

[Confirmed. I am running a search for matching tread.]

"Atta girl." Rome glanced up the street into the city. A pair of Madison PD black and whites rolled up, their lights bouncing blue and red off the sloped white walls of the incinerator complex. "Aldo..."

"Yeah, I know, I'm done."

Once a crime was reported inside city limits, it was technically hands off for pursuit contractors. Local LEOs got the call. It was up to them to handle the case. That said, nothing prevented drivers like Rome and info techs like Aldo from scooping up every bit of evidence they could prior to the cops' arrival, especially with a substantial bounty on the wire.

There were four officers—a stocky sergeant with thinning brown hair who looked as pale as the incinerator building, and three young guys who couldn't be any more than a few years out of the Academy. Two still had their heads shaved, while one sported a blond crew cut. Blondie had sideburns that reached all the way down to the base of his chin.

"Victor Two Two and Two Seven on scene," the sergeant said. "Ten Forty-Six."

Rome stood with Aldo, their hands clasped in front of them. His gun was in the Halcyon, as were both spazzers. No need to up any tension with the presence of firearms. "Morning, officers."

"Bronsky, you and Devereaux check on the victim."

"She's in shock," Rome said. "They cut out her implant and attempted a sloppy cauterization of the wound."

The sergeant's gaze dipped down to the badge on Rome's belt. "ID."

Both Rome and Aldo held out their wrists. A drone the size of a softball with the appearance of a flattened cylinder floated behind the sergeant, buzzing on tiny turbofans. It cast a red light on their implants. No happy chirps or vocal confirmation from that unit.

The sergeant looked at his own implant. Whatever it said about them, Rome figured it would not lighten the mood. The man's brow was so furrowed with lines Rome could take up farming atop his bushy eyebrows.

"Pursuit specialists." He said the last word as if it were a joke and a swear word rolled into one.

"Yes, sir." A "sir" never hurt, especially where city LEOs were concerned. "We're on contract with FTZ West to investigate and detain a group of drivers who have robbed several vehicles along the Ninety. We were tracking Ms. Sartorian as a potential victim."

The sergeant snorted. "Bang-up job. They got away."

"That happens." This guy qualified as a new entry on Rome's list of people he'd like to hit with the Halcyon. "I'd say you guys should go after them, but, you know…" he shrugged and smiled.

The sergeant headed for the car, stone-faced.

"Don't go anywhere," Blondie said.

"Wasn't planning on it."

After he left, Aldo chuckled. "Man. You just can't help it."

"Needling LEOs like that prick about the fact that they can't drive? Nope." Being polite didn't hurt. Cutting a martinet like that sergeant down a few notches didn't hurt, either. "Did Marcy find anything interesting?"

"Whoever their tech is, he's good. They put their own software into Sartorian's ride, but when they scrammed, it self-deleted. Marcy found a few bits of code that don't belong to the Talon. Might be able guess what it looked like, but don't hold your breath."

"Something's better than nothing."

"You?"

"Same bits of gunk as in Joe Brace's car, back in Billings." Rome dipped two fingers into his jacket pocket and tugged out the evidence bag. "Dump it on the seat."

"So Marcy can scan? Right." Aldo scratched his stomach with his left hand, while the right bumped against the glass. "Open Sesame."

The window slid apart a few inches. Aldo flicked the bag inside.

"Run a comparison, Marcy," Rome murmured.

[Affirmative.] This time, the response came through his implanted earpiece instead of the car's speakers.

"Sergeant Dickhead returns," Aldo said.

The sergeant limped. A slight mechanical whine with each step of his right leg told Rome it was a powered model, all the way up to the hip. "You boys give me access to your chase log?"

Rome folded his arms. "Not required."

"No, but it will make things easier for her insurance. The VIC says she had sixty grand in collectible coins with her. Those were the second to go, after the implant."

"Give me a moment for my comp to redact the contract specific data."

The sergeant appeared to chew on some words he'd like to spit Rome's way, but Rome knew he'd keep the exchange civil. The tiny, white and purple light blinking on his badge confirmed it. Everything about the conversation and the crime scene in general was being recorded—audio and visual—plus whatever kind of scans the drone conducted. Everything was streamed live to Madison PD.

"That would work."

"One second." Rome leaned closer to Aldo, and lowered his voice. "Everything related to their ride's scans."

"And our case notes. Got it." Aldo swiped in non-verbal commands to Marcy.

"Should have it in a moment, Sergeant," Rome said. "Anything else we can do?"

"Just one." The sergeant reached for the drone. It shuddered and spit out a slim rectangle of transparent plastic. Words and numbers skittered across the surface in black type lined with a blue glow. "Safety and navigation violations, at least eight, by our count. Pay them before you depart city limits."

Rome frowned. The one part of this gig he hated. Sure, he was authorized to drive when hardly anyone else was, and he could break the rules whenever he needed to in order to catch his target, but that didn't mean he got away completely clean. The fines levied by local municipalities and counties were independent of FTZ oversight. Part of the pittance paid so that FTZ alone maintained its say over how the Ninety operated. And it came out of his pay after taxes.

Rome took the slip. "Old school, Sergeant."

"There's a digital copy in your account now." The sergeant smiled with as much pleasantness as a man chewing on asphalt projected. "Your presence is no longer required at this crime scene." He joined his officers at the Talon.

An ambulance arrived. It was a white, oblong vehicle with pulsing red lines on all sides.

"This mean we're dismissed?" Aldo asked.

Later that morning, thick clouds gathered overhead and dumped rain on what seemed like the entire southern half of Wisconsin. It was pouring when Gabriela scooped them up in the Condor.

"You guys are going to have to re-color," she said. "Have you seen the Net?"

Rome rubbed his brow. "No. Please don't tell me what I think you're going to tell me."

She ran two vids from the display glass at her right. Both showed their Halcyon running after the thieves' truck while the rest of traffic went haywire, followed by the abortive EMP blast and Rome's barely controlled spin out.

"Nice move." Aldo took a huge bite from a pastry. A white, recycled paper bag sat on the console, its bottom soggy with grease. It was as wet as Aldo's shoes, which were propped on the same unit.

"Shut up."

"Aldrich! Get your gear off my console!" Gabriela shouted.

Aldo demolished half the pastry. He licked his fingers. "Okay, Rome, we're ever in Madison again we have to stop at that place. Best donuts, period."

Rome shoved his chair. Aldo's feet dropped to the deck with a bang, and his pastry fell top-down. Icing smeared on the metal. "Our car's image is all over the Net, thanks to our screw-up."

"Our screw-up? Hey, I didn't take a potshot at a freighter with an EMP in broad daylight."

"You were supposed to keep the Talon under our aegis. Somebody beat you to it."

Aldo scowled.

"Gabriela, send to FTZ West that we need a new set of registration numbers unlocked," Rome said. "I'm going back to run the re-color."

"Tell Marcy I'm not doing green again," Aldo called after him. "That last shade she picked was nasty... pea soup."

"Still with his stomach," Rome muttered.

It was louder back in the car bay, with the thrum from the Condor's engines and the hiss of the rain against the fuselage. Everything shuddered and bounced. Rome reached for a handhold, steadying himself as he gazed at the Halcyon. His expression stared back from the sleek curve of the hood—short black hair matted to his head by the rain, eyes as brown as soil, high cheekbones, blocky chin. There was a flash of light where his crucifix had come free of his shirt collar—simple gold on a black cord.

"Marcy, link with FTZ and get a new set of registration numbers," he said. "Should be in the pipe."

[Confirming. New registration acquired. Eleven more possible registration numbers also stored for later use. Shall I commence with color alteration?]

"Go for it, but no green. Aldo insists."

[Complying.] The car body became suffused with heat. The white slowly darkened and changed the hue to a deep maroon. Gray panels shifted to match the same shade.

They'd let that truck escape, but it wasn't his fault. Aldo fouled up his control software, somehow. Or was it because their opponents were that much better? Rome tucked the crucifix back under his shirt. No one gave them the slip like that before. Then again, none of their targets had ever sported a ride that could disappear.

Speaking of disappear, the Halcyon's registration numbers printed in black and silver on both flanks evaporated. A new set of numbers wrote themselves in black and gold.

[Reconfiguration complete,] Marcy said. [Registration is modified. Exterior color redone and holding.]

"Thanks, Marcy."

[You are welcome... I have results of the materials comparison, which you requested.]

"Spill it."

[The material recovered from the Lexus and from the Talon is identical. It is a silica rich soil fragment, comprised of—]

"Not interested in the specifics, Marcy. I need to know to what degree they match, and they need a location." Rome knew Marcy didn't really care, but he got the impression interruptions were considered a violation of her social etiquette programming.

[The two samples share composition to within 99.2 percent of each other. As for location...]

Rome's implant chirped. Marcy transferred the summary of her report there. When Rome triggered its receipt, a map that fit into the palm of his hand hovered a half foot over his wrist. He recognized the terrain, though it wasn't as familiar as the western region of the Ninety. "Appalachians."

[Correct. Specifically, the silica is found in farming soil used in this region.]

"Marcy, do you have any idea how many farms and agro-towers

there are in eastern Ohio and western Pennsylvania alone?"

[They number in the hundreds. Shall I audibly list them?]

"No thanks."

[The summary is compiled with the rest of my report.]

"What about the upholstery swatch? That coconut smell..."

[It is from a lotion used in sunscreen. Three brands of SPF 160 and greater add the fragrance to mask the pungent odor of the primary compound that blocks damage from ultra-violet rays. All three were created in the late 2020s after the predominant sunscreens were shown to increase risk factors for certain kinds of cancers by 25 percent.]

That was the problem with autonomous computers—they could amass and relay a ton of information, with astonishing speed and accuracy. But their ersatz personalities couldn't quite get the knack of withholding info when their owners found it tedious. "Narrow it down for me, Marcy."

Red splotches appeared throughout the holographic map. [These represent the areas where all three sunscreens are sold. Thirty-six overlap with known agriculture centers.]

"You can rule out the agro-towers. Sunscreen like this, it'd be used by folks working outdoors."

Several splotches disappeared. [I am left with fourteen possibilities.]

Rome considered them. A few were right smack on the Ninety—rest areas set up great distances from major population centers. Too many vehicles. Too many chances the thieves would get noticed one way or another—either themselves or their truck. How long could that thing run invisible? He wished Aldo would pester his Army buddy more for answers. "Marcy, how many of those fourteen locations have facilities that could accommodate a truck with the dimensions of the one we're chasing?"

Five more places vanished. That left nine blotches.

Rome smiled. Three were way too far off the Ninety to be of any use to the thieves—between sixty and one hundred miles away. That left six possibilities. "Highlight the six that are fewer that sixty miles from the highway. Start monitoring local communications. If they've got equipment powerful enough to jam the nav systems of multiple vehicles, then you should be able to get a whiff of their signal strength."

[Tapping into local communications networks. Shall I concentrate on the nav systems between cars and satellites, as well as their ground relays?]

"Yes, but don't discount other sources. I want anything anomalous."

[Understood.]

Aldo rapped on the frame of the bay hatch. "Hey. That's a good color."

"Not green." Rome doused the hologram. "We've got some matches from the samples we pulled out of Brace's and Sartorian's cars."

"Nice." Aldo brushed at his beard, dislodging crumbs. "So, I... uh... heard back from one of my boys in the Army National Guard. Michigan."

"Let me guess—they manufacture those stealth transports in Michigan."

"Yeah, outside Grand Rapids at Bacevich Arsenal."

Rome sat on the hood of the Halcyon.

"Seems one of the newest ones went missing. One minute, she was rolling out from under the robot arms, and the next—poof."

"You'd think the Army would notice something like that."

"That's the thing. They have." Aldo grinned. "My buddy tells me there's no report on the disappearance, no inquiry, nothing. He thinks the brass doesn't want word leaking out that something like this is driving around in public. His superiors are furious that it might have gotten sold overseas."

"No kidding. I'd hate to be the base commander who had to admit that the Superior Arms Embargo was broken."

"I know, right?" Aldo made a face. "Can you imagine selling a stealth transport like that to the Russian remnants? Or Greater Egypt?"

Rome shook his head. "Don't suppose your pal can send us any hard data."

"No way. His base's info flow is locked down. The security vids and holos at Bacevich Arsenal are all stashed on comps that can only be accessed in person. So, unless you can get the FTZ chiefs to snuggle up to the base commander…" Aldo shrugged.

"Yeah. We'll have to figure the best way to do that."

"Um, other than bouncing a signal to Director Cho?"

"He's got Thad following this case, too."

"Okay, that sucks."

"Yeah. Insurance, in case we foul up."

"What, and then he gets the bounty? No way."

"Look, Marcy's narrowing our search even further. We've got a half dozen possible locations for the thieves' base of operations. Get up to Gabriela, tell her we're flying for western Pennsylvania."

Aldo hadn't taken more than two steps before Gabriela's voice scratched through the intercom. "Hey boys? You've got a possible bounty. Unregistered driver, headed west toward Rockford."

"Alter course," Rome said. "We can nab that one on our way to—"

"Already done. I'll drop you in ten minutes." The Condor shuddered. "Assuming this weather doesn't get any worse. You might want to buckle in."

Neither one argued. Rome and Aldo got in the Halcyon and let Marcy set up the restraints in cocoon-like fashion.

Aldo grimaced. "Shouldn't have had that donut. I hate getting dropped."

Anchors lowered from the bay ceiling like tentacles. They sealed with the roof and sides of the Halcyon. The deck underneath rumbled.

"Marcy, do we have a lock on this unregistered driver?"

[Affirmative, sir.]

Rome nodded. "You know the routine."

Gabriela flew the Condor down through the low clouds, scudding at treetop height. She found a road not far from the Ninety off-ramp that was—for the moment—devoid of traffic. There were only fields and a handful of abandoned buildings, some of which were no more than burnt out shells.

The bottom of the Condor's bay cracked open.

Rome ran the engine and spun the wheels as the anchors lowered the car through the open hatch. Marcy's dash indicator showed the Condor's airspeed at a bare 80 miles per hour.

The Halcyon's wheels hit the pavement in a spray of water. Rome accelerated. The anchors snapped free and he sped toward the ramp. The car swerved for a moment, but he steadied her out.

[Road conditions are poor for pursuit,] Marcy said. [Exercise caution.]

"Noted."

The target car drew near to the ramp. The tracker had it bracketed through the tree line to Rome's left, even though he couldn't see any hint of it. Everything outside the windows was a blue and gray version of the normal mix of colors. Not a single set of headlights, other than the luminescent panels on the Famtracs, freighters, and other cars.

"I know the tactical reasons for what we just did." Aldo wiped sweat from his face. "Can I just say, for the record, that it sucks?"

"Also noted." Rome drove up the ramp. "Here it comes."

"I'm on it, I'm on it." For all his whining, Aldo already had a navigation co-option program prepared. "Acquiring the signal."

The car appeared, weaving amidst the cars. Even without the bracket and the dangerous maneuvers, Rome could have marked it as their target. Bright halogen lamps projected sharp beams of blue-white through the gloom.

"Moron," Aldo said. "He might as well put a tag on his roof that says 'Hey! Illegal driving going on here!'"

"Judging by his ride, he's not worried about being discreet." Rome watched the bright orange car with a yellow lightning bolt streak by—eye-watering neon among drab passenger vehicles. "Don't complain. An easy bounty's the best kind. You ready?"

Aldo grinned at the displays, his face suffused with green and blue light. "Oh, yeah, I'm synced. Say the word and we'll pull him over."

"Let's give him a chance to come quietly first. In this weather, we don't want to be chasing him all over Creation."

Rome got Marcy's confirmation to drive, and once he had control, he lit up the emergency beacons. He steered right onto the car's rear, two car lengths back, and broadcast the standard message.

"He might not want to give up the ride," Aldo said. "It's a 2017 BMW. Classic ride. Can't imagine where he found parts for it—must have had them custom printed. At least it got converted over to a power core."

The BMW accelerated, spraying water behind it in a thick cloud.

"Okay, so he's rabbiting. That's your cue," Rome said.

Aldo swiped in his commands. "Done."

The BMW immediately braked, and started toward the side of the road. Adjacent traffic automatically cleared out, making a hole as the vehicle crossed three lanes. Rome drove alongside it, making sure the cars around them gave a wide enough berth.

Marcy's proximity alert sounded. [A vehicle is approaching from directly behind, on intercept with the target. It is registered as a pursuit driver.]

"The hell?" Rome looked in the rear view display. Emergency lights identical to his sparked through the rain. The car was easy enough to see—a 2066 Panther, gray-blue, with gold running stripes. It barreled down on them with no signs of stopping.

"Watch out!"

Rome cranked the steering column. The Halcyon slipped back into the far left lane, and the Panther shot by, spraying the windshield with water. Something slapped against the door, on Aldo's side. Rome was just about to query Marcy for a scan when the internal lights flickered.

[Power drain. Core output reduced to 70 percent, and dropping.]

Just like that, his speed fell, too. Rome still had control. He steered toward the left side of the road, but no matter how he stomped on the accelerator or changed gears, he couldn't get any more power to the engine.

"Found it," Aldo said. "Pulse inflictor. Thing's latched right on the side of the car, behind my door."

He enlarged the miniature hologram of the Halcyon. A tiny sphere protruded from the otherwise smooth body. It was black with three gray stripes around it. Orange lights trickled across the center.

"It's gonna take me a few minutes to unlock it from our system," Aldo said. "Stupid thing is hardwired. See? Those tendrils extend from the sphere and punch directly into the command links between the power core and Marcy's CPU, and from there into the car's controls."

"We don't have a few minutes." Rome pulled over on the shoulder and braked. The car barely stopped when he popped the canopy. He stepped out into the pouring rain. His head and face were immediately soaked, though once he zipped his jacket, the clothing system dried his shirt and kept him warm.

There it was. The BMW was stopped a mile ahead with the Panther behind it. Small figures stood outside. Rome swore one of them waved.

His implant chirped. It was from Thad.

"What's that old saying? 'Snooze and you lose,' *amigo*." Laughter echoed through the speaker.

Rome glared at the implant. Aldo promised him the sphere would be unlatched in two minutes.

He walked to the other side of the Halcyon, ignoring honks from the pedestrian warning horns on passing cars. Aldo stared, wide-eyed, as he drew the Hunsaker. Two shots echoed like fireworks, shattering the sphere. The third was unnecessary to break the device, but it cleared the last fragments off the Halcyon. A ragged hole trailed ripped wires.

No wonder Thad was laughing.

Chapter Six

The forums for pursuit specialists across the states told and retold Thad's story of how he swooped in and scooped up the bounty from Rome. Aldo pointed out at least eight in which the details were far more dramatic than reality.

"Aldo, you show me one more, I'll spaz you and put a bullet through the holo generator," Rome grumbled.

Aldo switched the display to news about the flooding in Illinois and Indiana.

Rome slumped in the chair behind Gabriela. He stared out the cockpit. Sun gleamed across the canopy and he squinted in the second before it darkened to reduce glare. Up here, at 10,000 feet, the thick clouds of the massive rainstorm swaddling two states were as soft looking as cotton.

"Heck of a mess down there," Gabriela said. "I figured you guys would rather have the lift to Ohio and Pennsy than have to take about fourteen different detours."

"What, Thad didn't signal for a ride?"

She smiled. "He did. But, oh darn, I was already en route. Could be a few hours before I go back for him."

Rome smirked. "Thanks."

"Least I could do." Gabriela's smile faded. "You okay?"

"Okay as I can be when Thad steals from me."

"I thought pulse inflictors are illegal."

"They are. Since when has that ever stopped him? I've already lodged the formal protest with FTZ." That wouldn't be how to put Thad out of his way. The case was foremost on Rome's mind. He wouldn't let a petty thief like Thad rile him much when there was bigger prey out there. Besides, two could play at his games.

"I don't suppose I want to ask what toys you guys have stashed in the Halcyon these days."

Rome lifted an eyebrow.

"Like I said. Don't want to ask." Gabriela checked her console. "Should be over eastern Ohio. It's clearing out over there. You have any specific coordinates in mind or is this just a sightseeing tour?"

"Marcy's got all the details." Rome tapped commands into his implant. "Should be in your console now."

"Thanks." Gabriela reviewed the map of possibilities. "Are these in order of likelihood?"

"Proximity." Rome swiveled in his chair. "Aldo. Check on the—"

"Already on it." Aldo waved a hand through the news footage. Marcy's map replaced it. "You had her running the possible signals interference—the way the guys dug into Sartorian's car controls. She got a few results, though you can't make heads or tails out of most of them."

"That sounds bad," Gabriela said.

"Ah, it does, Gabby, but only if you don't take the extra step to narrow the focus on stuff that's intermittent, stuff that has a natural human tendency to show error." Aldo grinned. "Most of the signal traffic out there in the same wavelength is auto-regulated."

"Don't tease a gal, Aldrich."

He shrugged. "Okay, then. Voilá."

Aldo flicked his fingers at the display. It flashed. All but two of the red patches vanished.

"You got them." Rome crossed the cockpit to Aldo's console. "You're sure?"

"I'm insulted you asked."

"Got to be sure."

"I'm sure." Aldo pointed two fingers at the target areas. "First up: a rental business center, off a less-than-busy road, tucked back in a forest halfway between a small town and a main artery. Option two: a warehouse that prints bicycle frames twenty-four seven. Way less visibility, even than the rental center, but it has full-time robotic security. Drones on the perimeter, sensor pulls, you name it."

Rome frowned. "How about capacity? They need room to park that vehicle of theirs, and they can't keep it camouflaged all the time. Plus they'll require some kind of workspace."

"Either one would do. The business center has several storage units and garages on the back lot that could park a whole fleet. Same deal with the warehouse. It's got delivery trucks."

"Staffing for the business center?"

"None. Same for the warehouse."

Rome scratched at his chin.

"What's the plan, boss?"

"Gabriela, see if FTZ Central will task us a few drones to fly surveillance," Rome said. "If we can get IR scans of both places, that'll help. Anything that will show us heat signatures for bodies and machinery."

"I'll put in the request. We should have a few drones ready by the time we get over eastern Ohio." Gabriela input text into her console.

"Aldo, any difference in power draw?"

"Nope. Looks close to equal—at least, the difference is negligible. Could be that they've got shielded stuff. You know, like anyone else who doesn't want to pay into the power grid."

"Right. Come on. Let's strap in." Rome patted the back of Gabriela's chair. "Let us know when you're over the first target."

Gabriela smiled. "Shall we drop again?"

Aldo groaned.

The Condor set down on a field by an abandoned farm, its buildings long ago overtaken by the very plants it once raised. Marcy drove them through thick brown stalks, carving a path to a dirt road. The 3-D map on Aldo's display showed it intersecting with the warehouse's street by way of two winding connectors.

"Getting feed from the drones now." Aldo grasped a pile of flat image rectangles in his hologram, and spread them apart like he dealt cards.

Rome counted six images. Each one had a serial number hovering at the bottom. "Six drones total?"

"Yep. They're running IR on both buildings." Aldo split the rectangles into trios. "First up, business center."

The Halcyon bumped along the dirt road. Marcy steered them around the deepest pot-holes and largest rocks with grace. Rome drummed a beat on his legs.

"Why'd you pick this one?"

"The warehouse?" Rome shrugged. "Call it a hunch."

"The place is crawling with security."

"Security that's all electronic, all automated. You're good enough you could make it look the other way, couldn't you?"

"Of course."

"Well, then, these guys have shown the same aptitude."

Aldo frowned. "Too busy a place."

Rome just gestured at the drone scans. "Rattle off the results."

"Right. So…" Aldo enlarged the first three images. "Zip on the IR for the business center. Heat sources, yeah, but those come back as solar cells and a couple appliances. Oh, and a tiny biological signal."

"Biological?"

"Hamster. I think. Could be a guinea pig. Or a hedgehog. Hard to tell at this resolution."

Rome rolled his eyes. "Show me the warehouse."

"Same thing. Got lots of machinery." Aldo waved his hand at yellow shapes drifting slowly across all three of the other images. "Those would be the security robots. I'm getting specs uploaded."

"Look like Pikes, to me."

"More than likely." A new line of data spilled down the right side of the images. "Yep, score one for you. Pike VS Three-oh-Three."

The VS303 wasn't top of the line, but it wasn't bargain basement, either. The scan showed eight of them, patrolling in pairs on every side of the square warehouse. "That's the outside. Internal?"

"Can't access them." Aldo took a bite from a purple protein bar. It stained his teeth a pale violet. "Hmph. That's weird. I should be able to get something."

"Tell me about that." Rome pointed at a haze across the center of the warehouse.

"Could be ambient ground temps."

"Could be intentional interference."

"Maybe. We're not going to be able to tell from aerial drone scans."

Rome pressed a panel on the dash. "Condor Three Three, this is Pursuit One Twelve, copy."

"Go ahead, Pursuit One Twelve."

"We need tiny eyes on the ground in both target locations."

"Roger that. Re-tasking drones to deploy mites."

Among each trio of drones, one carried a full load of ten mites. Rome could fit three of the autonomous robots into the palm of his hand. On each set of displays, the drones watched from above as the mites deployed by dropping a couple hundred feet through the air into the undergrowth nearby to both the business center and the warehouse. When they finally scooted across the parking surface to the respective surfaces, all Rome could see were shadowy forms that reminded him of tailless rodents.

"Getting the secondary feeds from both locations." Aldo shoved the aerial shots aside. New imagery encased in circles appeared.

At the business center, the ten mites swarmed the building until they found ventilation ducts. They made quick work of the obstacles with two mites unlatching the vent covers and holding it open like a hatch for their compatriots.

The other team made slower progress. The Pike sentries were huge in comparison—great looming white bullets with optical rings that glowed red. They rolled along a perfect path 50 feet from the warehouse walls. Beyond them, the building was a citadel of sloped walls angled at 20 degrees, without visible windows, seams, or any other obvious ways in. If there were ventilation shafts, they were well hidden.

"Single shell construction," Aldo said.

"Yeah. Whole thing was extruded right in place, probably with the framework printed beforehand."

The mites at the warehouse slunk along the brush at the edge of the property until they found a place where the lot's surface was cracked by erosion. They scurried along the narrow trench, through a gap in the sentry's patrol.

"See?" Aldo grinned. "They got it."

"Hang on. The first team's inside."

Footage from the business center showed a bland hallway of beige walls, brown furnishings, and sectioned office space.

"Nothing on IR there," Aldo said. "Not picking up anything strange on EM emissions or signals, either."

"Send them into the garages at the back." Marcy's display told Rome the Halcyon was less than five miles from the warehouse. The terrain around the structure was largely forest. "Marcy, park us in one of those commercial zones, the more cars the better, a quarter mile out the service road for the warehouse."

[Altering course.]

The second team of mites reached the warehouse wall. They nudged along the base, prodding with writhing tentacles for a possible breach. Finally, a pair of them dug into the ground, tearing at the pavement, until they exposed a gap between the walls and the base.

"Drainage pipe," Aldo said. "Going for a swim."

The pipe, however, was empty—save for a trickle. Rome couldn't see anything on the display besides dark, curved walls.

An alert chimed. Aldo switched imagery. "Well, no luck at the business center."

Rome saw empty space inside the center's garages. "Keep them on site. Check for any subterranean passages. You know how these guys like to dig."

"Right. Hold up… the second team's entering."

The mites emerged from the darkness into a room aglow with pale orange lights. Rome spotted some machinery he didn't recognize and…

The images went static.

"What?" Aldo swiped at his controls. "Lost connection with the mites. The drones can't reacquire."

Marcy pulled the Halcyon into a parking spot outside a row of restaurants and storefronts. A broad canopy shielded the nearby slots and storefronts from rain. The whole lot would flood if not for the trenches that opened along the curbs, draining huge volumes of water through concealed grates.

"You got a cause for it?" Rome asked.

"No. Could be a glitch. Could be a dampening field, more likely. Whatever it is, the signal's toast."

"Let's go." Rome turned his seat 180 degrees, facing the back bench and storage compartments of the Halcyon. He unsealed one long box with his handprint. Inside was an FN Toro, half the length of a rifle, with a collapsible stock. It had a spazzer mounted underneath a long, slender barrel. A curved magazine projected from behind the trigger in bullpup configuration, and a power pack for the spazzer glowed on the right side.

Rome checked the magazine—7.52mm tracker rounds. He grabbed a second magazine of standard 7.52, tucked it in his coat, and a magazine of 10mm for his Hunsaker pistol.

Aldo was already out of the car with just a spazzer. He had a black cap pulled snug over his head. "Getting wet out here."

"Here." Rome tossed him a 10mm magazine.

"Thanks." Aldo opened his jacket, and tucked it alongside the Hunsaker he, too, carried in a shoulder rig. "Ready for a walk?"

Rome's senses buzzed at everything around him—the pitter-patter of receding rain on the branches, the cool touch of the mist on his face, the crunch of his boots on the pine needles, the soft whirr of the Pike sentry bots on their patrol.

They had to be quick. The Pikes should accept their badge authority, but if there was anyone inside the warehouse, they'd have a moment to gain entry before the sentries alerted law enforcement. Rome counted on the fact the sentries had likely been tampered with, so they thought the building was vacant too.

Trouble was, nobody knew who or what was inside. If anything.

He and Aldo walked swiftly across the paved lot. Aldo handed him a sensor-eye and fit one over his right eye. The patch was curved, made of a transparent green material. It reminded Rome of a seashell, albeit a flimsy one. He pressed it over his socket and felt prickles around that part of his face as it adhered to his skin. It stretched, crawling across the bridge of his nose until it covered his left eye with a smaller, rectangular patch.

Aldo's scanner, the same one he'd used on Joe Brace's Lexus, hovered ahead of him. Whatever it picked up was transmitted directly to the sensor-eyes. It ghosted over Rome's vision. He saw the path taken by the mites as well as thermal readings from the interior of the building, though only about 20 feet deep.

The nearest pair of Pike bots wheeled around, converging on the two men.

[Identity.]

Rome winced. Why'd they have to be so loud? He held up his implant.

[Confirmed.] They repeated the process for Aldo.

"Your turn," Rome said. "Sentries, confirm human occupancy of the building."

[Vacant.]

"Grant access."

The robots escorted them to the warehouse's main door. It towered a good ten feet over their heads. Beside it was a smaller, normal sized door with the sign "Great Gears Inc." that glowed in blue neon. One of the robots flashed a light on the inset access panel next to the door. It slid open.

[Access granted.]

Rome glanced at Aldo, who nodded back. Rome entered first, gun held ready.

The building was dark inside, lit only by the glow of blue, red, and green lights on the printing machinery. Massive extruders—five of them—sat end to end. Each one rumbled along, the stench of heated plastic and metal filled the air. Automated arms removed bicycle parts as they were completed—gears, chains, seats, frame tubes, and tires. Farther along, more arms reached down from the ceiling and out from the walls with great spidery limbs that pieced together bicycles of all shapes and sizes. Airbrushes hissed from behind plastic sheeting—the painting booth.

The necessity for stealth hushed their words and prevented the activation of their sleeve beacons. The sensor-eyes took the night vision data from the scanners and modified the visual range, which made it as bright as a late afternoon. Rome led them left of the fabrication units to the wide-open garage space.

Aldo's scanner flew low to the floor. Mercifully, its volume and lights were muted. It moved back and forth over the rough gray metal. Rome's sensor-eyes gave him a clear view of bits of mud, scattered pine needles, and splotches of water.

Aldo glanced at Rome. "Tracks," he mouthed.

Rome nodded. He knelt—watching the area around them—and placed a bare palm on the metal near the tracks.

Warm.

He leaned a couple feet away from the debris and touched the floor nearer the fabrication units. Cooler by 8 degrees, according to his sensor-eyes.

He frowned. He got a full read on the entire floor section by rocking back on his heels and widening his gaze. The scanner's results were clear. There was a large rectangle that was warmer than the rest of the warehouse, completely indistinguishable to the naked eye. However, nothing penetrated beyond the floor. The scanner returned only a warm haze.

"Shielded," Rome mouthed to Aldo.

Aldo rolled his eyes.

Rome found the line where the temperature change occurred. The slab they sat on was cooling, slowly turning blue from a bright red-orange. He felt along one of the many grooves and indentations in the floor.

There. That one wasn't full of gunk like the rest, and it stretched a long way.

Aldo sent the scanner over. It hovered by Rome, bobbing along the crack. The results were instantaneous.

Airflow.

Rome glanced back at the door. He took in the orientation of the debris, the rough shape of the tracks that abruptly ended, and the outline the scanner determined.

A hatch. A Freight elevator.

So where was the door?

Light flared around him with such brilliance it was as if the roof had split open. Pain stabbed his eyes and he squeezed them shut. Aldo swore. A split second later, the sensor-eyes turned transparent, deactivating the night vision mode. They shaded to give Rome's sight time to adjust to the sudden change in illumination.

When he finally blinked amorphous blobs away, he saw shapes moving. People—among the fabrication units.

He saw a gun.

"Down!" Rome shoved Aldo to the floor. Bone cracked on metal.

Gunfire exploded above them. The breeze from its passage told Rome he'd brought them out of the line of fire just in time. Bullets spanged off the walls with sparks. The staccato informed his ears that whoever was in here carried fully automatic weapons.

He and Aldo scrambled for cover behind the nearest fabrication unit. Rome reached for the trigger of the spazzer mounted on his Toro.

"How many?" Aldo hissed.

"Four. At least." The sensor-eye showed them as red outlined bodies clad in black suits, each one an obsidian copy of the woman they saw on the security video from Joe Brace's robbery. "Stealth suits."

"Oh. Right, those." Aldo fiddled with the power level on his spazzer until its gauge reached red. "Any idea whether those things will stop a focused neural burst?"

"You're the one with the Army, pal. You tell me."

Quiet, measured footsteps. Whoever moved was disciplined. They were not some thugs, shifting cover.

Rome leaned to the edge of the fabrication unit and peered around.

The figure bolted across an aisle and ducked behind a support beam.

Rome made eye contact with Aldo. He pantomimed shooting, then repeated the gesture lower with his hand positioned near his waist.

Aldo grinned. He scooted into the same aisle, firing the spazzer as he moved. Ripples of air, like heat waves over pavement, shot out, tracing along a faint white stream of plasma.

Rome thought it looked like clouds surfing a lightning bolt. The metal steamed where the bolt struck.

No sooner had Aldo made it to his new hiding place, then a black-clad figure leaned out and fired what Rome's sensor-eyes helpfully identified as a Dragge Arms Javelin-60 rifle. The shots hit Aldo's support beam. Each one moved closer to his actual position without penetrating the metal. The shooter never changed his stance.

Great. They had trackers, too.

The man—Rome could tell by the sheer bulk of the shooter—was mid-firing when he shot him center mass with his spazzer. The plasma discharge skittered all over his body, crackling like tongues of fire. Grunts emanated from the mask. The man twitched, and then collapsed.

Rome burst from hiding and hurried toward him. It was good to know the spazzers disabled a person's voluntary nervous system through the suits.

Except, the man didn't stay down.

He staggered upright. His left hand propped against the support beam. The right aimed the J60 at Rome's chest.

It didn't matter.

Rome shoved the muzzle skyward, pushing the man's right arm against his left. Shots fired. The sound was deafening to Rome, making his left ear ring. He swept the stock of his gun across the man's mask. There was a hard clack of teeth against teeth. Rome let go of the man's J60 rifle and struck him again across the right side of the face. That time, he toppled like a tree.

Aldo joined them. He slapped magcuffs around the man's wrists and secured his ankles with a zip strap.

More footsteps echoed in the plant. Behind the rumble and hiss of the machinery, Rome heard voices shouting.

"So much for spazzers," Aldo muttered.

"No kidding. I had mine set on max, just like yours." Rome passed Aldo the J60. "Hold this for me."

"Um… yes, please. Did they bio-lock it?"

"Nope."

"Morons." Aldo tucked the spazzer into its holster and hefted the rifle. He examined the magazine. "Trackers?"

"Yeah."

"Super."

"Don't worry too much. With all the obstacles in here, it's a Hail Mary to even use one." Rome hurriedly tapped at the selector on his gun. "Program for appendages."

[Sir, Pilot Soares has contacted FTZ Central authorities and local law enforcement for additional support.]

Marcy's pleasant, normal-volume voice made Rome start. "Hell, Marcy, dial it down!" he hissed. "Tell them these people are heavily armed. If local PD's coming in, they're going to want their heavy gear, like a patrol mech!"

[Understood, and already determined from the sensor results.]

Figured Aldo would have fed her everything from the scanner drone and the sensor-eyes from the moment they stepped inside. "Where are you?"

[Approaching the perimeter of the property.]

"Stay put until I signal. You're not a hundred percent bulletproof."

[Observing safety protocols.]

Suddenly, an overhead view of the warehouse appeared in the corner of Rome's right eye. It was imaged from somewhere high up. He realized Aldo's scanner hovered at the pinnacle of the ceiling. Rome clearly saw the three remaining attackers. Two men, one of whom was 20 feet to their right, and the other who was on the far side of the warehouse moving toward the entrance Rome and Aldo had used. The third was a woman. She could be the one from the video, unless there were more underneath.

Another shout. The woman and the furthest man aimed their guns straight up… at the scanner drone.

"Move!" Rome shouted.

They swept from their hiding place. Rome led them right toward the nearest man. He must be the one who gave the order, because he didn't shoot at the drone.

Rome targeted him.

The man hid behind a six by six foot column of processing material that glowed pale green. As soon as they reached it, Rome and Aldo split up, moving to either side.

The black suit leaped at Aldo, brandishing a gun.

Aldo tumbled behind a conveyor belt. Bullets stitched a line across the top, each one curving closer to the edge.

Rome aimed for the man and fired.

He had his back in his sights, but having programmed the gun's tracker projectiles, the shots went for their intended targets—the man's arms. Rome wanted him disabled, unarmed, and in pain. They pierced his shoulders, and ripped through the elbows. There was no spray of blood. Instead, sparks and hydraulic fluid spattered the man's suit.

The man turned around, face still hidden by a featureless mask.

Rome did the only thing he could from that range—he barreled into the guy. He successfully knocked him down, though it took twice as much effort as Rome judged necessary for a man of that stature and build.

It also hurt a ton—like he'd hit the support beam instead of flesh.

The man slapped Rome aside. The J60 lay discarded beside him.

Rome brought himself upright, onto one knee. "Pursuit specialist! Don't touch the weapon!"

The man ignored him and reached for it.

"Head!" Aldo shouted. "Shoot him in the head!"

Rome adjusted his aim and fired.

The man's head exploded into plastic, wires, and circuitry. His body slumped, as dead as a bot with its control shorted.

Aldo emerged from hiding, face red and dripping sweat. "A bot?"

"Android frame." Rome pulled a chunk of the fabricated "skull" off. A blinking blue light greeted him, mounted on a thin black wafer. "Remote operation."

Shouts from behind Aldo drew their attention.

The remaining man and woman came at them. They moved in tandem, laying down suppressive fire with J60 rifles.

Aldo took a round to the thigh. He screamed as his blood sprayed out the other side. He went down, writhing and grasping for the wound.

Rome took shelter and fired back, hoping to halt their advance. It worked temporarily, but he knew his gun didn't carry nearly the capacity as the J60 magazines.

The entire front door of the warehouse flew up. A pair of familiar cars skidded to a halt just inside, near the lip of the lowering elevator—the Halcyon, and the blue-gray Panther. Behind them, four police black and whites raced up, accompanied by a bot that rolled on triangular tank treads. It stood twice as tall as the car, with a pair of mounted spazzers on both shoulders and two arms as long as Rome's body. It, too, was painted black and white, sporting the same emergency flashers as everything else.

Overhead, the roof shook with the reassuring sound of Condor 33's engines.

"Attention!" The voice boomed from a speaker.

Thad's voice. Rome ground his teeth.

"Put down your weapons and come out with your hands up!"

All gunfire stopped. Rome took a chance and slid over to Aldo. "You okay?"

"Yeah, great." Aldo's teeth were clenched. He'd torn a strip of cloth off his shirt and tied it near the wound. "You know what? Feels like somebody shot me."

"Hold still and quit whining." Rome tugged a First Aid sealer from his pocket. "Use this."

"Thanks. Anybody tell you you've got the bedside manner of a med-drone?" Aldo applied the sealant to his wound. Foam oozed out. He sighed as the pain reliever seeped into his system.

Rome moved in on the suspects. Both knelt with hands clasped behind their heads, their guns cast aside. Rome reached for his magcuffs.

"No one move!" Thad was there, with Enrique. Both had spazzers, and though Enrique looked as bored as if he collected groceries, Thad wore the most blinding smile. "Good thing we arrived when we did, Roman. A collaborative effort, yes?"

Rome replied by placing his magcuffs on the two suspects. He'd be damned if he shared the bounty with Thad Mancos.

The woman muttered something, her words distorted.

"Speak clearly." Thad tugged the mask away.

Brown hair spilled out, strands sticking to a sweat streaked face. Her eyes were blue as the waters off Seattle. She ignored Thad, focusing instead on Rome.

Rome stared, his brain not quite catching up to the image. Talk about lag.

"Not unlike you to be struck dumb, Roman," Thad said.

Rome cleared his throat. He only had one awkward thing to say. "Hey, Sara."

She shook her head. "Not what I envisioned for our next date, Rome."

Chapter Seven

The room on the second floor of FTZ West headquarters was labeled "Confidential Interviews." Rome had been inside one often enough to know it for what it was—interrogation space. The similarity to a police interrogation room, however, ended with the name.

This was no barren square of concrete and drywall. It could have been an FTZ staffer's office, denuded of art and plants. The floor was the same polished stone as the lobby and most other rooms in the building. Walls were a uniform shade of eggshell white with soft blue highlights. Light panels in the walls suffused everything with a warm glow.

There was a single, oblong glass and metal table in the center. Three people sat on one side—the crew of thieves, including Sara to the far right. Rome and Aldo sat opposite them.

"Where is he?" Rome leaned back in the chair, hands folded in his lap. His seat was as comfortable as the Halcyon's upholstery, and it contoured to his body even better.

The three responded with stoic glares. The guy Rome had knocked out sat in the middle, his jaw sporting a bruise the size, shape, and color of a plum. He was a tall, powerfully built Latino with a buzzcut and thin moustache. ID came up as Jorge Cuellar. The man to his right was shorter, blond, his hair thick and matted from being inside the stealth suit. He was tattooed all over. He, Robert Brand, and Cuellar wore identical black sleeveless shirts.

Sara glanced at the men, but her jaw was shut tighter than security for Director Cho's office. Rome did his best not to stare at her—Sara Haig. She, too, was clad in black, though Rome found her tank top far more flattering than either of the men's. The curve of her neck was way too distracting. The last time Rome saw it, the graceful body that went with it was totally naked beneath the sheets of his bed.

Almost a year ago. He hadn't heard a word from her, until Thad ripped that mask off. He kept his face studiously neutral.

"Think these guys like playing dumb, Rome." If Aldo had noticed his partner's introspection, he didn't let on. "Funny, though. Their records can do all the talking. Between local LEO charges and stuff from the other FTZs, you fellas—and one lovely lady, I should say—have had enough scrapes to fill… well… three criminal records."

"Stop trying to be funny, Aldo."

"I'm not trying. I am. And if my humor's glitching it's because, wait for it, I got shot by these dopes. Okay, let's see. Aggravated assault. Forgery. Larceny. B&E. And the big boss of them all, robbery. Plus, you know, theft and possession of federal property. Namely your cloaked ride, and Special Forces stealth suits."

No one gave evidence for surprise or chagrin—or any other outward emotion for Rome to detect. "There's a fourth person on your crew. Someone was in control of that android, we know that much from the booster in its skull. Tell us who's heading this up and we'll cut a deal with FTZ."

Sara stared at him, her expression cold. It was a far cry from the laughter and amusement he'd seen over glasses of wine.

"FTZ is not going to let this slide. If you don't cooperate, you're looking at reconditioning at the best, and cryo at the worst."

"There's always the lunar mines," Aldo added cheerily.

Rome nodded. "Hear they're always looking for fresh help."

He had to give this crew credit. They were not about to turn on their fourth member, which only reinforced his suspicion that the fourth one was the leader.

"Where's the truck?" Aldo asked. "Security and LEOs swept the building top to bottom."

"Found the mites in the basement," Rome said. "Quite the Batcave you had down there."

Aldo frowned at him. "I don't think we found any biologicals that big on the scans, did we?"

"Big as what?"

"Bats."

"Never mind. Look, we know the truck went somewhere. Give us the location so the Army can have it back, no mess." Rome was better off talking to an old car—one of those pre-automation classics.

The room's door slid open. Director Cho came in, flanked by Thad and Enrique. "Driver Jasko, Mr. Burns, a moment, please."

"Sure thing." Rome smiled, rather than do what he really wanted to, which was kick all three of them out of the room. Once they were in the hallway, Aldo voiced a similar opinion.

"What are you doing?" he scowled. "That's our interrogation! Sir."

Cho's composure never slipped. "The disposition of the bounty has yet to be determined, Mr. Burns, and as such, Driver Mancos needs to be in on the questioning."

"There shouldn't be any question about the bounty," Rome said. "Aldo apprehended one suspect, I cuffed the other two. We tracked their location, we got into their base of operations. All within the specs of the contract."

"You two would have been perforated if I hadn't brought in the local police," Thad pointed out. "That capture is as much mine as it is yours."

"Strange definition."

"Ah, but public perception is stronger than legal definition." Thad presented his implant flourish. The holographic projection showed the messages and titles of eight news items, which scrolled into even more. Each one of them made some mention of the arrest of the robbers.

"The Ninety Bandits?" Aldo made a gagging sound.

"Director, that's a clear violation of procedure." Rome's hands tightened into fists. "Leaking arrests prior to the formal filing of charges… should be enough get Thad kicked off his contract."

"I never said anything about Driver Mancos having his own contract."

So, it's like that. Rome had been lied to, straight to his face, on more than one occasion. It was especially galling when he knew the truth ahead of time—and from Freddie, who would have the inside story. "Not going to argue that point. Whatever's going on, Thad's got no call to step in on my questioning."

"I'm not stepping in, señor, I'm taking over." Thad flicked imaginary lint off Rome's shirt. "How do you think it will look if Driver Jasko is known to have a romantic interest among the suspects?"

Aldo choked—and this time, it was real. He'd produced a granola bar from his coat and ate halfway through it. The man's stealth with obtaining snack food was on par with the thieves' ability to go invisible. "His what, now?"

"Ex-interest. Sara and I were… together. It's been a year."

"Ten and a half months. But who is counting?" Thad smiled.

Cho looked less than enthused. "If that's true, Driver Jasko, we're going to have to re-evaluate your access to the suspects."

"There's nothing to worry about. Sara… Ms. Haig and I are no longer involved. Does it look like I've been going easy on her? I've run all the offers from FTZ as per your authorization. But you've seen that on the HD feeds, no doubt."

"I have. This casts a new light on the questioning, however," Cho nodded at Thad. "You and Mr. Bassa conduct the negotiating from here on out. Standard offers apply. We want the stolen goods returned to their owners—or barring that, arrangements for financial recompense."

"Yes, Director." Thad clapped Rome on the shoulder. "Sorry about that, *compadre*."

Rome grabbed his wrist, stuck his foot under Thad's ankle, and had him pinned to the hallway wall in a blink. He pressed against the back of Thad's neck with his forearm. "Don't know how you knew about Sara, but here's fair warning. My personal life? Not your hobby. You got that?"

"Indeed I do."

Rome released him.

Aldo whispered at his side, "Ease up. Cho's goon squad's waiting."

And they were, 15 feet down the corridor.

Rome smoothed his jacket. "Good luck in there. You'll need it."

Thad brushed his hair with the heel of his palm. "Doubtful."

As soon as they were in, Cho departed. His goons fell into formation behind him. "We'll meet later to finish out your contract for the assignment," Cho said, without looking back. "Expect my signal."

Rome glared after him. Damn Thad and damn Cho.

"Come on, man." Aldo chomped down the rest of his granola bar. He brushed crumbs off his jacket onto the immaculate stone floor and scuffed at them until they smeared flat. "I got something that'll cheer you up."

Marcy had parked the Halcyon in one of the repair garages for a power core recharge. Dome Four was divided into six wedges, with a central common area for parts and power stations. Overhead skylights let the gloomy, mid-afternoon light into the stark, gray and tan slices.

The entrance scanner of Pursuit 112's rented bay checked in Rome and Aldo via their implants. A small timer tracked the hours and minutes of use, adding the cost to Rome's account. He grimaced. Never let it be said that FTZ was anything other than precise when it came to bookkeeping. There was an upside. Their slice was completely free of surveillance. There were no sensors, no cameras, no nothing. Security was the scanner at the door and at the main entrance to Dome Four, but it was up to the Driver and info tech to safeguard the rest.

Aldo limped for a cabinet—one of several locked, gunmetal gray units—and opened it with his implant. "So. Sara. You never mentioned her. I never even saw a pic."

"Nobody's business but my own." Rome waited for him by a table laden with all sorts of computer innards, most of which he didn't recognize.

"Yeah, but Thad knew."

"He saw Sara and me at dinner once. Didn't say anything to either of us. I didn't think he'd noticed. Apparently, he had."

"You know he pinged our tags, right? That's how he found us."

"Hell." Rome ground a dirt clod into the concrete floor. "Drivers aren't supposed to do that to each other."

"Guess the rules don't apply to our buddies at Del Norte." Aldo brought a tiny, white circle with trailing blue wires to the table. "Okay, clear out."

Rome slid farther along. "Not seeing how this will cheer me up."

"This bad boy is going to data hunt, and he's going to look in here." Aldo pulled a thin black wafer from one pocket and a battered silver lump from the other.

"Is that from our android ghost?"

"Yep—the receiver used to operate it remotely, and its CPU. Such as it is." Aldo connected blue wires to both the wafer and to the silver lump. "That thing had fewer brains than a cheap vacuum. Wasn't meant for independent use."

"You think whoever's at the top of this gang was dumb enough to leave incriminating data on the CPU?"

"Not really. But I figured, since Thad gets to do the questioning, we should dig on our own while he's wasting time." Aldo tapped at his implant. Green lights flickered on all three objects lined up on his table. "Okay. Well, good news is you didn't completely blow the brains out of the android when you shot it."

"You're welcome."

"Hey, not complaining. Bad news? There's not a lot stored in the CPU besides the basic commands—evade, shoot, et cetera. What I'm hoping for is… ha! Bingo."

A set of numbers scrambled by strange characters trickled across the interface. Rome frowned. "Encoded."

"Yeah. Give me a sec." Aldo glanced at the car, and when he spoke again, pitched his voice louder. "Hey Marcy? I'm sending you a stream. See if you can decrypt."

[Receiving data. Running decryption… stand by.]

Rome's implant vibrated. He checked its display. Kelsey again.

<Friday, 7 p.m. Please be there. I have seats set aside.>

There was still time. It was only Tuesday morning. Marcy could drive them the whole way. Even better, they could fly. Gabriela was good for a favor or two. A quick hop on the Condor would give him even more leeway.

He brought up a still image from his implant's memory. Himself, with less gray and a big grin, plus a younger Kelsey and two kids—an impish Vivian and gangly, smiling Jake. He had the same black hair as Rome, hazel eyes like his mother, and the barest sprinkling of freckles. Those were inherited somewhere along the genetic line on Kelsey's side—a great-uncle, he thought.

"You, uh, busy?" Aldo flipped through projected screens of information.

Rome showed him the image. "Six years ago."

"Oh. Pre-Sara."

"Pre- lots of things. Adultery, fights, divorce…" Rome shrugged. "People change. She didn't understand that, about me or herself."

"'Least you get to see the kids."

"I'm their father. That's the deal. I could be closer, but since she moved to Massachusetts… well, I'd be hard pressed to find any work near there."

"No kidding. Not without taking a 20 percent penalty."

"Think they call it a 'Safe Roads Fee.'"

"Yeah, or you could call it what it is—tax on Drivers," Aldo grumbled. "Makes me glad for the idiots who go around breaking the law every day. Keeps us gainfully employed." His implant chirped. Before he could check out the results, Marcy said, [Decryption complete. Partial recovery only.]

She wasn't kidding. The gibberish resolved to a set of instructions, and a broken string of numbers. Rome recognized the latter immediately. "Latitude and longitude. Looks like there's missing digits."

"Probably damaged. What about those instructions? 'Rally barn and steady. Silence. Phase Two imminent. Scapegoat marked.' That's weird."

"No kidding. Lock all that away."

"With the case files?"

"No. Set up your own storage for sensitive information." If he stored it in the case files, there was the chance Thad could get his hands on the data, and bringing in the fourth member of the thieves' team might cinch him the entire bounty.

Aldo smirked. "Already got one. Consider it done."

"Okay. So, the coordinates—they look to be East Coast, or near there. Narrows it down to the last third of the Ninety."

"Could be anywhere within a few hundred miles north and south, though."

"That's why you and Marcy need to rebuild the missing digits. There has to be a remnant somewhere in there, right?"

"Maybe. Not that simple..." Aldo snapped his fingers. "But, hang on. If I can get the receiver working again, maybe I can use it to ping the transmitter. Find out where that is."

"Good. You get cracking on the receiver and have Marcy crunch the numbers." Rome thought of another possibility, and started for the door.

"Hey, where are you going?"

"To continue my questioning."

He was right. Thad had separated the prisoners. Now it was just a matter of waiting.

After forty-five minutes of sitting on a couch in a reception corner stocked with a holo projector that displayed baseball stats and game highlights, Rome saw Enrique lead Sara from the interrogation room to a holding space down the hall. Their backs were turned to him.

Rome watched the baseball announcer, though it had been years since he'd been to a game. Hockey was more his speed where the guys flew around the ice, fast as cars. Never standing still. But, by watching the holo, he saw Enrique and Sara's reflections in the transparent divider that separated a table and four chairs from the rest of the waiting area.

Enrique and Sara went in, but Enrique came out with Cuellar instead. They went back to the interrogation room. As soon as that door hissed shut, Rome moved.

He reached the door to the holding room. The security plate on the wall scanned his badge and implant before it slid open.

A young man in FTZ Security tans sat just inside the door, his cap perched on the corner of a low table. He read something on the table's display surface. The other two walls had four doors with opaque panes in their centers. Two glowed a soft yellow with blurry silhouettes visible. The others were dark.

"Pursuit Specialist Jasko, here to see one of the suspects," Rome said.

The young man nodded, eyes never leaving his display. "Badge and implant clearance."

Rome presented his badge and let the guard scan his implant… again… which the kid did as numbly as a bot.

"You're clear. Which suspect?"

"Sara Haig."

The kid looked up. "She just came back from questioning."

"Sure did. Now she's in for Round Three. Open the door."

As soon as the door unlocked and opened, Sara was on her feet. Rome stepped through.

"I didn't think they allowed conjugal visits here," Sara said.

Rome held his finger to his lips until the door slid shut.

"There's nothing for me to say to you, Rome. I know they've got listening devices, probably all over this place."

"I took care of that." Rome tapped his implant. "Driver's prerogative—privacy in questioning. Only thing that will record is my implant, which will then pass it along to FTZ Security, but I disabled the function."

"Oh." She rubbed her hands together. Rome noted scrapes across the knuckles of her right hand and a long bruise on the left. She had a series of bumps and scratches all over her arms.

"Sara, what's going on?" Rome stood in front of her, hands on his hips. "Last time we talked you were working on boundary disputes along the Texas border."

"I was. Satellite demarcation, automaton reinforcement. Unfortunately, the Republic doesn't subscribe to the infallibility theorem where comps are concerned. Every square foot I mapped was challenged." Sara smoothed out what few bunches there were in the skin-tight black pants. "Didn't help that I had armed men shadowing me the entire way."

"Okay. Fast forward a year and here you are. With thugs like Cuellar and Brand, ripping doors and implants off luxury cars."

The corner of her mouth twitched. "Change of scenery."

"No doubt the money was good."

"Is good. And yes, I enjoy the challenge."

"The challenge of being a modern-day train robber? Come on, Sara. Where did you meet up with your crew?"

"The Net."

"Where did you get your equipment?"

"Trade secret."

"This isn't a game, Sara. I need you to tell who's in charge of this thing. Any cooperation you can give means the consequences will be less severe down the line."

"Less severe? Than what? Having no freedom?" Sara's expression twisted away from the charming smile.

Rome searched his memories from their months together for a time when she looked this bitter, but he came up blank.

"Maybe you're more like them than I thought, Rome. Do you like having your electronic shepherd taking you everywhere you need to go? Making all your decisions for you?"

"What are you talking about? I'm a Driver, Sara. I get paid to do what everybody else can't."

"Yet you probably still rely on the machine every second you get." She gestured with her wrist. "You're hooked into those."

Rome glanced at his implant. "Are you serious? My family lives half a continent away from me. How else am I going to stay in touch?"

"You're so trapped in society's mindset you can't even see what's going on. Everything that makes us human is being stripped away. We're not individuals anymore."

"So that means you get to assault people and steal their belongings."

"We need funds."

"Dammit, Sara…" Rome rubbed his chin. It was his fault for letting her drag him into some nonsensical discussion about philosophical ideas. Got him riled up. He took the images in his head of Kelsey, Jake, and Vivian and pushed them aside. "Enough of this crap. Tell me who's your boss."

Sara glared at him. She folded her hands in her lap and rested against the wall.

Unbelievable. "Look. I'm trying to give you a chance. We owe each other that, don't we?"

"You know what? You don't owe me anything. We had our fun. I've moved on to something bigger. Something more important."

"What are you—"

The lights flickered and died.

The cell plunged into complete darkness. Rome felt a whoosh of air behind him. The door popped open as part of the safety protocols enforced by the building computer. In the case of a fire or outage, no one would get trapped.

Something hard rammed into his gut. He went down, smacking the back of his head against the frame. Sara's hands were all over him, but not in the way he'd like. Whatever she was searching for, she didn't find. He lashed out at her, swinging wildly, but hit only air.

Distant footsteps and she was gone. The kid guard shouted but the only reply was a blow. It sounded like his nose got broken. More footsteps… hushed whispers. Rome's head spun. He breathed slow and deep, trying not to vomit.

When the static in his brain finally cleared, everything was cast in dim, red lights. Emergency backup power?

His implant flashed. "Aldo."

"Rome! What's going on?" Tinny shouts filled the signal behind Aldo's voice in Rome's earpiece. "Everything's out. We're trying to open the garage doors but the thing's locked down."

"Grab Marcy out and get over here!" Rome staggered. He slapped a hand against the wall. Okay… good. He didn't pass out.

The building shuddered and swayed. Something rumbled like thunder. As it faded, a steady roar grew, muffled by its distance.

The guard lay slumped by his desk, curled in the fetal position. Rome felt for a pulse. Weak, but there.

He took the guard's spazzer. Unlike lethal weapons, it was not bio-locked. Good thing. Rome realized Sara had grappled with him to get ahold of his gun, but Rome had left it back in the Halcyon. Standard security for FTZ West's holding cells.

A pair of security men jogged down the hall. They shouted overlapping conversations into their implants. Whatever was going on, it wasn't good.

"Talk to me, Aldo."

"We're headed to the HQ building. Got some lights on around the compound, but Marcy's running us on IR. There's…" He trailed off. "Uh, Rome? There's a Condor hovering right outside the garden between the towers… and it does not look like one of ours."

Rome skidded on the carpet and altered his course. He shouldered a fire escape door and took the stairs up, two at a time. "You're sure?"

"Well, it's missing the FTZ logo, its internal lights are red, and it's painted black, so… yes. Not one of ours."

"Stay sharp. I'm headed up there now."

A sickening buzzsaw sound made the air tremor from somewhere above. Rome knew the noise.

"They're shooting up the entire garden!" Aldo shouted through the signal. "Don't know who's up there but, unless they've got their heads down, they're dead!"

Rome burst from the stairs onto the seventh floor and sprinted down the corridor toward the garden. The noise was even louder here. It jarred his teeth. A handful of security guards—two men, a woman, and a pair of Pike robots—were hunkered behind furniture. Beyond them, the door to the gardens was open. Rome counted two bodies—torn and bloodied scraps—and the shredded plastics of more Pike robots.

"Stay back!" The female guard—a slender Chinese woman—had both hands pressed to a wound on the abdomen of an Asian guy. "They've got a heavy MG out there."

"The suspects! Where are they?"

She waved a hand, its palm slick with blood. "We chased them in from both ends. Had them boxed until that thing started shooting up the garden."

The steady stream of machine gun fire died out. Rome got up from his crouch. "Cover me."

"With what?"

It was a fair question. A quick inventory revealed the guards carried only spazzers. Rome felt ridiculous stepping through that door, shoes crunching broken glass and squishing ripped leaves, with only a weapon that could incapacitate a person.

"This a bad time?" Aldo's voice muttered inside his earpiece.

"You could say that." Rome swept his spazzer in an arc. The men on the floor were both dead, no question. He didn't need a scanner—there wasn't enough left of their bodies. His heart hammered from the adrenaline and the gnawing anger. The ache in his chest grew. These guys with whom Sara was involved, they weren't just petty thieves and robbers anymore. They were killers.

The garden was a long corridor with high transparent ceilings and walls. A rock slab walkway wound through the center, flanked by phalanxes of rhododendrons, ferns, and a whole bunch of greenery Rome didn't recognize. He just knew that, under other circumstances, the brilliant greens and rainbow of flower colors, coupled with the heady aromas, could be far more relaxing than any virtual reality program.

The pitch of the Condor's engines changed. Wind blew through a jagged hole in the right side of the corridor where a 20-foot section was broken. Two figures stood framed in the opening. Sara was one of them, her hair whipping around her.

"Sara!" Rome called.

The man in front of her leaped out. She looked Rome's way with terror in her eyes, and jumped, too.

Gone.

Rome's race downstairs was a blur. People shouted, alarms blared, medics scrambled into the building with flocks of med-drones—the little winged robots with flashing red lights and boxes of emergency supplies slung underneath. Then he was outside. The damp air immediately soaked him.

The Halcyon sat there, engine rumbling. Rome threw himself into the driver's seat. "Where is it?"

"Headed east, but not quick. I don't know what they're doing but they're not shooting out of here." Aldo winced. "Sorry, bad choice of words."

"Marcy, switch to pursuit."

[There is no illegal driver case indicated. Target is needed—]

"The aircraft headed on the vector you and Aldo tracked!" He slapped his hand to the dash. "Override and confirm!"

Marcy lagged. [Free Travel Zone emergency status confirmed. Bypassing standard pursuit protocols.]

A few seconds later, Rome had them out on the main ramp to the Ninety. Traffic peeled away from them. The Condor was highlighted on the windshield, a dot far ahead and descending.

"There's no aerial response from FTZ." Aldo shifted in his seat. He rubbed at his leg, where the bullet left its mark. "Localized EMP. Blew out everything. Good thing the garages are hardened against that kind of crap."

"Good thing. Marcy, triangulate the possible landing sites for the aircraft."

[Affirmative.]

"Looks like we're first out of the gate," Aldo said. "Everyone else is catching up. Gabriela says she should be airborne in five."

Rome nodded, but didn't say anything. The skies cleared out, the grays splitting open for blues to cut through. The Halcyon's tires hissed across the wet highway. It helped him calm himself.

Two men dead.

They reached the landing site, but too late. The Condor sat in a vacant lot by a half-demolished building. A hulking deconstruction robot pulled chunks of concrete and strings of rebar free, dumping them into reclamation chutes. The mech made Rome think of a gorilla, only two stories tall and yellow, with arms as big as the Halcyon.

"Tire tracks." Aldo marked them on his holo display. "Off southeast... think we can trace them. Marcy, scan everything you can."

Rome got out of the car. The smell of hot materials drifted across the lot. Why would they leave the Condor sitting here? Its hatches were wide open. "Doesn't make sense."

Another set of engines whirred overhead. Rome glanced up. Finally, Gabriela.

His implant chirped. Simultaneously, Aldo said, “Um, what’s he want?”

It was Director Cho. His tiny visage was grim, his tie loose. “All FTZ and contracted units, be on the lookout for Pursuit One Twelve. We have reason to believe they are affiliated with the criminals who escaped FTZ custody. They should be considered armed and dangerous. All units are authorized to pursue and apprehend.”

Rome stared, uncomprehending.

“Please, don’t move.” Gabriela’s voice echoed from the sky, angelic and forbidding all at once. “I have to take you in.”

Chapter Eight

Nope.

Rome floored the Halcyon out of the parking lot. Aldo was shoved back into the seat. “What are you doing? Did you hear them? We’re suspects!”

[This course of action is not recommended,] Marcy said.

“Both of you, shut up!” The car skidded across the lanes of traffic, cutting through at least a dozen vehicles’ paths. Their automated systems veered away from Rome’s rampage with inches to spare. A flurry of warnings splattered on the dashboard.

“Slow down! Slow down!” Aldo gripped the sides of his seat.

“Quit freaking out and get into the nav systems,” Rome said. “Disable everything.”

“Everything?”

“Tags, trackers, our signals in and out—anything that can be used to lock down the car.”

“But Marcy… she won’t let…”

It was too great a risk for Rome to say any more—what he’d said already could be too much. But to his credit, Aldo stopped yammering. His face went pale. “You got me?”

“Yeah. Yeah, I do.” Aldo doused his holographic display and unhooked his restraints. He contorted himself in his seat so that his back was on the floor and his head under the dash.

[Sir, we are operating at unsafe velocities.] Marcy’s tone was sterner than Rome had ever heard it. She brought to mind his mother when he was caught guessing her PIN for the family accounts. [Please re-engage your restraints.]

"Sorry, Marcy." Aldo's voice was muffled. "This is gonna suck."

[Refrain from accessing hardwired systems. They should only be altered by a certified Free Travel Zone technician or other—] Marcy's voice hiccupped.

Aldo pulled on wires, removed and reinserted circuits, and disconnected feeds. Rome couldn't see everything he did—he was preoccupied with not getting them killed as they hurtled down the Ninety—but Marcy's voice was swamped with static and interruptions.

[Accessing safety broad... band. Contact... authorities and override... override...]

The wheel twitched under Rome's grip. The Halcyon's speed dropped by 15 miles per hour. "Aldo, cut her off."

"What the shit do you think I've been doing down here! Yoga?"

Rome struggled against the steering controls, but the car kept lurching toward the side of the road. The nav display showed Gabriela's Condor high above and very, very close behind. Warning messages accompanied by red lights streamed across his dash until they suddenly vanished.

"Got rid of that," Aldo muttered. "Hang on."

"Hurry up." The shoulder of the road was one lane away. Rome jerked the controls left, buying them a few feet and a few seconds, but Marcy's programming made her inexorable. She would do the safe thing—the thing that saved the greatest number of lives and avoided the most damage. She would turn him and Aldo over for arrest to the same people who—up until a few minutes ago—they were contracted with to chase illegal drivers.

Thad's Panther gained in the rear view, breaking away from the herd of Famtracs and freighters that slowed down several miles back. A pair of dull, tan cars joined him—escorts from FTZ West Security. By the way they maneuvered, Rome could tell they were Drivers. Comps wouldn't go that fast—even Security models—and their drift toward either side of their lanes confirmed it.

Additional cars pulled to the sides of the road around them, even going so far as to leave the center lane and cut across Rome's path toward the edge of the pavement. He recognized the pattern. It was only used in extreme cases… for dangerous fugitives.

His car slowed down every passing second, against everything he willed.

"We got company?"

"Yeah." Rome wrested the controls around a freighter as it made for the right lane. He accelerated, cutting up on its right side. The freighter swerved, attempting to steady its path. It drove back to the left and then braked, putting it directly in line with Thad's formation.

"Okay, okay. Marcy, you could make this easier and shut down, you know."

[Not authorized. Illegal… action not condoned. Not condoned.] Her tone was more strident. [External command is attempting override.]

Not what Rome wanted to hear. "Aldo…"

"Relax. They won't get in from our signal receptor."

"You're sure?"

Something small and black landed on Rome's lap. It trailed two severed wires.

"Nice work."

"Going to be a colossal inconvenience to fix if we ever want to talk to someone farther away than the windshield. But hey, you're welcome."

A light exploded across Rome's rear view. The freighter suddenly drifted to the left, sparks covering it in a web. Thad missed his target. Rome grinned. "Never was that much of a marksman."

[Compensation confirmed,] Marcy said.

The Halcyon skidded, shooting to the shoulder at such a great rate of speed, Rome knew he couldn't prevent an impact. He struggled with the controls until his arms shook.

"Got it!" Aldo wagged a red and gray striped wire from under the dash.

The Halcyon veered, diving across to the left lane. The freighter ahead dodged right, accelerating out of their path. They were close enough Rome made out the chips of paint missing from the advertisement on its rear fenders.

[Control… broke quarantine.] Marcy's voice was faint. [Unable to… update contact broken.]

Thunk.

Aldo twisted upright into his seat. He cradled a small, squashed object about the size of an apple in his hands. It was black with copper-colored lines that traced random patterns on a knobby surface. Green lights flickered around two axes, their frequency increasing as they turned gold, then orange, and finally dark red.

Aldo stared down at the lump. His knuckles were scraped red. "It's… Marcy."

The ache in Rome's chest surprised him. What was the problem? It was the autonomous computer programmed to safely navigate the car. Ten years ago, it didn't even exist.

Aldo reached under his seat. He pulled out a rag from some compartment that rattled with tools. He covered the object, and wrapped it snugly.

The lights faded completely.

Aldo tucked Marcy into the tool compartment. He exhaled, his eyes rimmed red. "Okay. So, she's disconnected."

"Okay. I need you to reconfigure the systems she used to run. Navigation. Telemetry. Countermeasures."

"Got it." Aldo activated his holos and dove into the work, face rigid and near unblinking. "Charge the EMP?"

Rome eyed the Condor closing in on them. "Yeah, probably going to need it."

They worked in silence for a few minutes—Rome driving, Aldo reconfiguring. It wasn't until the nav system chirped its familiar proximity alert that Rome stopped trying to think of this as a leisurely drive. Well, that and the rumble of the engine pushed to its max.

"Company." Aldo snorted. "Guess."

"Thad?"

"Bingo."

Traffic thinned ahead until only a handful of cars were left on the road.

Aldo frowned. "Where'd everyone go?"

"They cleared them out." Rome tightened his grip. He flicked his gaze from side to side. There were no exits. "Give me the locations of the nearest off-ramps."

"Okay. This is good, right? No obstacles for us."

"None for them, either." Rome pointed skyward.

Aldo's eyes widened. "Oh."

"Yeah. That."

The sky flashed. Light burst ahead and to their right, rippling out. Sparks skittered along the pavement.

Rome steered clear with tires squealing. He kept from overcorrecting and put the Halcyon into a higher gear. The speedometer ticked upward.

"EMP blast!"

"I noticed. What's our charge time?"

"Uh… ten minutes."

Way too long. "Make it faster. Reroute power from the core as long as it doesn't siphon off my speed."

"There's an old saying in there about not being a miracle worker, Rome."

Gabriela's Condor zipped ahead. Its wings angled sharply as it banked into a turn.

Coming around for a second pass?

Sure, enough. She stopped as if on the proverbial dime, hovering a couple hundred feet over the road where it crested a hill.

"Okay, maybe I should," Aldo said.

A signal pinged on the dash. Rome recognized the origin.

Gabriela.

"Tell me you unhooked the comms from the other onboard systems."

"Ah, one sec." Click. Aldo straightened, a pair of wire cutters in his hand.

How many tools did he have stashed under the seat? Rome had never thought to investigate.

"Done and done. Speak freely without fear of us getting hijacked."

Rome acknowledged the signal.

"Rome… Aldo… it's Gabriela." Her face appeared semi-transparent on the windshield. Her eyes were bright with tears and her jaw was tight as if she held something back behind her teeth. "Just do what they ask. Pull over and park. Step out of the car and put down your weapons. I got a read on your system before—well, I assume you cut Marcy out. That's a felony, don't you realize? Please. I've targeted you with the EMP. I don't want to use it again."

Aldo focused on his displays. As far as Rome could tell, he never even looked up at her face.

"Sorry, Gabriela. We can't. You know we didn't break those people out. I'm not letting them lock me up." Rome killed the signal.

A bright light exploded from the underside of the Condor.

"Incoming!"

The EMP burst reached them in a second. Even reacting as fast as he did, Rome couldn't avoid the entire hit. Sparks rolled across the windshield, up, and over the Halcyon until the entire right side of the car was covered in electric vines.

"Cascading failures," Aldo said. "I'm doing what I can with the backups. But if the power core goes into flux…"

Rome kept them centered with the Condor. They shot past underneath, dunked in darkness by its wings. "Don't worry. That was just a graze. Didn't affect the engine. Not yet."

The Halcyon sped below an underpass, which momentarily kept

Gabriela at bay. It did nothing against Thad and his escorts, all three of whom slowly closed the distance.

"Someone's trying to get into our nav!" Aldo yelped.

"I thought you severed all the connections."

"I didn't sever all of them. That'd be stupid."

"Not when the people trying to arrest us can use them to stop our car!"

A large shape loomed at the bottom of the slope between the hill they'd crested and the next tree line. It was way too big to be a freighter.

"Definitely Enrique, Thad's stooge." Aldo grimaced. "Can't believe how sloppy a tech he is. You see that signature? Might as well have put a VR ad into our brains that told us everything he had planned, up to and including the pathway he's taking."

"That's great. How about you concentrate on shutting him out."

"Already doing that." Aldo's fingers maneuvered commands in his holo display.

"Not there. Cut another wire."

"Hey, I wasn't just doing that because cutting things apart is fun—which it is. If I sever any more connections we're not going to be able to communicate with the nav map, let alone any other cars, and… oh, hey."

The sensors finally identified the vehicle ahead. It was a house transporter—a massive vehicle comprised of three, interconnected sections with six wheels each. Every section was big enough to straddle two of the three lanes. A pair of chase Famtracs, each one painted white with neon orange caution stripes, drove in the leftmost lane.

"Enrique's trying to override our power core settings," Aldo said. "Sloppy, but smart. If he can dip the power levels enough, they can close in for an EMP shot."

"Noted." Rome braked.

"Wait. What are you doing?"

"Prodding Thad." Rome watched the rear view. "Come on."

"Uh, this is a bad idea."

"Only if it fails."

The three cars shifted formation. One of the escorts raced ahead, leaving Thad back in the center lane with the other FTZ Security vehicle as a wingman.

"Told you. I know Thad," Rome smiled. "Always ready to have someone else do the dirty work if he can take credit. Siphon off the EMP charge to the grapples."

"Okaaaay." Aldo didn't argue, at least. Progress.

The house transporter grew ever larger ahead. Rome ignored it, for now. His eyes were fixed on the FTZ ride.

It was a 2053 Halcyon, an older model with subtle differences in the wheel covers and front fenders. It had the same general chassis. Same pros and cons as Rome's model.

The pursuer got within 100 feet. A hatch below the fender pulsed with light.

"Grapples?"

"Good to go."

"Hang on." Rome spun the car 180 degrees and deployed them.

The projectiles slammed into the front of the pursuing car. One even impacted halfway up the hood toward the windshield.

"Reel him in, top speed."

"That'll put a major drain on the power core—"

"Do it!"

Both cars snapped together like the ends of a rubber band, albeit the Security vehicle moved three times as fast. When it was less than ten feet away, Rome cranked the controls.

The Halcyon whipped into a turn, wheels skidding and smoking in a maneuver that Marcy would have instantly overridden and corrected, citing highway safety protocols. With her brain removed, the Halcyon was significantly dumbed down and let Rome do whatever he wanted.

Just like the old days.

The two cars spun about each other, equal weights on the end of an invisible line, until Rome hit "release." They shot backward toward the house transporter.

Rome threw the Halcyon into reverse. The Security car did likewise, hurtling back down the Ninety the way it came. The Driver managed to correct, but not before he smashed into the front left corner of the other Security Halcyon. Inflatable barriers exploded between them, cushioning the collision.

Thad managed to swerve around them, wheels bouncing along the median, and back onto the highway.

Aldo whistled. He enlarged the holo scan of the two cars, now immobile at the side of the road. "Well, that worked. So, good idea."

"You're welcome."

"Umm..." Aldo glanced over his shoulder. "That house transporter's not gonna move out of the way, you know. Too big."

"I know."

"Also, we're still backwards."

Rome drove as fast as he dared, hurtling wrong end first down the left lane of the highway. Their straightaway ended a couple miles up, where the road started a series of turns into the mountains. Thad's car gained.

"He hits us with that EMP, it's gonna hurt a whole lot more than just sliding off the road," Aldo said.

"No kidding. Where's Gabriela?"

"Coming up, above Thad." Aldo swiped through a menu. "EMP's charged, whatever you want to do with it. I'll target Thad."

"No. Lock on Gabriela."

"You're kidding. We can't shoot down an aircraft, Rome!"

"There should be plenty of power behind it."

Thad's car was less than a quarter mile out.

"Yeah, I get that, but I meant there was the problem of... oh, I don't know... the launcher can't pivot more than 10 degrees from the surface of the road!"

"Aldo, shut up and lock the target."

Whatever Aldo muttered was lost beneath the alert chimes from the dash.

Yes… the house transporter was way too close—near enough Rome saw the warning holograms dance along the rear bumper.

Yes… Thad locked his EMP on the Halcyon. As close as he was, he wouldn't miss. And if Rome fired his EMP now, he'd lose the chance to knock the Condor out of the sky before it could turn their car into a rolling brick.

Rome reached for the window release.

"Hey." Aldo frowned. "Hey, what're you…"

The panel slipped back and down into the hatch panel. Wind blasted into the car, swirling around Rome with a rush of cool freshness. It was a welcome relief from the car's mingled air—food, plastic, and human body stench.

He kept his right hand tight on the steering control. With his left, he drew the Hunsaker from the center console and aimed it out the open window. He thumbed the targeting module.

"Rome!"

He ignored Aldo's protest. The proximity chime rang, its tone almost lost beneath the rumble of the engine and the howl of the wind. Thad's car was so close he saw two silhouettes through the windshield above the glowing discharge port for the EMP.

Rome didn't want to kill Thad. He didn't want to be caught, either.

He fired, emptying the magazine.

The tracker projectiles sparked off the bullet resistant hood of the Panther, arcing downward, toward the pavement—

Until the last three blew the front right tire apart.

Polymers shredded in a puff of high-pressure gasses and slate gray fragments. Red flashes lit up the exterior lines and internal spaces of the Panther. It skidded into the center lane, straightened out for a few seconds, and then angled back to the left. The Panther launched down an incline just as the road curved south, going airborne over a 30-foot stretch. It slammed onto the grass. Bits of the body cleaved off as it scraped among rocks.

Aldo grabbed Rome's right arm. "You shot him!"

"Get off!"

The Halcyon skittered madly, back end swerving. Rome lashed out with his elbow, the impact shooting pain clear up to his shoulder. Aldo cried out. Rome let the empty gun fall to the floor and seized control again. He spun the car around, changing gears. It growled madly. A new, unsteady whine echoed from the power core.

The rearmost chase Famtrac for the house transport was 40 feet ahead. Automated, no passengers.

Rome accelerated again. Just as he neared its bumper, he manually toggled the front collision bags. They exploded outward, shoving the back end of the Famtrac. Rome pressed on, using the Halcyon like an old-school bulldozer. The Famtrac went into an oddly graceful, yet ponderous turn, then tumbled off the side of the road. It bounced along the embankment, following the incline to a stand of trees.

Smoke drifted up in Rome's rear view. Good thing it was unoccupied.

"Okay, look, relax." Aldo's voice shook. His hands had a worse tremor. "We can get off the Ninety up ahead. There's a turn-off."

"Show me it."

Aldo widened the hologram. Yeah, it was a standard ramp—and something in Rome's mind clicked.

"Gabriela's closing," Aldo said.

"I know."

The Condor came in low to the road, soaring only 60 feet above the pavement. Rome threaded a path around the house transport. The Condor matched it, banking sharply. Engine exhaust made the warning holos on the transport waver, but Gabriela didn't alter her course or put more distance between herself and the roof of the prefabricated home.

"Wow, she's good," Aldo muttered.

Rome never had any doubt.

The exit ramp was only a minute away. He pushed the Halcyon to top speed. If he could time it right, they could get Gabriela off their backs and gain some time to think.

If he screwed up... well... they'd be dead.

"FYI, Rome, exit ramp speed is 45." Aldo didn't bother with his displays. He held on tight to the sides of his seat. "If we're gonna make it..."

The Halcyon shot right by the exit.

"So, yeah. You missed it."

"Nope. Hang on." Rome cranked the controls.

The Halcyon left the highway.

Tires reconfigured to match the rocks and grass clods. Rome fought to keep the car straight as the terrain tugged at the wheels. They barreled down the embankment. Pine branches scraped at Aldo's window. Aldo yelled his head off.

They bounced hard up a ditch and across two lanes of a small connector road. A tow truck braked hard, skidding sidelong. Rome caught a glimpse of the warning message flashing across the windshield as two bearded men in vests and caps stared.

Rome drove up the opposite embankment, the wheels spinning dirt, grass, and pine needles.

"No, no, no! Don't get back on the road!" Aldo hollered.

"Ready the EMP!" Rome snapped.

"It's been fully charged for the last five minutes!"

All Rome wanted to hear.

Gabriela's Condor roared by, its wings twisting as it angled into a turn. She overshot them. Rome knew she lined up for a repeat of the EMP burst.

If she had the chance to fire.

The embankment was a steep incline the last 30 feet before it met the Ninety. The Condor dipped lower. The Halcyon's proximity warning blared.

"She's got us!" Aldo shouted.

"Sorry, Gabriela." Rome triggered his EMP.

The shot was perfect. It caught the Condor across the left leading wing, spreading electrical discharges across the entire fuselage. Turbofans stuttered and died. Nav lights winked out.

The Condor went into a slow, flat spin.

The Halcyon leapt the last 20 feet. For a moment, Rome didn't feel the comforting presence of the road beneath his wheels. The power core took on a high keen.

When it slammed back down, everything in the Halcyon shook. Even Rome's teeth rattled. They bounced around, but the seats and the restraint held them fast, absorbing as much of the impact energy as possible.

Aldo craned his neck. "Is she down? Can you see the Condor? Did she make it?"

He could see. The Condor's nose bent up the last second before it hit the ground. She skidded along, throwing up sprays of dirt in an open swath between a small cluster of buildings and the highway. The wings crumpled. Foam sprayed from external ports as the plane attempted to soften the landing. Finally, it halted, chin up, a wounded bird broken on the ground.

Broken, but not destroyed.

Rome didn't look away from the rear view until he saw a tiny figure emerge from the hatch. Only then did he breathe again.

The Halcyon raced on the highway until the three lanes merged to one. Rome kept his eyes on the road, in front and behind. So far, no more pursuit. So far, they were free.

"Traffic our way's bottled up behind that house transport five miles back," Aldo said. "Nothing else to report."

Rome nodded.

"So…" Aldo shut down all his displays. He stared at the road in front of them. "We're fugitives. What now?"

Rome took a second to stare, too—at the green and white of the mountains, the mirrored blue surface of the lake. He loved this route. Loved this drive.

Not anymore.

"We run," Rome said. "And we disappear."

Chapter Nine

Aldo held up his hands. "Nope. No. Again, no."

"Don't be a baby. It's a razor, not a machete."

It was two hours since they'd escaped capture. The weather cleared out as soon as they crossed the mountains, and on this eastern side the sun beat down on Rome. Heat rose from the Halcyon's hood. The landscape around them was burnt brown for miles, shades of sienna and ochre.

Aldo found them a dry gully to stop in. It provided enough shelter from prying eyes for the time being. Local Net info said this was a prime area for off-roading.

Sunnyside.

Rome would have found the name funnier if it hadn't been so bleak. Sunny, all right—way too much of it. There was a hint of green on the horizon, in the town proper to their east. There were also dozens of abandoned homes that littered the landscape.

Rome had a small battery-powered razor in one hand. Part of his toiletry kit for when they traveled. He preferred to be clean-shaven, but if they were going to get out of this mess, he'd have to forgo that comfort. Aldo, on the other hand… "It's got to go."

"No way!" Aldo clutched at his chin as if Rome were a vampire and his beard was the cross to ward him off. "Not shaving a single hair. This is me."

Rome grabbed him by the collar. "That's why you have to shave it off! Everything about us has to go—implant data, tags, names, faces. They're going to look for every sign of Rome Jasko and Aldo Burns they can pick up. We can't let them find anything."

Aldo stared at him, blinking.

Rome let him go. He raked his hands through his hair, his fingers came away sweaty. Must be the heat, combined with the strain. He shouldn't have snapped at Aldo like that. "First thing's first. Re-color."

"We're stuck maroon," Aldo said. "Unless you want to hook Marcy back up."

"No. Can't you get in and alter the programming?"

"It's gonna take a while."

Rome squinted at the sun. The sky was a bold blue, without a hint of cloud—or a speck that could be a drone, either. "Make it work. Even if it's green."

Aldo shook his head. "This is crazy. They think we helped those guys out."

"Yeah."

"Why?"

"I have no idea."

"Don't you have—I mean, isn't there someone you can talk to?"

Rome's mouth twisted. "Too big a risk to contact Freddie right now. Or anyone else. Staying off the signals is our best bet, at least until the initial pursuit winds down."

"What are we gonna do?"

Rome twisted the crucifix on the ends of his fingers. "We discuss our options."

"Options. We ran out of those." Aldo ticked off points. "Ninety FTZ West has a warrant out for our arrest. Every contract Driver on the Ninety—and probably those on any of the other major FTZs we happen to hit—is going to be after the bounty. Never mind the cred that comes with nabbing someone with your record."

"I'm flattered."

"Whatever. Also, Thad Mancos—who personally hates your

guts—is without a doubt sniffing down every crumb left on every road between the Cascades and the Rockies right now. You think we won't spark off a bounty race among the rest of his Del Norte buddies? Oh, and let's not forget we've got a car that we've got to wire back together because you made me break it!"

"It isn't broken. It's modified."

"Modified?" Aldo shook his head so vigorously Rome pictured it splitting clean off his neck. "No. Nope. Broken is an error message from the nav system or a faulty sensor that lets you bounce off the fender of a Famtrac in front of you. We deliberately crippled our car to the point of making it the automotive version of a coma patient."

"Upside, Aldo, is that she's a Halcyon." Rome patted the hood. If he left his hand on its surface he figured he'd burn it. "Unless someone manages a very up close and personal scan of her power core—which is decidedly not stock, thanks to our investment—she'll look like all the rest. Once you get the re-color done and the registration numbers changed..."

"Yeah, I get it. I can rig something. But it'd be simpler if we plugged Marcy back in."

"Right. Marcy." Rome's stomach tightened. "That's the other thing we have to deal with, before anything else."

"What about her? She needs the AI equivalent of CPR," Aldo muttered.

"She's tagged."

"Duh. So are we." Aldo waved his wrist. The implant was black as stone, and deader looking than one. "Thanks to yours truly, we're blocked out of the Net for a while. But it won't take the FTZ techs too much longer before they figure out how to access our tags. You owe me lunch for that."

"Relax, we'll eat."

"Okay." Aldo deflated somewhat. He tugged at his beard. "Marcy's tag could be a problem. Theoretically, a tech with enough skill could reactivate it remotely."

"How much skill?"

"A whole lot more than me."

"But it is possible."

"Maybe. Okay, yeah, there's a decent chance. But I can alter the connections. If I can bypass her failsafes that prevent physical tampering—"

"Aldo." Rome drummed his fingers on the hood. "We need to leave her."

Aldo frowned. "Leave her… alone? Stashed away in the tool compartment?"

"No. Here." Rome scuffed dirt. "Right here. Buried."

"What, in the middle of nowhere? Rome, this isn't a busted implant module or a comp panel." Aldo reached into the car, and brought out the neatly wrapped package. "This is an automated command and navigation computer with base level AI that cost a fair bounty with a whole bunch of zeroes! What if some kid rolls up and grabs her for parts? What if we can't find her when we come back?"

Rome put his hand on Aldo's shoulder. Aldo's eyes were wide and getting red around the edges. His hair was mussed, his beard scraggly where he'd tugged at it. "We're not coming back."

Aldo stood, unmoving.

"You're scared, and frustrated. I get it. But that's not going to help us get out of this. I need you at your best. Promise me that."

Aldo looked down at the bundle in his hands. "It's—she's our partner, Rome."

"She's a danger now. She could lead FTZ straight to us. They think we're in league with the crew of thieves, and they just killed two Security men back at West headquarters. In FTZ's eyes, we're accessories to manslaughter at best."

"I know. I know. But…" Aldo swallowed. "Okay. Let me take a shot at unhooking her tag. Please?"

Rome considered the package Aldo held, and his partner. It was part of their team—she was part of their team. She'd kept them safe for thousands of miles and hours. She was just as much their companion as Gabriela. The same Gabriela who'd immediately turned on them when her bosses issued the warrant. But, unlike Gabriela, Marcy could be reprogrammed. Maybe.

Rome blew out a breath.

"Come on, Rome. It's worth a try." Aldo's grin was half-hearted. "We all make a better crew that way."

It would make it a lot easier to hide them, using Marcy to recode the Halcyon.

Rome reached for the crucifix again. "All right. You make sure the tag's inaccessible remotely, and plug her back in—but limit her access. Only the re-color and the false registration number. Don't let her near anything that can reach the Net."

"You got it. Don't forget about the guns." Aldo eased into the car, favoring his uninjured leg.

Rome heard the bundle unwrap. Aldo started murmuring to himself.

Himself, or Marcy?

Rome checked his implant's time stamp. Tuesday afternoon. The concert was Friday. He grimaced. Odds were, Kelsey had already seen the news.

He hoped Vivian hadn't.

The basics. They needed food. And Aldo was right. The guns had to be tossed.

Rome volunteered to ride to town while Aldo took care of Marcy. It wasn't far. Just a couple of miles.

The Halcyon had room in its storage trunk for a single, foldable bicycle made of a lightweight carbon fiber nanotube structure. It had 700c rims, so the whole thing only took up three feet on either side. Rome had it unpacked and locked together in minutes. He loaded up a backpack with their guns.

It was a long time since he had a quiet ride, just to relax. It gave him time to think about everything… about nothing.

Wind whipped by, tossing up dust devils. Rome shielded his eyes. His implant flashed a message about dust levels in the valley. Drought warnings, too. What else was new?

He stopped alongside a collapsed, dry riverbank. It took a couple minutes to dig a trench, then another to put their guns in—the submachine gun he'd used against the thieves, plus his and Aldo's Hunsaker pistols. All three were tagged with benign tracers, which—under normal circumstances—did nothing but confirm the legality of ownership. Since Rome and Aldo were fugitives, however, he knew the tracer was active. As soon as they passed the nearest law enforcement drone or station, the tracer would alert authorities to the presence of illegally owned weapons.

Rome would rather take his chances with nothing but a pair of spazzers.

He removed his badge from his belt. Sunlight gleamed off it as bright as chrome on one of those old classic rides—the combustion models from a century ago that collectors outfitted with power cores. It wasn't tied to his implant. The badge was just a decoration, albeit one that displayed basic identification about the holder. It couldn't be interrogated like an implant.

Easy enough to remove the data board from the badge and keep the dead reminder in his pocket. For all his grumbling about removing Marcy from the Halcyon, Rome wasn't ready to part with the memento. He'd given up too much else.

Rome mounted his bike and headed down the road. He passed an older couple riding nearby. They waved, and smiled. Rome nodded back.

Closer to town, there were more occupied homes. The change from sparse brown weeds to green fields was startling. Most were protected under domes, each held together with octagonal frames. Moisture beaded on the inside.

Rome pedaled past the crumbling remains of a sidewalk. It improved the nearer he got to the dense neighborhoods. Houses became more clustered, scattered trees appeared—though they were gnarled, stunted versions of the mountain conifers. Cars drove by. A family of five passed, the father pushing a toddler in a stroller while the mother guided twins who could walk. An older woman led a simple, automaton carrier that lugged bags of groceries, following her like some stupid, chrome ogre.

Downtown, there were a few shopping choices. Rome ignored the automarts. They all had sensors in their entrances that marked the tag in a customer's implant. This town still had a couple of regular stores—the ones where he could use the banknotes in his pocket. Okay, so Aldo was right. It was a good thing they'd stopped for a withdrawal before their accounts were frozen, no matter the risk.

Rome gathered a bag of the basics—freeze dried meals, protein bars, and desiccated fruit. He grabbed a small case of water and made a face. It was more than twice the cost in Seattle. It doubled the price of everything else he'd just picked up.

The clerk was a young man with swirling tattoos on peach skin. His hair was shaved down to bristles dyed neon green. Rome concealed his befuddlement. Why bother, then?

The kid gestured at the white arc that curved like a duck's neck over the counter. "Tag."

"Here." Rome piled a few banknotes.

"Oh. Uh…" The kid frowned. He held the paper under the scanner. It beeped, accompanied by a green light. "Okay, I guess that works. I need to know what bank these came from. And your ID."

"Not how it works. The banknotes are legal tender without ID."

"Well, yeah, but the store policy—"

"Just give me the change, kid, and I won't make a scene," Rome smiled. It wasn't meant to reassure the clerk.

The kid's face paled under his tattoos. "No, no. That's not a problem. They're good. You're good."

Rome waited, resisting the urge to drum his fingers on the counter as the kid printed off change slips of similar shape and size to the banknotes. The transaction numbers were identical. They could be traced, yeah, but weren't linked to any person.

As he left the store with bags in hand, Rome caught a glimpse of the kid's reflection in the sliding glass doors. He talked on his implant, back turned.

Probably not good.

Rome wheeled his bike to the other side of the street. There was a crosswalk strip on the road, but he didn't bother with it. Cars on either side of him halted, their sensors arresting progress until he was safely clear of the minimal traffic. No one in either set of vehicles looked up at him. None of them even turned around in the backward facing seats.

So far, he hadn't seen any LEOs.

There was a car dealership down the block made of concrete and glass walls, with row after row of cars gathering dust on the corner. The window nearest to Rome blurred and ran an ad. It showed a sleek Halcyon, spinning its wheels down an immaculate stretch of paving, with countless shining cars around it.

"Get where you want to go. Do what you want to do. Don't worry. I'll keep you safe. I'll be there for you, wherever we are." The voice was seductive, feminine—a sultry version of Marcy, he realized. Or at least, it was meant to be. The voice didn't seem as halting as the comps he'd dealt with. Slicked up, no doubt, to better sell the vehicles.

It didn't do anything to improve his mood. He started riding. Thoughts of Aldo pining over a damaged and potentially lost Marcy faded into the background.

Come on, Rome. Think.

Sara was in the wind—literally—with the thieves. Whoever their leader was, had stayed hidden. Two men were dead, and significant property damage done at FTZ West. Warrants for his and Aldo's arrest. Gabriela tasked with bringing them in—likely carting Thad around, too.

But why him? It didn't make sense. As a contracted pursuit specialist with approval from the feds and FTZ to operate the interstate highways, he wasn't the person he'd pick to set up as an accomplice.

The next thought slammed into him with all the force of the Condor hitting the ground in a crash landing.

FTZ. Someone knew. Someone inside had access to his personnel records, and used his past against him. It made sense. With that kind of history, he'd make a tempting scapegoat.

His implant blinked. It was Aldo, sending a text only message.

<News. You.>

"Hell." Rome pulled over and activated the Net, hoping Aldo's tricks kept him invisible in the process.

There it was. Sooner than he'd expected, but they'd put it all out there.

"—suspects are Pursuit Specialist Roman Franklin Jasko and Information and Support Specialist Aldrich Harold Burns, independent contractors operating as Resolve Interception, Inc., licensed and based in Philadelphia with U.S. DOT permission. Unnamed sources confirm that Jasko was a habitual illegal driver, with multiple counts of—"

Rome cut off the signal. Perfect. Just perfect.

<Get back ASAP.>

Rome glanced over his shoulder. A police car rolled by slowly, and one of the officers inside watched him from behind mirrored sunshades. The sight made him wish he'd gone ahead and shaved his head, just like he'd badgered Aldo to get rid of his beard. Anything he could do to throw off facial recognition scans would be good.

Yeah. He'd better.

He spotted the car's fender in the sunlight about a quarter mile away, tucked down inside the dry riverbed. The dark maroon shimmered, taking on silver streaks, but seemed to hiccup. It didn't transition entirely to the new color. Whatever Aldo was doing with

Marcy had hit a glitch.

A high-pitched buzz tickled his senses. It came from the northeast, spindly and white with blue markings. Rotors spun into blurs on the ends of four wings, each one slender and tapered at the tips. Patrol drone.

Great. Rome had no idea whether it saw him. Those things carried at least two omni-directional cameras. It didn't appear to be one of the more advanced models that came equipped with IR or basic facial recognition. He watched it stop midair and change direction and altitude, before continuing a slow, deliberate path.

He knew that pattern. Standard search, prompted by something nearby that had drawn its attention.

It would ignore him, for now.

Rome stopped his bike by the mouth of the creek bed where the terrain began its descent between dusty banks. He toggled his implant. "Aldo, I'm here. We've got company."

"You think? Yeah, I noticed." Aldo's voice was as high-pitched as the drone's rotors. "Can't tell if it's spotted us—Marcy's got it tracked on passive scans."

Marcy was operational, then. "How's she doing?"

"Clunky. My fault, for severing as many connections as I did."

"Don't worry about it. We had to cut her off, you know that."

"Re-color's not going so hot."

"I noticed."

"And the new registration number won't upload."

Rome crouched low, and picked his way down the bank. Using brittle roots as handholds helped delay his slide. "I've got eyes on the drone. Do what you can about the registration. Cover it with your jacket if you have too. Anything to keeping it from reading the Halcyon."

"Well, it won't get anything from the comp, that's for sure. We're disconnected from everything. I've double-checked..."

Rome didn't like the way he trailed off. "Aldo?"

"Um."

"What is it?"

"We're transmitting a locator signal."

"Aldo…!"

"I don't know how! I thought I used every possible precaution."

Rome rubbed at his forehead. "You have to be kidding me."

"Don't worry, I'm on it. I'll block whatever the carrier signal is and…"

"Forget that. We have to take care of the drone." He saw the entire length of the Halcyon now. The maroon was nearly gone, having faded to a pink hue behind the new silver exterior.

Aldo cracked open the door, and pulled himself out, dragging his jacket.

"Get the registration numbers covered."

"I'm on it." Aldo staggered around the back of the car. He flung the coat like a matador's cape.

The buzzing intensified. Rome didn't bother looking for the drone. He ran for the car, churning up the ground. His mind moved faster. The drone would look for registration numbers first. Barring that, the make and model of the car. Of course, whatever signal was leaking from the Halcyon could give the drone everything it needed to positively ID them both.

Twenty steps to the car.

Aldo was back in his seat. Whatever he did on the displays was invisible to Rome, blurred by privacy blinders at that distance. The drone noise grew louder until the spidery craft appeared, stark like a manmade cloud against the cobalt sky.

It immediately banked for the car.

"Okay, it saw us," Aldo's voice reverberated, carried both on the wind and on Rome's earpiece. "That's bad."

"Toss me a spazzer."

"You're kidding, right? They're tuned to the human nervous system, and only then to a specific—"

"Shut up and give me the gun!" Rome slid into the side of the car, and popped open the driver's side hatch.

Aldo tossed him the spazzer. Rome caught it one-handed.

"I'm jamming its signals as best I can," Aldo told him. "'Course that means I had to open up our signals again—which, with Marcy unhooked, isn't easy."

"If you're angling for a commendation, save your breath." Rome powered the spazzer up to its maximum level. He raised it skyward.

The drone buzzed down, the black dome of a camera swiveling on its underside.

Rome fired. The air rippled around the energy discharged, distorting everything, including his view of the drone. Its rotors stuttered and its body shuddered under the touch of the bolt. Rome didn't deviate his aim. He kept the drone centered in the pulse, even as the power indicator flashed yellow and then blood red.

"You're gonna fry the thing!" Aldo said.

"That's the idea!"

"Not the drone, idiot, the spazzer!"

Rome fired a second time. A steady vibration increased. Heat stung Rome's hands. He gritted his teeth. Sweat broke out on his face and chest. The air around the spazzer poured off hot. He fired again.

Sparks exploded from the drone. Its rotors stopped, whirred at top speed one last time, and then the entire vehicle spun in a lopsided spiral down to the riverbed. The impact severed half its arms and crumpled the underside. Smoke twisted into a gray tendril.

Rome dropped the spazzer at the same time. It sizzled where it hit the dirt. He fell to his knees and shoved his hands deep into the dirt. The cooler layer soothed the burning sensation.

"You okay?" Aldo crouched nearby. He prodded the spazzer. "Man. I told you."

"Yeah, thanks." Rome examined his palms. They were red, but otherwise looked undamaged. "The jamming—"

"No problem. If the drone got anything out, it may have emitted a distress beacon before you fried it. Don't think they know anything about who it was."

"Won't take FTZ long to figure us out, though. Let me stow the bike and we can get out of here." Rome stood up.

"Wait." Aldo caught his arm. "That news on the Net. What they said… they're spamming, right? It's just a thing to make us an even hotter bounty, isn't it?"

Rome frowned. "Look. I haven't been clean with you. What they're saying about me—that I was an illegal driver—it's true. I ran modded cars twenty years ago, starting in high school. Got a lot of people hurt that way—in wrecks, in fights. I didn't give it up until a Driver caught me."

"Freddie?"

"That's the one. The best. Trained me and a bunch of other Drivers, and was a great mentor before retiring from pursuit contracts and taking up a desk job at FTZ. We learned how to use our love for the freedom of driving to do good, to do right by the law and for the safety of others." Rome leaned on the fender. "Not long after, I met Kelsey and found out a man could love more than himself. That became more true when Jake was born, and then Vivian. Now it's all crashed."

"Not everything is. Marcy's good. That whole time we were running? She was crunching numbers for the decryption from the android's CPU. And she got them."

"You're serious."

"Serious as ever. Got it all uploaded to my comp-panel. We can go after them."

Rome nodded. "That drone could have tipped someone off."

"I know." Aldo didn't meet his eyes. He seemed more interested in the tips of his shoes. "The tag—I was wrong. Thought I had it severed. But she has a backup transmitter. I never even knew it was there."

"Probably built in by the manufacturer."

"Yeah."

Windblown dirt stung Rome's face during a moment of silence. "You know what we have to do, then."

Aldo's expression was pinched, but he nodded.

He buried Marcy in the side of the ravine.

Funny. As Rome stood there, he folded his hands in front and recalled an echo of the liturgy he'd always known. May the Lord bless you and keep you…

Crazy. Marcy was just a comp.

Aldo patted the last bit of dirt over the shallow—grave?—he'd dug. He set a milky white lump of quartz over top. "Sorry, Marcy, that we couldn't do better. You were a good partner."

He didn't say anything else when they got back in the car, or when they started off down the road, past Sunnyside, or when they got onto the Eighty-Two South toward Oregon. Rome drove as steady as possible with the auto-steering engaged. It was a backup to Marcy's navigational programs, but nowhere near the same level of sophistication. No regular traffic and nav updates via their signals, but at least the proximity sensors operated.

But Rome was still at the controls. He darkened the windows and windshield as much as possible to avoid attention. They'd have to come up with something more permanent.

Aldo sat slumped in his seat. No holos, no displays. He had the electric razor in his hands. "Where are we going?"

"To see an old friend."

"I thought Freddie was with FTZ."

"Freddie can't help us. Not until I can find a secure means to communicate. We're headed to Wyoming. There's someone we can trust there."

Aldo nodded.

He hadn't even eaten anything.

Chapter Ten

The Eighty-Two and the Eighty-Four were smaller connectors, linking the Ninety with the Eighty Free Travel Zone. Patrols were correspondingly lighter. A few times, Rome started from a sleep when the Halcyon chimed that drones overflew their position.

Once it was a Condor.

But Aldo had them disguised for the time being. The Halcyon was a deep, shining chrome, and its registry numbers were an amalgam that—as far as FTZ was aware—Rome and Aldo did not have in their databanks. Aldo had fabricated a new set from scratch in the first hour and a half of their 13-hour trek.

The next half hour, he'd rigged up his comp-panel so that it could drive the Halcyon.

It wasn't nearly as responsive as Marcy, but at least Rome could stow the steering column and the other cars around them would register it as driverless. Plus, Rome had no desire to drive clear through the night. He leaned into the headrest and watched out the window as the dim white and yellow glow of passing vehicles made traffic a stream of fireflies.

They drove into a 30-mile stretch of wireless induction charging panels and the Halcyon immediately lit a graphic of the power core's level. It had dipped below 40 percent. Rome's eyes blurred as he drifted into sleep, giving him double vision of the charging progress.

Aldo shaved. Red hair rained onto his jacket, which he'd spread out on his lap as a makeshift apron. It still got all over the floor, dusting his shoes and the seat, too.

Rome didn't have the heart to bother him. Every whine of the razor, every clump of fiery hair, must cost Aldo.

The Eighty FTZ across southern Wyoming was barren as Rome had ever seen a highway. Sure, vehicles passed them every once and a while, but the bulk of them were freighters, huge convoys of them. Eight passed them end-to-end, doing 100 miles per hour. The Halcyon synced with the local Famtrac and passenger car traffic, which held at a steady 90.

The rolling landscape around them was bathed in blue—pale, powdery shades for the dry hills, dark navy for the sparse vegetation and shadows. Suddenly, a dark shape barreled alongside the Eighty, its cockpit lit up with a yellow beacon. Tiny red lights marked the ends of hundreds of containers—some boxy, some cylindrical, others spherical—all streamlined for high-speed rail travel. The train blasted by the Eighty traffic at 184 miles per hour—so the Halcyon told him, its basic nav sensors registered the speed at too dangerous for road travel.

Rome blinked at the red numbers on the dash. 2 a.m. A faint green glow encased Aldo's side of the car, silhouetting his seat. He was turned toward the window.

"Can't sleep?" Rome's mouth was as parched as the ravine at Sunnyside. He dug down by his seat, and located a hydrator bottle. He drained a third of it, clean and cold.

"No. And I'll clean up the mess whenever we get where we're going."

"Don't worry about it."

Cheyenne was a thick cluster of lights on the otherwise dark plains. Warren Air Force Base clung to the side of the city, its lights and fences demarcating its boundaries. Rome squinted. Could be there were mechs on maneuvers, bounding across the hardscrabble terrain.

Could also be that there were armored vehicles parked there, just like the kind stolen by Sara and the band of thieves.

The Halcyon exited onto a main road lined with hotels, restaurants, and boxy storefronts. Some were still under construction—skeletal frames next to which a pair of construction bots slumbered like lethargic giants. Some appeared to date to the last century.

Five minutes later they were in a parking lot, empty except for the Halcyon and weeds. The building was a flat, one-story with smoky brown glass for windows and rough textured walls that mimicked adobe. There were six business spaces, each one big enough to fit two Halcyons side by side: a Thai restaurant, a pet store, two vacant fronts, a cybernetic parts dealer, and…

"A church." Aldo's lip curled. He looked as if he might be sick.

"That's the one."

The air outside whipped along, cold and dry. Even with the glare of city lights, Rome made out countless stars.

"Well, that's just great. We won't have any trouble with one of those." Aldo shook out his jacket and brushed hair off the seats.

The sign read "Greeley Lutheran" in plain black letters on a pale blue panel. Unlike the rest of the business signage, it was not lit, nor did it feature a hologram as the cybernetic parts shop did. A disembodied hand of metal and plastics swiveled as Rome walked by.

"You planning to scan in? At two in the morning?" Aldo shrugged on his coat. He sealed it, and wrapped his arms around himself. It took a few seconds, but eventually an orange glow emanated from the cuffs and collar.

"That is the plan." Rome's jacket likewise adjusted its warmth to match the outdoor conditions.

"Dumb plan."

There was a flat black panel mounted outside the door. Rome placed his palm on its surface. It lit up red around the edges. When he removed his hand, the message "Occupant Notified" scrolled across the panel in amber text.

Rome waited for movement inside.

Aldo tucked his hands into his pockets. “Crap. Has to be below zero out here. In April!”

Rome’s implant told him it was 40 degrees. No doubt the wind chill made it feel worse, but not as bad as Aldo intimated. “Welcome to Wyoming.”

A light appeared through the window. Rome made out the silhouettes of chairs, arranged in six rows of ten each, plus a pulpit and several closed doorways. A man’s shape filled one of the doorways—a black shadow on a gold rectangle.

“I should mention now, Wyoming has next to no gun laws,” Rome said.

Aldo patted down his jacket. “My spazzer.”

“Relax.”

The door slid open on a powered track. The man standing there was huge, nearly 7 feet tall with arms as thick as trees and the body of a professional bot fighter, wrapped up in a flannel robe. He was balding with a thick gray beard and skin more like leather.

“Saints above.” His voice was a rumble of thunder. “Here Cath thought the home comp was mixing up its data. But it really is Roman Jasko standing outside my sanctuary.”

“Good to see you too, Andrew.” Rome hugged the man. He would have been less crushed by the grasp of a bear, but it was such a familiar embrace that Rome could be twenty years younger. Burdens evaporated.

“You brought company.”

“Andrew, this is Aldo Burns, my info tech. Aldo, Pastor Andrew Gold.”

Andrew clasped Aldo’s palm with both hands, smothering it. “Blessings, friend.”

“Uh, yeah. Likewise.” Aldo jerked a thumb. “I’m gonna go, maybe check on the car, see if it’s… there.”

“Stay put,” Rome glared at him.

Andrew laughed. “Boy looks like he’s got to recite catechism,

Rome."

"Can you blame him? You're probably the first pastor he's ever seen."

"True, true." Andrew gestured for them to come in. "Please."

Rome and Aldo followed him through the darkened sanctuary. There was a wooden cross inset on the wall. Aldo whistled.

"Don't fret. You can't see it from the street, as per the ordinances." Andrew opened the door ahead of them.

Beyond was a decent sized apartment. The corridor had two rooms to the left, an office, and a vacant bedroom. To the right was a large living space with furniture arranged around a stone-topped table. Tattered books jutted between the legs. Past that was a kitchen, and adjacent the kitchen was another set of doors. One revealed a bathroom, and the other a bedroom, both dim with orange lights set into the floor.

"Rome!" The woman stood in the bedroom entrance, dressed in a kimono-type nightgown, shimmering green with brilliant flowers all over it. She rushed him, and hugged him near as tightly as Andrew had. She was a head shorter than he and Aldo, with curly brown hair streaked with white. Blue eyes filled with tears. "It's been so long!"

"I told Cath she didn't have to get up." Andrew dropped his frame into a blue chair with metal legs. It creaked under his weight.

"Nonsense. If you boys are in trouble I'm not snoozing away the night. Sit down and rest. Go on. I'm making tea." She pushed them both in the direction of a long couch with matching upholstery, then headed to the kitchen. "We've got enough water left on the day's ration."

Rome wondered what they'd think if he told them about the constant deluges in Ohio or the fog in Seattle.

"So, was Rome on target?" Andrew asked.

"Not kidding," Aldo said. "You are the first."

"Disappointed?"

"Kinda." Aldo plucked at his beard—or rather, made the motion at air since his beard was gone. His cheeks reddened. "The way they talk about the churches in school, you'd think you guys were all either gun-toting militants or chanting monks."

"Hmm. Well, close in some cases, I'd reckon. But not all. If I were to—hypothetically speaking—own a gun, I certainly wouldn't tote it. But let's talk about you fellas." Andrew raised an eyebrow, each one as bushy as a dog's tail. "If you're here, it's bad."

"Seen the Net?"

"Certainly. I'm no Luddite. Most of my congregation gets my sermons that way, and when we can't meet—" Andrew shrugged. "It isn't the same as the body of Christ gathering in one place, but in spirit, it's close enough. I should hand it to you, Rome—when you get in trouble you don't do it by half-measures. I should comment on the FTZ tip site."

Rome leaned back onto the sagging couch. The antique didn't even adjust to his contours. It just sat there like a sullen pet. He ran his hand along the arm of the sofa. Yeah, the bare patch was still there. "Sure would help you with your taxes."

Aldo crossed his arms and scowled at them both.

"Take heart, beardless child," Andrew rumbled. "I'm not turning either of you in. I'd no sooner turn my back on one of my former congregants than I'd delete my Scriptures."

"Right."

"Seriously, Aldo," Rome said. "I was joking."

"You know what's not a joke? The bounty on us!" Aldo waved his implant between them. The holographic numbers blurred into a green smear. "Same as what we were gonna get paid for bringing in the thieves! Except we don't get it, or even half if we'd have to share with shit-brain Thad!"

Andrew winced.

"There won't be any of that talk in my home." Cath approached with two cups of tea. Steam swirled off the tops, carrying a hint of plum. She handed one to Andrew, and one to Rome. "You keep that dirty mouth running and you'll be waiting in the car, and I don't care what the FTZ does."

Rome shook his head.

Cath kissed Andrew on the cheek and patted Rome's arm. "I've got to be up for my shift at the med center early. Goodnight all."

"'Night, darling." Andrew watched her leave. Then he regarded Aldo with the curiosity of a man inspecting a strange insect. "You must like danger."

"Drive with him, don't I?" Aldo slumped into the couch. "So, what, I don't get tea?"

Rome sipped it. Piping hot, the best. "Aldo's got a point, Andrew. FTZ hasn't found us yet but I'm running short on banknotes. I wouldn't fault anyone for thinking they could make some bucks off our capture."

"Won't argue that. But some things are of far greater value than money. The soul, after all." Andrew winked. "Since you mentioned money, though…"

He handed his tea to Aldo. "Do not drink it, boy."

Aldo held it, staring.

Andrew crossed the room and lifted a photo set of himself, Cath, and several children, all of whom appeared to be in their twenties. Behind the photo was a wall safe. He pressed his face near to a tiny strip of black and white plastic to the right. Gold light played across his eyes.

The safe opened with a barely audible hiss.

"Ah. Thank God." Rome joined him.

"Don't make light, Rome."

"I'm not. Meant both words." Rome reached inside the safe. He removed a pair of bags—both black, and both longer than his arm. "You kept them."

"I did. They're your property, and I promised you they'd be ready when you needed them most."

"Good thing." Rome set both bags on the floor in front of Aldo.

"Christmas presents?" Aldo held Andrew's tea. The cup trembled.

"Next best option." Rome unzipped the first bag. It was packed full of stacks of banknotes, dozens of them. There were also twenty packages of coins, gold and silver, stamped with the insignias of several different mints. Rome nestled one container in the palm of his hand. It held six silver coins.

"Holy—" Aldo cut off the rest. Andrew glared at him. "That's, um, a lot of money."

"Eighty thousand. I've been stashing it for years. Every bounty we got, I'd take a percentage, cash it out, and send it to Andrew," Rome smiled. "Kind of a pain, too."

"What, did I ever complain about having to drive to seven different post office boxes in Wyoming, Nebraska, and Colorado?"

"Until now? No. So thanks."

Andrew chuckled. He retrieved his tea and took a long sip. "Well, it was my pleasure. The second bag, I made sure to open and clean the contents every so often. Nothing like proper maintenance to ensure proper performance."

Rome unzipped the bag. He drew three J-60s. Stuffed in the far end of the bag were 21 magazines.

"Amen to that," Aldo muttered.

Rome finally convinced Aldo to get some sleep, but only after he moved the Halcyon around the back of the business buildings. By the time he came back in, Aldo was curled up on the couch. He snored a few times. To Rome it sounded like a belching dog.

"Boy could resurrect the dead," Andrew muttered.

He and Rome sat in the darkened sanctuary where Aldo's snores were more faint. "Yeah, well, he's had a rough couple of days."

"Where'd you find him? FTZ assign him to you?"

Rome nodded. "Four years ago. He was a rookie—never even been with someone driving a car before. Hell—sorry, heck, I don't think he'd even seen anyone do it. But he's skilled with the comps. About as good as having a second one aboard."

"What's with the beard? He looks like he just shaved. Badly."

"Made him ditch it. I've got some dye—he'll have to go brown for a while."

"Makes sense. He's as bright as Santa Claus on top. And I see you're carrying scruff on the chin, too."

"Anything easy we can do to throw off facial rec."

"Makes sense." Andrew took another long sip. His eyes didn't leave Rome.

"Okay, what's wrong?"

"What do you mean?"

"You're a good man, Andrew. The best. But you won't lie to me. And you just repeated yourself, which means something's bothering you that you won't say." Rome gestured toward himself. "Download it for me."

Andrew set the mug aside on a vacant chair. He leaned forward, elbows perched on his knees with his hands clasped. "The Lord's clear enough about worry. We're not supposed to, even when it pertains to the future. Got enough trouble for the present."

"Won't argue that," Rome murmured.

"That said, I'm worried about you, Rome."

"Me too."

"Now, be serious. I know you boys are on the run. What kind of plan do you have?"

"Can't tell you the details, Andrew. The less you know, the less you have to answer for if anyone finds out we were here." Rome frowned. "But, bare bones: we're changing our looks, Aldo will forge us some new electronic credentials, and then we'll stay hidden."

"I don't suppose your family realizes this."

Kelsey. Vivian. Jake. The concert was on Friday. It was very early Wednesday. There was still time, if they drove as non-stop as possible…

What, was he kidding?

"I haven't been in touch. Being on the run puts a crimp in Daddy sending a signal."

"The people who've done this to you. You're going to stop them. Correct?"

Rome shifted in his chair. He suddenly felt tired and knew the past 24 hours caught up with him as the adrenaline wore off. He wanted nothing more than to sleep. "There isn't much I can do. It doesn't feel right."

"Feel right? Feelings have nothing to do with it, Rome. It's either right or wrong. Day or night. Can you look at what's happened to you, to the innocents who've been hurt, and tell me otherwise?" Andrew retrieved his mug. His wedding ring pinged against ceramic. "I can't make you do what needs to be done. Not even God will force you. But there is a drive in you toward the light—I've known it since the first time you crept in our back door. Deny all you want, but the truth… the right, will pursue you with far greater diligence than any drone and driver."

"I just want to hang it up." Rome's admission was a surprise, as if he heard himself voice-cloned by an AI. "To go see my kids, put all this in park, and walk away."

"You can't."

"Why not? I'm entitled to the rest. I've paid my penance."

"Not arguing that. But what will you tell your kids when you've given it all away? That their father no longer cares about pursuing what's good, right, and salutary? You can rest when those who do wrong and hurt others are brought to justice." Andrew reached over and slapped his leg. "I'm going to bed. You'll need your sleep, too." He left, the darkness was interrupted by a brief splash of light from the apartment door behind them.

Rome leaned in the chair, ignoring the half-full cup of stone cold tea. He wished it was a lot stronger.

Six a.m.

The sun turned the sky from black to pale blue, then rose streaked with fiery orange. It colored the tiny bathroom the same shade. Rome's face was cast in bronze.

He stood in front of the mirror. He already had decent stubble of black and silver growing. Give it a day or so, and he'd be halfway to a beard.

Rome ran a hand through his hair again. Wouldn't be him, as Aldo inferred. Did that make such a difference? Changing his looks didn't mean changing him, the person. Did it?

Did he even want to be Rome Jasko?

He flicked on the electric razor. It hummed, his fingers vibrating to its motor. Rome cut through the hair on the right side of his head, strip after strip. Coal black clumps fell to the white tile. His scalp was shockingly pale. The buzz of the blades intensified with each pass.

Rome glared at himself in the mirror. Hide? That wasn't him. Neither was the pity party.

The facts of the case—and the fiasco it had become—filled his head. The gang of thieves had a leader, someone with access to a Condor lifter and military tech that included stealth suits and a disappearing truck. Bacevich Arsenal in Michigan might have lost one of those, but it was being hushed up. Someone was after more than just a simple scapegoat for the whole mess. They'd targeted Rome for his background, for his status as a Driver, and all the liability and publicity that went with it.

Rome didn't care who he was up against or what they wanted. As far as he was concerned, the person behind everything was a killer—certainly the deaths of the two FTZ security guards were on his or her hands, along with the pain suffered by the victims of the robberies. Whoever it was, they took Rome's life away… and Aldo's, too.

Right or wrong. Black and white. They had the coordinates for the location used by the thief leader to remote control the android decoy.

Rome didn't feel sorry for himself. He brushed off his self-pity's attempt to gain a second audience.

The only man he felt sorry for was whoever had crossed him.

Chapter Eleven

They got past the Chicago Restricted Coast without having to hit any sensored checkpoints. Rome spotted a stream of small freighters coming out of the South Gate, stamped with Red Cross icons. More relief supplies, no doubt. The sporadic traffic entering the CRC consisted primarily of military transports.

"Think they'll ever get it put back together?" Aldo's face was lurid red with the local travel warnings.

"It's been eight years. I'm not optimistic."

It wasn't long after entering Indiana that Rome saw the familiar car in the rear view.

"That isn't Thad… it can't be!" Aldo stared at the image, gazing through his holographic displays.

"It sure can. Run the comparison." The car was black instead of Thad's trademark blue and gold, but Rome was sure of it.

No emergency lights, yet. No alerts to local traffic. So, Thad hadn't taken manual control. Nobody watched the road, period. Not when the comp took care of the safety notices. It made Rome feel like a stranger in a room full of friends. Like now, when he saw everything suffused in the golden light of the sun as it dipped low on the horizon. He bet he'd be the only person on the road to remember it.

"I'll overlay." An image of the Panther appeared in Aldo's display. It drifted onto a second car of near identical features. "That's—huh. It is him. Same chassis, same contours, different color and registration."

"No surprise there. We did the same thing."

"But how'd he find us?"

"Could've tracked us since Sunnyside. Could have picked up a facial recognition hit when we passed Cheyenne, or when any number of drones flew by."

"Yeah, okay, but we still look like all the other Halcyons out there, and without the same registration. How's he going to—"

Red and blue lights erupted behind them. A light pulsed on the dash.

Aldo scowled. "Bet that call's for you."

Rome killed the signal. "Nearest exit?"

"South Bend. You want to take it?"

"Point us that way." Rome eyed the map and looked again at Thad's speed. "We'll make it."

Road construction lined the highway for twenty miles. They were finally approached the end of it. Hulking assembler robots hefted girders, while other, squat robots extruded paving. Crews of ten to thirty people—mostly men, ranging in age from their late teens to their fifties, though Rome saw a woman for every eight workers—dug out culverts, laser-lined railings, bolted down ramp fittings, and generally scurried around the robots as if they were the masters and the humans mere attendants.

"Infrastructure Rebuild Corps sure is busy here," Aldo said. "You'd think there wouldn't be anything left to fix after running non-stop for thirty years."

"There's always old bridges buckling or roads falling apart," Rome groused. "And there's the jobs—last count was 4 million employed. Pales compared to the five times the number working for IRC across the country in the 2020s."

"Oh, no doubt. Things were a wreck back then. But now we've got more bots. Seems like fewer people is the word of the day."

"My dad did that work—still consults from his engineering firm. Grandfather was on one of the first crews as a designer and supervisor."

"What, you didn't feel the urge to play with concrete and carbon fiber all day?"

"Too slow."

They took the ramp with a dozen other cars and Famtracs, streaming single file down the ribbon of road cutting across a green slope. It dumped them into a two-lane road where incoming cars merged seamlessly with the other traffic.

Thad's car slowed far behind them, stuck behind a line of ten more vehicles.

"Okay, do a comparability scan."

"Comparable to what—" Aldo grinned. "Ah. Gotcha. No problem."

"I figured that."

"One scan of silver Halcyons, coming up."

Within thirty seconds, Aldo's scan results pegged eight Halcyons with similar color schemes, all built in the past five years. He transferred the results to the dash and the windshield, where the car's sensors ghosted red outlines over the nearest vehicles.

"Beautiful." Rome triggered the manual controls, and kept the Halcyon as steady with the other traffic as he could. There was a trick to maintaining the appearance of a car run by comp—drive cautious, but react with lightning reflexes. When he'd worked for his first interception company, they'd taught their trainees how to do it seamlessly, but after several years on the road, the skill was lost on most Drivers.

Rome's hands sweat. He was in that majority, but he practiced now and then. He hoped Andrew was praying back in Cheyenne.

He guided the Halcyon into the mix of cars, now slowed to 40 miles per hour. Amber lights hovered above the lane, far ahead. Familiar amber lights… "Great."

"What?" Aldo craned his neck. "Oh. More construction."

"Yeah."

The vehicles around them continued to slow in near unison. Rome followed their lead and mimicked their moves. He and Aldo wouldn't have any warning of approaching construction zones. Should have seen that coming. Without their link to the surrounding cars, they were guiding themselves, receiving only basic proximity warnings from those vehicles.

The rear view showed Thad still stalled several cars back. He scooted into the left lane when a small gap presented itself, but then couldn't get any further.

Rome grinned. Count on comps to keep their vehicles running as close together as possible, at speeds and reaction times that precluded lane switching in tight quarters.

"Ain't gonna keep him stuck there forever," Aldo said. "You want me to try to route some construction bots into his path? That'd overload him."

"No. No sense drawing more attention to ourselves, and if you go out playing with navigation systems, Thad's pal Enrique will probably catch you."

"I'm insulted." Aldo frowned at his reflection in the window. "Not as insulted by this hair color. Plain old brown?"

"Shut up." Rome glanced left. The side of the road was thick with trees, but every so often, there was a road. He glimpsed identical homes, white and tan, plus parked cars. "Got a residential neighborhood, left."

"Ah…" Aldo swiped through his holos. A square of mapped terrain sprang up three times its original size. "Check. No access though. This road runs parallel to the one on the side of the neighborhood, and there's four side streets heading east off of—"

Rome cranked the steering controls. The Halcyon cut left, in front of a Famtrac. He saw the backs of two adult heads behind a smoky gray windshield. A little blond boy between them stared, eyes wide as the moon.

"Hey!" Aldo dropped a grain bar on the floor. He scrambled for it, cursing.

Rome was glad to see he had his incessant appetite back, but it'd serve him right if he got hair all over it. There were still scattered remnants.

Their car bounced across the narrow median, wheels lifting them up and tread adjusting to the off-road surface. In a second, they were on the parallel street at the edge of the neighborhood. Rome steered left, heading opposite the way they came.

They shot past Thad's Panther. Its windows were dark enough that all Rome saw of his pursuer was the silhouette that turned toward them.

Aldo flashed them the finger.

Rome cut down one of the side streets. A red outline blinked into view.

"Got another one," Aldo said. "Same model, different make. Color's near enough you can't tell the difference unless you've got top-shelf scanners and a tech better than me."

"Good enough." Rome drove past, braked, then backed up with one hand twisting the controls. He got the Halcyon within two feet of its counterpart.

"Umm…" Aldo looked over his shoulder. "So, we're gonna wait here for him?"

"You are." Rome grabbed the black bag from the back seat. He popped the door. "Stay put and play dumb."

"Yeah, okay, or I could just run, too!"

"Can't. I need you to distract Thad," Rome smirked. "Pretend you're panicked."

"Pretend? Oh, sure! I'm not freaking out or anything."

Too late. Rome was out, jogging across the yard. The ground squelched underfoot with each step. He made for the hedge that formed a barrier between it and the neighboring property. It was only 30 feet from the parked cars, but tall enough to provide cover.

Rome ducked behind it. He drew the J20 out of the bag and checked the magazine. Good, trackers.

The rumble of an engine alerted him. The Panther shot onto the street at the same speed and near same recklessness Rome exhibited when he'd cleared the median. It slowed to a crawl in the middle of the street.

Come on, Thad. Roll on by. Rome sighted on the Panther's tires. He felt a twinge of remorse about doing the same thing to the same, very nice vehicle within the past couple of days. Only for the car's sake, though.

The Panther jumped forward, then skidded, its back end turning out. Thad stopped it so it crossed a T to the parked Halcyon.

Smart.

"Vamos!" Thad and Enrique were both out of the car, leaning over the doors. They aimed spazzers. "Get out of the car, Roman! You and your tech!"

"Hey, hey!" Aldo exited, hands reaching for sky. "He bolted! I don't know where he is."

"Get down on your knees. On your knees!" Thad snapped.

Aldo complied. Even from this distance Rome could see the tremor in his hands.

Enrique reached him first. He patted Aldo down, one hand along each side. "Unarmed." The man's voice was a gargled whisper.

"Where is Roman?" Thad tucked the end of the spazzer under Aldo's chin.

"Dunno. I told you!" Aldo pointed right, across the street—in the opposite direction of Rome's hiding place. "He took off that way. Jumped right across the hood! He left me sitting here with nothing to do but wait for your sunny faces to show up."

"You expect me to believe you did not take the opportunity to escape?"

"I'm not certified," Aldo said. "Can't drive. Not legally or even illegally."

"Small wonder you two lose contracts to Del Norte."

Rome fired.

The gunshot cracked like thunder. The Panther's front left tire exploded, heaving the front end up.

Thad pivoted, spazzer up, and shot back. The pulse rippled through the air, causing only a tremor in the leaves where it breezed through the hedges.

Aldo hopped up, bringing his shoulder into Enrique's gut. The man's breath expelled loudly, as if he dry-heaved. He staggered back, clutching his abdomen. The instant his spazzer hit the pavement, Aldo scooped it up.

Rome moved in a duck walk. Thad bounced around in the J20's sights, but green indicators flashed on the target as soon as the tracking software got a positive lock. Rome fired again with a three-round burst.

The first two bullets went high. The third struck Thad's spazzer dead on. It shattered, leaving Thad with a spray of sparks and a broken handgrip. He swore and dropped it. His hand dipped behind his jacket.

"Don't." Rome stopped 10 feet away. He adjusted his aim so Thad's head was bracketed. "I won't miss, Thad. Bring out your hand. Slowly."

Thad stayed motionless. Behind him, Enrique was on his knees, glaring at Aldo. The spazzer hummed. "Yeah, I'd do what he says, boys," Aldo grinned.

"You have lost your mind. Gone completely loco." Thad drew his hand out. The blade it held was at least four inches long, serrated, flat black with an orange handle.

"Drop it."

Thad squeezed the hilt. The blade retracted to a quarter its length, narrowed, and folded into a compact orange container. He let it fall.

"Aldo?"

"Check." Aldo stepped in with his spazzer still trained on Enrique. He snatched up the knife. "What do we do with them?"

"Make it difficult to follow."

"You already shot out my tire. Again." Thad scowled at him.

"Yeah, somehow that didn't work as well as I thought, because here you are. I'll give you that much—you're persistent."

"You're—"

Aldo's spazzer discharged. Enrique grunted and slumped to the ground. His arms and legs slapped the pavement, splashing in a puddle.

"Aldo!" Rome snapped.

"What? That's what you meant, right?"

"I meant I wanted you to disable his comp!"

"Oh." Aldo scratched the back of his head with the spazzer. "Well, yeah, okay. I'll go do that."

"Do you think it will be so easy?" Thad snarled. "Touch my car and a spazzer strike will feel like a woman's kiss by comparison."

Aldo froze, hand hovering over the frame.

"Anti-personnel measures," Rome said. "You're prepared, too."

"And you're a fugitive. You shouldn't have run, Roman. Why did you bother? You know you'll be caught."

"Funny. I don't hear any air support."

"You put down my air support. She was your friend, remember?"

Remorse turned Rome's gut. "Gabriela. Is she okay?"

Thad tilted his head aside. "She is unhurt. Physically. Her heart, though, is not so well, *amigo*."

"I'm not your friend, Thad."

"No. But you are a Driver. All this—" Thad waved his hands in a rolling motion. "Is pointless. You cannot outdrive us."

"I'm doing pretty well so far. Here's the deal. Stay off my tail. I'll explain it all later."

"Is that a threat?"

"Yes."

Thad frowned. "You run me off the road and shove a gun in my face, you accost me and my tech… for what? Why delay the inevitable?"

"I think you're pompous and dangerous, Thad, but I never had you tagged as stupid. Come on—we both chased after those thieves. Why would I be in with them? Why would I stand by while FTZ boys got killed?"

"You are aiming a lethal weapon at me right now."

Rome lowered the gun. "I won't tell you again. Don't come after me."

"You want me to leave you be. So you can do… what?"

"So I can find out who's really behind all this."

"That is a lot to ignore when the bounty on your head is so deliciously sweet."

"Aldo? Get me the other bag."

Aldo was already back in the Halcyon with his nav and communications systems up and running. He rummaged in the back seat. "Got it."

Rome took it from him and pulled out a container. It held a handful of gold coins.

Thad's eyes widened. "*Madre Dios.*"

"Don't trust you a bit, but I know you'll abide by a contract. Consider this ours." Rome handed him the container. "Ten thousand. Untraceable. Let me slide, you get the rest."

Thad glanced at Enrique. The tech was immobilized, staring skyward. He snatched up the container. "You are crafty, Roman Jasko."

Rome shrugged. "I make do."

"You realize this is not a full ten thousand dollars. I have to repair my tires."

A low buzz grew louder. Drones? Thad hadn't been entirely honest about the lack of aerial support. Shocking.

Rome got into the car. He started the engine. It was a tight spot between Thad's Panther and the Halcyon behind them. "Best offer I can make. Keep my road clear." He backed up, bumping the other vehicle. It skidded. Suddenly a warning appeared on Rome's dash. Rear impact cushions burst.

Aldo just shook his head.

Rome put the car into drive and took off the down street. He made sure not to run over either rival. The last he saw of Thad, he was staring at the container in his hand.

They drove east. Staying on the Ninety allowed for higher speeds, but Aldo reprogrammed the route to occasionally include rural and less traveled state roads. Those weren't monitored as often and with less vigilance than the main highways. It helped that most of their next leg was in the dark. Rome let Aldo's comp do the driving so they wouldn't need headlights active.

"Drone must have gotten off a signal with our image before you spazzed it," Aldo said.

"I figured. If it was during the re-color, Thad and Enrique would have had a baseline to work off of—and if they had our rough direction of travel, that would have made tracking us easier."

Aldo's displays lit the interior of the Halcyon with a series of flat maps and 3-D terrain views. Coordinates streamed down the middle. "New York. The signal operating the android dummy came from there. I'm checking to see if there's anything still coming out of there."

"You think they wouldn't have shut it down?"

"They'll have shut down the link to that android, yeah. But my guess, whatever transmitter they're using has to be for more than just one purpose. No sense in having a one-shot transmitter, right?"

"I'd have one. Break it when I was done." Rome drummed his hand on the window. The ghostly glow from passing cars and charging sections illuminated the dark landscape. It was soothing—the lights, the sounds of the engine, the whisper of the tires on the road.

"Well... okay, so it's a theory. I'm running with it."

Rome eyed his implant. No contacts. Not surprising. It was off-line. If he were looking for a message from Andrew, or Kelsey...

Hours passed. It was late. Midnight. Rome's body ached as he fought back the dizziness from the conflicts that swirled in his mind. He needed to clear his head. He wanted to stop, get out, and stretch, but Aldo snored beside him, his face lit green and blue by the holos. The program ran what he assumed was a search, judging by the endlessly spinning icons and the flicker of light. Rome couldn't stay in the car another moment.

When the nav system highlighted the next exit, he reached for Aldo's comp panel. He entered a new location that was 20 minutes out of their way. He didn't intend to wake Aldo. Let him rest.

The Halcyon drove over the river onto Goat Island. Even this late, they passed a handful of cars. Rome overrode the window lock and lowered it far enough to let the cool night's breeze into the car. He smelled it—wet earth, damp grass. A steady rumble overwhelmed the car's faint engine sounds.

Rome left the car in a lot away from the nearest light globe. The path to the river's edge was deserted. He walked quickly, aware the time index on his implant glowed from his wrist. He should make it in time.

Niagara Falls spread out before him, a churning beast of frothing water. The roar from more than 3,000 tons of it cascading over the rock and plunging nearly 17 stories to the rest of the river below sat deep in his chest. The falls were aglow with blue and green lights from Ontario, projecting the illusion that it was a wall of ice or some hidden chasm of the Antarctic—or whatever might be left of that half-melted wasteland.

Rome leaned his elbows on the fence and let the mist wash over him.

This was his sanctuary. His chapel. Far better for him than any pew. Nothing against Andrew and his breed.

The moment was gone far too fast. One by one, the lights blinked out until the falls reflected only a hint of the city's glow in the distance. The thunder stayed.

He removed Thad's knife from his pocket. One gentle squeeze and the blade extended, growing its signature serrations. Rome considered its razor-sharp edge, its obsidian color blending perfectly with the night.

Footsteps. Rome glanced back.

"Hey." Aldo stretched his arms wide and yawned loud, shattering any semblance of tranquility. "You freaked me out."

"Didn't think you needed a note."

"Me? Nah. I enjoy waking up abandoned in the car in a dark, empty parking lot. Should do it more often." Aldo tucked his hands in his pocket. He wiped his face. "Wet."

"Yeah."

"Once I saw on the nav where we were, I figured you'd be out here. Kelsey?"

Rome nodded. "Our first anniversary. Long time ago."

"I take it that's why we stop here every spring, if we happen to be on FTZ East."

"You're not leaning as bad on the leg. Better?"

"Isn't worse. They knit it up pretty good before we sped out of FTZ West headquarters. It ached the first day or so, but it's fading. I'm gimping less, so, hooray."

Rome watched the torrent before him. Relentless. Driven. He put the knife away. "You come out here because your beauty sleep was up?"

"Nice. Yeah, and plus, I got a hit on my search." Aldo rolled his eyes. "Thing's slower than a kitchen comp's cleaning algorithm."

"What've you got?"

"A transmission source. Like I figured."

"Huh. So… you were right."

"He said it!" Aldo bounced his fists off the rail and whooped. "Roman Jasko, you've admitted I'm right, which makes you… what's that 'w' word?"

"Shut up." Rome backhanded him in the chest. "Where's it located?"

"Between Batavia and the Lake Ontario shore. Can't be more precise now, but the closer we get, the more accurate the trace."

Rome rubbed at his eyes. Images blurred. "Okay then. Let's go find it."

The drive ended at a turnout hidden in the trees on the north side of the Erie Canal.

Aldo peered out the window onto the glassy surface of the waterway. "This is it?"

"What was once the most efficient way of moving goods across rough terrain, now a piece of transportation history."

"It's a ditch."

Rome scowled. "Ditch? That's like calling the Ninety a long driveway. Aldo, the canal is the predecessor to our highways. Swift transportation."

"Okay, sorry, preach on."

Rome switched to manual and nudged the Halcyon through the undergrowth that poked up through crumbling asphalt. He drove only with running lights on, no headlights. The sky was full of stars, so he had enough illumination to prevent steering off the road.

It curved just a quarter mile back into the trees. Every foot was more overgrown than the last. For the final hundred yards, branches scratched at the car doors.

"Up ahead," Aldo whispered. "You see it?"

He did. Even if the Halcyon's proximity sensors hadn't outlined it in red, Rome wouldn't have missed the tall, slender tower of gray and green. It barely topped the trees. The clearing it sat in could accommodate a car or two, but that was it. It was well concealed. The camouflage netting that draped the clearing was a nice touch, too.

They approached the tower on foot. Aldo found an access panel on one side. He didn't touch anything with his hands. Instead, he used his autonomous scanner. It hovered by his side and cut apart the panel with a tiny laser torch that hissed like a snake.

"Okay. This isn't as bad as I thought." Aldo peered inside. He tapped on his implant. The scanner shone white light from its underside. "Hmm. Yeah, much better."

"Better than what?"

"Better than there being an EMP in place or something else to fry it if we mess with it."

"Can you hook us in?"

"Yeah."

"Good. Because I want to see every signal they send. I want to know where they are and what they're doing."

"You got it. Give me an hour, maybe two, and we'll be set."

An owl hooted in the treetops nearby. An answering hoot came from far off.

"What do you need?"

"Tools from under my seat. The whole batch." Aldo tapped in more commands. The scanner extended spindly arms into the guts of the panel. Nothing in the mess of wires and modules was familiar.

Rome retrieved the tools from the car, and brought Aldo the entire mess in a satchel that was bent and twisted from being perpetually jammed under his seat. He leaned against the fender and watched Aldo work, guiding the scanner, removing and crossing wires, and occasionally shoving the scanner aside so he could do something himself.

"Rome."

"Yeah?"

"You're, uh, creeping me out. Why don't you rest? Bet you've slept way less than me."

Rome rubbed his head and was startled when he felt bald scalp—not a trace of his hair save for tiny bristles. He forgot. "Good plan."

"I know, right? Don't want you shooting me or… say… anymore cars. Bad enough you do that when you're rested." Aldo dug a folded pouch of hazy gray material from his jacket. He scooped out dried cranberries and crammed them into his mouth. "C'mon."

"You're the boss, Technician."

"Mmph."

Rome swiveled his seat around until it faced the rear of the Halcyon and laid it into a sleeping position. He expanded the foam headrest to a more comfortable pillow size and zipped his coat. Within a few seconds of relaxing, the jacket adjusted its ambient temperature to better enable sleep.

He drifted off to the conversation of the owls, interrupted only by Aldo's soft cursing.

The transport truck ripped away from him, dragging him out of the car and into midair. His shoes skidded on the pavement. Pain shot through his legs.

Sara held out her hand and yelled.

The man behind her aimed a gun, and fired…

Rome jolted. The sound was deafening.

"Hey!"

Again, the noise. This time it was subdued. Aldo rapped on the door's frame. It must have been what triggered the gunfire in his dream.

Rome rubbed at bleary eyes. "What? What time is it?"

"Six-thirty." Aldo had deep circles under his own eyes, but his grin was manic. "I've got them."

"You what?" Rome adjusted his seat upright. He started the engine and activated all systems.

Aldo already climbed into his seat. "They're coming up the Ninety, like we did, along the Lakes. Got their coordinates and everything. I'm shadowing their signal."

"Shadowing. You mean they're using their signal to override someone's nav system."

"Just like we saw when they went after the Sartorian lady."

"How far out are they?"

"Maybe an hour. Less, if you floor it."

Rome put the car into a tight K-turn, missing an oak by a hand's breath. They took off, bouncing down the access road.

Chapter Twelve

The Ninety along the Lakes' shore was crammed full of vehicles. Maneuvering would be a challenge this close together, especially undetected.

"There is no way we are not getting spotted the second you put it back into manual," Aldo said.

"Tell me about it." They moved at a decent 90 miles per hour clip and blended well with the surrounding traffic. Rome knew Aldo was right. The autonomous vehicles would detect a vehicle moving under manual guidance and immediately steer clear of it while contacting all adjacent cars with a safety warning. That safety warning would travel up and down the lanes faster than the wildfires that swept the plains every summer.

Rome drummed his fingers faster. It was a risk he was willing to take.

"They're five miles ahead of us. No sign of them on sensors, but the signal's coming in loud and clear."

"Pinpoint it for me."

"Can't yet. But I got something better." Aldo pulled a list from thin air—a glowing sheet of text that filled the space between his knees and the dash. "Voilá. Roster of possible targets for our merry bandits—same one I pulled Sartorian's name from. Uploading it into the nav system."

"Right. If we find a target in the vicinity of the signal—"

"Then we find our magical disappearing truck." Aldo snapped his fingers and pantomimed shooting Rome.

Rome rolled his eyes.

Within a half a minute, more than two dozen red outlines draped themselves over cars in the stretch of three-lane roadway ahead of them. The glare from the morning sun shot up over trees, bathing everything in a sharp-edged light. Rome squinted. He tapped the controls for the window dimmers, darkening them further.

"Okay. Got three possibles within a quarter mile of the signal area."

"Give me the center of that signal area."

"It's hazy," Aldo said. "Can't be more precise than that quarter mile."

"Better than nothing."

Three cars pulsed red while the rest of the thieves' potential targets faded to yellow.

Rome frowned.

There were six gaps in the traffic large enough to accommodate the truck. Without the more advanced sensors Marcy used to operate—and that would definitely tip off the Halcyon's presence as a pursuit car to FTZ Security—he relied on anything else he could get. "Program nav. Get us into that first gap."

"You're kidding." Aldo stared at him. "We go in there and the truck's there, you know what will happen?"

"The proximity sensors won't pick it up and we'll ram it."

"Oh. You do know."

Rome nodded.

"And… that's your plan."

"Dammit, Aldo! Just do it!"

"Okay, all right!" Aldo entered new coordinates, smacking the surface of his comp panel with such frustration that Rome was certain it was meant for him and not the device.

The Halcyon switched lanes—staying within traffic laws—and nudged toward the gap behind the rumbling freighter.

Rome's stomach churned. If they hit it too fast…

Nothing.

Aldo exhaled. "Wow. No stress there."

"Quit whining." Rome ignored the thunderous beat of his heart. It was a gamble. "Line up the next one."

He heard a hissing noise. Spray spattered the windshield. Water?

Rome craned his neck. They entered a stretch of the Ninety that appeared to have been rained upon recently. The freighter must have hit a puddle. There were several shallow ones scattered across the highway.

Perfect.

"What're you—"

"Hang on." Rome leaned forward.

Up ahead, a huge puddle stretched across the two outer lanes. A freighter splashed through it, followed by a Famtrac, and one of the luxury cars Aldo had highlighted. Then water sprayed up for no apparent reason.

"That's it." Rome switched control to manual. "Mark the coordinates."

"Got it, got it." Aldo swiped frantically at his displays as the straps cinched around him and Rome. "Okay, bringing up the specs from our last oh-so-friendly encounter."

A wireframe of blue appeared on the windshield, filling the gap in traffic with the digital representation of where Rome's guess overlapped Aldo's signal trace.

Rome grinned. Gotcha.

Cars peeled off around them as he accelerated. A raft of safety warnings skittered across the dash. The luxury sedan, a black Monaco SR with silver trim and burnished gold windows, drove along the center lane as if the automaton in charge hadn't a care in the world.

The gap in traffic aligned to the Monaco's right. Air currents rippled.

"Charging the EMP," Aldo said.

Rome let the targeting reticle drift over the wireframe outline of the thieves' truck. The EMP would take too long to fully charge. The best chance he had was to fire off at 30 percent and hope it knocked out a critical system. Then what… magnetic grapples? The truck outweighed the Halcyon. They'd get dragged along.

The truck suddenly solidified as a black lump on the highway. The Monaco attempted to brake and switch lanes—at least, that's what it looked like to Rome. He labeled it an "attempt" because the Monaco swerved back to its original position.

The left side of the truck opened. Its docking collar extended and latched down to its top.

Rome saw his last option.

"Charged to 25 percent—ah, Rome?"

"Get ready to control the car from your comp panel." Rome accelerated, coming up in the center lane behind the Monaco. It was only a few hundred feet away.

"What's the plan?"

Sparks and smoke sprayed off the top of the Monaco as the thieves cut into the passenger compartment. The docking collar bounced, hanging between the two vehicles. Its bottom was less than four feet off the road.

Rome eased the Halcyon until she straddled the delineator stripe between the center and right lanes. He lined up with the collar as best he could. Then he gave it speed.

"Look out!" Aldo braced himself. "Rome!"

In the seconds before the dark gray ribbed surface of the docking collar filled the windshield, Rome had time for a fleeting thought: This might have been a bad idea.

The Halcyon ripped through part of the material, which turned out to be reinforced fabric. The shredding sound was worse than the cries of a wounded animal. They were stuck between the two vehicles, hurtling down the highway at 100 miles per hour. The destroyed section of the collar banged at the sides of the Halcyon.

"Oh, man!" Aldo yelped. "I think they're pissed."

To the right, a figure in a full stealth suit aimed a J20 rifle at Aldo's window. To the left, a female shape in a similar suit whipped around. A slender knife blade shivered in one hand, and a tiny plasma torch glowed purple-pink in her other.

Beyond her, Rome saw a well-dressed man yelling. A woman and a child—a little girl with short red hair—held onto each other, locked in place by their restraints. All three wore short sleeves. The lights on their implants were plainly visible.

"Take it!" Rome opened the window. Wind blasted in and fabric slapped his arm.

"Okay, okay!" The Halcyon momentarily swerved as Aldo gained control through the comp panel's link. The steering column melted back into the dash.

Rome grabbed the window frame and hauled himself into the tattered remains of the docking collar. A narrow track bottom center was sturdy enough to stand on. Good thing. A runaway dirt bike would have been more stable than this thing bouncing around. Rome staggered forward and launched himself at the woman.

Sara. He knew as he collided with her, even before he ripped off her mask. It was the smell of her hair and the way her body moved as she twisted out of his grasp.

There was a flash of light—metal.

Rome jerked away. The knife blade tore a gash along his jacket. He bounced on the interior wall of the docking tube. It shuddered.

Sara fell to her knees, but didn't lose the knife. This time she jabbed out with it, like a swordsman thrusting for the kill.

Rome moved closer and grabbed her arm with both hands as the blade shot past. He slammed her arm down on his bended leg. Her scream was muted by the wind roaring around them and the car engines adding to the cacophony, but it must have been enough pain because the knife disappeared, lost on the blur of pavement visible through a rip in the collar.

"Rome! Your six!"

He spun. The figure inside the opposite end of the docking collar opened fire with the J20.

Rome dove into Sara. They tumbled out the end of the tube where Rome found his face suddenly jammed between Sara's jumpsuit and plush gray leather.

"Get out! Get the hell out of my car!" The man facing them was pale, balding, and dressed in a shirt and pants Rome knew had to cost far too much to be practical. How was he still bald if he could afford that? Didn't have enough for gene therapy?

"Sir, calm down. I'm a pursuit driver. My job to stop these guys." It would have been a more impressive proclamation if he wasn't extracting his face from beneath Sara's arm.

He checked her—eyes glassy, unfocused, breathing shallow. Gasping. The wind knocked out of her, probably.

The ceiling of the car shredded under the impact of the J20 rounds. Black and gray materials sprayed all over. The man shouted obscenities. His wife and child screamed.

"Rome! He's coming down the tube!"

"Then do something about it!" Dammit! Why wouldn't all these people shut up for five seconds so he could think?

Gunfire of a different pitch broke out behind him. Rome saw Aldo shoot at their assailant. The man was on the other side of the Halcyon, facing back the way he'd come from the truck. Aldo made good use of the Halcyon's bullet-resistant glass as it blocked the man's shots, but the increased spider webbing told Rome the windshield couldn't stand much more from the fully automatic weapon.

"My knife." Sara winced and pushed Rome off.

He thwacked his head against the dash. Pain lanced down his neck. That would hurt worse, come morning. "Sara, get off! Your knife's in the wind."

"In the wind?"

"Get. Up." Rome heaved her into the lap of the car owner. "Hold her there."

"What are you talking about?"

Rome launched off the dash, aiming for the middle of the assailant's backside. His target turned just as he closed the distance.

Rome kept his head down and arms folded. He knocked the man over. They sprawled across the Halcyon's windshield.

The J20 spun off and onto the road. That was a plus, but Rome didn't dwell on it. He was busy, scrabbling for purchase on the windshield. Might as well have been grabbing the water rushing over Niagara Falls.

The man in the stealth suit latched onto Rome, half in the tube and half out. For a brief, bewildered second, he wondered why the guy was trying to save him. That was before the man punched him.

A hand caught hold of his jacket, wrenching him away from the pavement. Rome's legs slapped against the Halcyon as he held onto the open window frame.

"Hang on!" Aldo shouted.

With Aldo holding his arm by the sleeve, and the man pounding on him with his fist, Rome was torn by pain from both sides. He freed his right hand and dug around in his pocket.

"Give me the other hand!"

Rome found Thad's knife. He triggered the blade, swept it up, and buried it up to the hilt in the man's knuckles. The guy screamed and immediately forgot he hung on with his other, uninjured hand to the interior of the docking collar. Rome pulled back on the knife as hard as he could and sent him headfirst onto the road below. There was a burst of crimson and the guy was gone.

"Hot damn!" Aldo's eyes bulged. "Did you see that?"

"Yes!" Rome hollered. "Pull me up!"

Aldo tugged on Rome's arm until he could get a hold with both hands. Rome dragged himself up, bracing himself on the frame with his knee. "Give me the 20."

Aldo passed him the gun.

"Don't go anywhere," Rome ordered.

Sara was still groggy and the passengers still yelling. He looped an arm around her waist. "Call emergency services. They should have police waiting for you at the nearest exit."

"Are you insane?" the man yelped. "I've been on the line with FTZ Security!"

Rome dragged Sara back to the car.

"You need help?" Aldo asked.

"That depends on traffic. Why the hell aren't you driving?" He eased Sara through the window.

Aldo caught her boots and directed her into the back seat. "Um, I am, or the comp panel is. And it doesn't matter because we haven't had any traffic around since this fiasco started! Also, FTZ Security's coming up the lane behind us."

"Which lane?"

"All three."

Rome got into his seat. He propped his own J20 out the window. "Watch your ears." He fired at the tattered remnants of the docking collar until it broke completely free of the passenger car. The stealth truck rumbled off, its body shimmering as it started its disappearing act. Shredded tube material scattered across the highway.

"I blocked them out of the car's nav system," Aldo said. "No way they're getting back in. Judging by the way their comp reacted, I think they were a tad surprised."

"Good work."

The car drifted into the median of the highway.

Safe.

Rome exhaled.

However, the rear view showed three FTZ Security cars—all Halcyons—accelerating behind them. No Thad, though.

"Let's get going." Rome glanced over his shoulder at Sara. "I got what we came for. Secure her."

Aldo clamped magcuffs on her wrists and seat restraints secured around her body quick enough that he was back in his own restraints before she came fully to her senses.

"What? Rome! Get me back there!" Sara squirmed. "My crew needs me!"

"Your crew's the least of your worries."

"Jorge can't explain to our boss why Robert and I are gone. He'll..."

"He'll what? Who is he?"

Sara kicked the back of Rome's seat. That neck pain he anticipated flared up much sooner than expected. "You have to let me go."

"I don't have to do anything you say, Sara." Rome switched lanes, cutting in front of a line of freighters. They braked with robotic precision. Three of the automated cargo carriers spread out in the center lane, giving Rome the safe distance to maneuver in the left. Their caution also gave Rome a screen of vehicles between himself and the three FTZ security cars a half-mile back. "You're the wanted person."

"So are you!"

"Yeah, and that's why I'm taking you with us. I want answers." Rome glared at her in the rear view. "Who's your boss? The fourth member of your gang—the one operating that android decoy we put down."

"I can't tell you that."

"Can't or won't?" Aldo said.

"Can't." Sara wriggled in the safety harness holding her firm. If Rome had been thinking, he would have had Aldo bind her ankles together, too. "I never saw him."

"How's that work?"

"You expect me to just spill everything on them? To betray them?" She kicked again, this blow more vicious than the first, but Rome pulled himself forward at the last moment. "You killed Robert!"

It was Brand who'd gone nose-surfing down the road behind them. That left Cuellar driving. And the fourth. "The man tried to kill me. If you're looking for me to get on my knees and beg your forgiveness, it isn't happening."

Sara sagged against the restraints. Tears welled up in the corners of her eyes. Her jaw could have been set in carbon fiber.

"You've got to help us. Someone's framed me and Aldo, and the bounty on you…" Rome paused.

"It's gone up. By triple." Aldo frowned over a raft of data spinning by the map that floated in his holo display. Most of it was highlighted red. "Also, they're… um… lifting safety restrictions on the methods used to bring us in."

"Us?" Sara snorted. "We're not together in this."

"Far as FTZ is concerned, we are. And they're willing to break their own rules to haul everyone in. Sara, I don't know what kind of point you hoped to make with these thefts, but this isn't a game anymore. You aren't Robin Hood. That guy, your boss, he killed people."

Sara stared out the window.

An approaching exit blinked on Aldo's map. Rome waited until he caught up with the next batch of traffic just under a quarter mile from the exit ramp on the far side of the right lane. The FTZ Security Halcyons sped up the left lane, having circumvented the freighters. They were human driven—Rome could tell by their sloppy lane shifts and the way they drifted over the lane markers before jerking back onto course.

Amateurs.

He stomped on the accelerator and shot the Halcyon across two lanes.

"Easy easy easy!" Aldo held onto the sides of his seat.

Cars all around them either braked or accelerated to get out of the way of what their sensors classified as an illegal driver endangering the lives of their passengers or the value of their cargo. Either way, the gap gave Rome enough room—with mere feet to spare—for the Halcyon to slip through traffic and zip down the ramp.

The FTZ cars were a set of red and blue flashing lights that continued down the Ninety—at least, until they found a place to double back.

Rome smirked. Manipulating comp-controlled cars was one thing. Suckering a live driver? No wonder his heart pounded like a drum line.

"Hey." Aldo tried to tug at his beard, but scowled when he remembered it was gone again.

"Yeah?"

"Who's Rob and Hood?"

"Who's—no, Robin Hood."

"Yeah, him. Did you bust him for illegal driving back before I joined you?"

Rome just shook his head. He got them onto a state road headed south from Ashtabula and put the Halcyon into comp control. It settled on the road with a half dozen cars around. After the frenetic pace of the Ninety, it was soothing.

"Rome?" Sara's voice was thick with emotion. Fear? Regret?

"Tell me what you know."

"I can't. I want to, but…"

"But nothing, Sara." Rome disengaged his restraints and turned his seat. "These aren't your friends."

"What does that make you?"

"Not your enemy."

"You don't understand. If I tell you anything, they'll—they said they'd hurt someone I care about."

"Who?" He didn't have time for this. People hunted him. Who knew how long his truce with Thad would last, or even if it had worked? And his family—the thought that he'd have to stay farther from them killed him.

"You, moron!" Sara folded her arms.

Rome stared at her. Whatever he expected, this wasn't it. They'd parted friendly enough, but he'd assumed their relationship was done. No contact. Nothing.

"Awkward," Aldo muttered.

"Sara…" Rome reached for her hands, still bound, and put them between his. "You don't have to worry about me. Don't let their threats frighten you. We need your help. Those people out there, the ones you've robbed and hurt—you can help them, too."

She wouldn't look them in the eye. She watched the trees and fields blur past.

"Uh, Rome?"

"Hang on, Aldo."

"No, really. We need to talk."

Rome blew out a breath. "Aldo? Not. Now."

"Yes, now."

Proximity alerts chimed. Rome spun around. Proximity? There weren't any cars around, not near enough to trigger the warning.

Aldo cleared his throat. He enlarged one of his displays, and pointed at the roof.

Oh no…

The distinctive whine of a Condor's engine vibrated through the car.

"I told you!" Aldo slashed through the holos, distorting all the imagery. "She tracked us down!"

"How?"

"Well it could be some complex search algorithm and her own dogged persistence—or, I don't know, maybe our buddy Thad told her what we were driving!"

"But you switched the registration numbers again!"

"Shut up and drive!"

Rome switched to manual control and spun them down the nearest side road. The Halcyon dove into a wilderness area thick with trees, interrupted with ponds and pathways. A pair of does sprinted from their path the second before Rome would have rammed into them.

The Condor dropped down between the trees, wingtips snapping off branches. The turbofans lashed at the woods all around.

Rome hit the brakes, but even as he did, he knew it was too late.

A flash of light exploded around the front of the Halcyon. Aldo threw up his arms and cried out. His holos winked and died with the rest of the car's displays. Every system shut down.

EMP.

Rome got out, the J20 in his hands. The Condor settled to the ground. Its hatch opened. Gabriela was out, striding across the road before leaves stopped swirling.

"Gabriela, listen." He lowered the gun. No way he could shoot her. "We don't have time for—"

She slapped him. The sting stunned Rome. Not the blow itself—he'd been punched worse—but never by Gabriela.

"I can't believe you ran, you idiot." She bit her lip. Then she hugged him.

Rome hugged her back, his cheek still stinging.

Chapter Thirteen

"The head of our group goes by the name 'Reno.'"

They were gathered in the cockpit of the Condor, soaring out over the Great Lakes. Gabriela had demanded a destination but Rome didn't have one for her, not yet. Instead, she plotted a loop among the clouds, keeping clear of the regular commercial flight routes.

Sara sat in one of the extra seats. Aldo was at his usual perch, feet up on the console. Every bounce of his shoes sent tremors through the raft of holographic displays that surrounded him like a set of sunroom windows.

Rome leaned against the bulkhead behind Gabriela's seat. "Reno."

"Like the city?" Aldo asked.

"I'm assuming it's after the first successful train robbery gang," Sara said.

Aldo made a face. "Pretentious."

"Start running a search for anyone using that alias, or anyone who has it as part of his or her real name."

Aldo jiggled a foot. A long list warped around it. "Duh. What'd you think I was doing?"

"Sitting on your ass and screwing around, per usual."

"Okay, see, that's just hurtful."

Sara rolled her eyes. "I can't tell you if that is his real name, or her real name, or even what Reno's face looks like, because I've never seen him. Or her. All of our contact is on the Net—or through drone android proxy."

Aldo mimed shooting with his thumb and forefinger. "Don't suppose this Reno goes in for facial reproduction. You know, a drone that looks like him. Her. Whatever."

"No. Why would he do that?"

It was Rome's turn to frown. "That'd be stupid."

"Hey, I didn't know! Criminal masterminds make mistakes. Don't they?"

"Not many. Hence the 'mastermind' part." Rome ran his hand over his scalp. "Where's the new base of operations? I assume FTZ is still watching the business center."

"They are. Completely shut down. Fortunately—well, for us at the time—the truck was off-site. Only Reno knows the new location. He sent a command for it to drive to him. He said it was for upgrade purposes."

"When was that?"

"Less than 18 hours before you two showed up."

"That's convenient."

"I wondered about it… before we were questioned… and during. But I knew Reno would come back for us. We're a team." She slumped her shoulders. "We were."

"Not much of a team when the boss leaves you stranded."

Rome glowered at Aldo.

"What? I'm just saying."

"What've you got on the search?"

"Big fat nothing so far." Aldo reached into the display, and pulled apart two screens of text and images that spun by at an alarming rate. He drew out a single long column of blue wording. "There's a ton of Reno out there—never mind narrowing the search to exclude historical people and place names. I'm scrubbing for Net chat, but if this boss of theirs is any good, he—or she—is going to watch their words. Employ a bot-writer to mix up phrases and figures of speech so that when Reno talks online, it doesn't sound like the talk he'd actually use in person."

"Right. We can't identify he or she based on what his or her public profile goes by."

"Also, I vote we call Reno 'he' unless proven otherwise. This gender bender is killing my brain."

"Agreed. The immediate problem is finding the truck again."

"That would be no problem, actually. Still got their signal marked, remember? Next time they try to take over another car's system, we got them."

"Yeah, except if they don't and go into hiding instead..."

"Oh. Right." Aldo rummaged in his pocket. The fruit bar that emerged was blood red and half eaten. He crammed the remainder into his mouth. "Mmph. Lemme work on that."

"Just because I'm glad to see you doesn't mean I'm going to let you make a mess out of my lander." Gabriela swatted at his shoulder. "Clean up."

"Yeesh! Picky." Aldo swept up as many crumbs as he could. He glanced about for a refuse port until Gabriela gave him a disposable bag. He dumped the crumbs. She tucked the bag into the port by the hatch leaving from the cockpit. The smell of burning biodegradables wafted out.

"I don't understand. Finding the truck won't find you Reno. It will lead us to Jorge, but..." Sara shrugged. "The truck is untraceable. That's the point of a stealth vehicle."

"Not entirely untraceable, as Aldo demonstrated." Rome drummed his fingers on his arm. "But that wasn't what I meant. We know from where it was stolen, and we know its theft was kept off searchable records at Bacevich. Which means either security was taken offline for its removal—"

"Or that data was partitioned away where Bacevich personnel couldn't get to it," Aldo said. "Either way, intentionally hidden."

"Right. Who could do that?"

"Tech like me."

"The base CO would have top authority," Gabriela noted. "And some of the guys I served with had both the know-how and access to keep watch on the data. Saves on personnel needed to operate the base."

"Okay then. We need to go there."

"To… where? I need a more specific course than 'there,' Rome."

"The base. We have to get the data ourselves to prove personnel were involved with the theft, and hopefully find something more that leads us to Reno."

"A military base." Aldo stared at him. "You want to break in. During… daylight?"

"We don't have a lot of options for time." Selfish as it was, he could see in his mind's eye a clock ticking down the hours until Vivian's concert. Having Gabriela on hand made for much swifter transport—and much more clandestine. She kept the Halcyon off the roads. Once FTZ got wind of her unauthorized activities, that window would close. Had to be narrow enough now. "Aldo will feed you the coordinates, Gabriela. If this is going to be a problem for you…"

"As far as FTZ knows, I'm transporting Thad to his next patrol, on the hunt for you." Gabriela smiled. "What's funny is the difficulty I've been having with my transponder. You know, the one the Condor uses to mark the registration of every vehicle I take back and forth so that FTZ can bill the contractors for transit costs. Just one of those problems I can't seem to fix on my own, and the bot crawlers can't deal with a comp error. It has to wait until I get back to FTZ West headquarters."

Aldo blinked.

"Atta girl." Rome squeezed Gabriela's shoulder and smiled.

"I still can't believe you shot me down."

"Hey, in all fairness, you shot at us first."

"Like three times!" Aldo insisted.

Gabriela shook her head. "The last time was after you guys made me crash."

"Listen up," Rome said. "We've got another problem."

"Bigger than having FTZ hunting you and trying to break into military base?"

"Yes. It's the car."

"What about—oh." Aldo polished off his bar.

"Yeah, 'oh.' Without Marcy to run through the protocols, I can't generate a new set of false registration numbers. Can't do a re-color, either. If I tried it by hand, it could be… bad."

"How bad?" Sara asked.

"Bad as in, the core could go into permanent shutdown, or the comp—the bits left over that weren't part of Marcy's operating system—could fry."

"*Madre Dios,*" Gabriela said. "There's got to be someone else who can help you."

"Well…" Aldo rubbed the back of his neck.

"No," Rome said.

"Come on, man."

"She's a criminal."

Sara cleared her throat.

"Not you," Rome said. "This is different."

"Yeah, okay, but Rome, it's our only option. Can't deny she's amazing at her job. We'd be in and out of her shop—" Aldo snapped his fingers.

Rome sighed. Knee-jerk reaction aside, he knew Aldo had a point. Unless they did something drastic, they weren't going to get into that base. Their proof of collusion between this Reno and the base commander—or whomever had helped him steal the truck—hinged on it. "We'd be adding another illegal action onto our record, you know."

Aldo shrugged. "You shot at a contracted pursuit driver. Twice."

"And downed one of FTZ's aircraft," Gabriela said. "Don't forget."

"Yeah, thanks, Gabby," Aldo muttered.

"This is going to take hours away from us," Rome said.

"Yeah, I know, but I still say going in daylight is stupid."

"I'm going to agree with your partner here." Sara's tone was even and quiet. "Night gives us a lot of advantages."

Rome frowned.

"Not that I'm taking sides, but it makes thing easier for me, too, if I have darkness as a cover," Gabriela pointed out. "Since I assume we're going to sneak out. Or at the very least, need a fast escape and avoid pursuit."

"We can go at night. But as for Jocelyn…"

"There's no other way, Rome."

Rome ground his teeth. This was not going to be pleasant. "Fine. Give Gabriela the coordinates for the shop."

Aldo grinned. He swiped through screens on his implant. A flash of light from Gabriela's console drew her attention back. "Done and done."

"Shouldn't take us long to get there," Gabriela said. "Two hours, tops. What is it?"

"A mod shop," Rome said.

"Oh. You know the lady who runs it?"

"Lady is a stretch. And yes. We brought her in. Three times."

"You're saying she won't be looking forward to our arrival." The pitch of the Condor's engines rose as Gabriela steered it onto the new course.

"We'll be lucky if she doesn't run us over," Rome muttered.

Gabriela dropped them deep in the Appalachians, far from the major FTZ routes, on back roads that were pockmarked with grass. Whether they were in West Virginia or Kentucky, Rome didn't much care. Sure, the scenery was beautiful if he looked where the pines still swathed the mountains in green. He just had to ignore the dull brown tops shorn of forest and sloughed off for the mines, and the patches scorched black by the spring fire season. A pall of smoke hung heavy in the valleys through which he drove.

"I sent another signal." Aldo glanced up and down from his displays. Then again. "Okay. Nothing back yet."

"Aldo."

"Yeah?"

"Hold still or I will punch you."

"Hey, excuse me, but the last time we saw Jocelyn she said she'd skin us both and dump us in an acid reservoir. Remember? After we busted her for illegal driving along the Eighty cargo routes."

"I remember."

Aldo rolled his eyes. "This would be a lot easier if you were scared instead of unflappable."

Rome shrugged. He was nervous. No denying it. But he doubted Jocelyn would kill them. She'd never resorted to violence in her crimes. Not even the threat of it.

Of course, that was three years ago. If she were sufficiently scared...

The Halcyon topped a steep hill. Ahead of them, the road opened onto a clearing. Dilapidated houses spotted the area, huddled around a creek. None of them appeared occupied—most had broken windows, a few had roofs that were caved in. No lights. No signals. No signs of habitation.

Rome stopped. He got out and inspected the ground.

Aldo sniffed the air. "Smoke. That what you're looking for?"

Rome picked at the grass. "Tire indentations."

"Ah."

"Any drone footage for us to rope in?"

"Nope. I checked. FTZ doesn't have any records of any flybys in recent months. I only just lightly perused—didn't want to dig any further and get ourselves tagged."

"Good idea." Rome squinted. The afternoon sun was bright, even through the haze. "Well, if she's here, she'll come out and say hello."

An engine rumbled. Then a second. Two trucks burst into view—one from behind a sagging barn and the second from around the porch of a two-story home. Both were Ford Bison—older models painted over with a rough mix of brown and greens, interspersed with gray pixelated patterns. Each had two people inside.

Each had a Driver.

"That's, okay… that's bad." Aldo reached into the car.

"No! No guns."

"What?"

Rome smiled, but he faced the oncoming vehicles, not Aldo. "Put your hands out, anywhere they can see them. No guns."

"Okay." Aldo put his hands on the door. "If I die, you get to clean out my tool stash."

"Shut up." Rome kept smiling and waved.

The trucks stopped, one on either side of the Halcyon. Three men got out, two of them as big as bears and with expressions just as friendly. They were black men with curly hair and identical beards—in fact, Rome realized everything about them was identical. The third man was shorter, slimmer, and clean-shaven.

The fourth occupant—the driver of the first truck—was a woman as tall as Rome and lithe as a mountain lion. She strode up and stared him up and down with icy blue eyes. Her skin was mahogany and her hair as short as the men's. She wore a camouflaged tan jacket, plaid button-down shirt, and dark blue jeans. Rome was more interested in the ornate gun belt that drooped across her hip. A Hunsaker .50 caliber Goldbreaker gleamed among the leather.

"I'll be." Jocelyn Moses's voice had a husky drawl. "Roman Jasko."

"In the flesh."

"Comm boys told me the signal was from you. You brought Aldo into this mess?"

Aldo grinned. "Hey, Jocelyn. How've you been?"

"Eking an illegal living modifying cars, when I'm not making snoopy visitors disappear."

Aldo's grin disappeared.

"Look, Jocelyn, we're not here on any official business."

"So I hear. You're a fugitive." Jocelyn smiled, all teeth. She still reminded Rome of a mountain lion. "That's a mighty big bounty you've got."

"What I've got is money, and someone I need to catch. I need your help to do it."

"That makes you desperate."

"I am that. How much?

"Boys, go see what our old pal keeps in his ride."

The men pushed past Aldo and rummaged through the back seat of the Halcyon. They came up with Rome's stash of coins, the extra guns, even their food.

Jocelyn nodded. Rome didn't think she could look any happier unless he'd given her the car, too. "Load it all up."

"Wait a sec," Aldo said. "We need that stuff! You take all our food and money, how're we supposed to eat?"

"Use your implant." Jocelyn made a show of snapping her fingers. "Oh, right. You probably can't pay for anything because your accounts are frozen and FTZ's tracking your every digital financial transaction. Wow, that must just be a terrible hardship for you."

"Enough crap, Jocelyn." Rome yanked one of the bags away from Jocelyn's men. When he lunged for it, Rome planted a shoe on his chest. The man wound up slick with mud.

"Don't piss them off, Jasko. They don't take well to people who cross me."

Jocelyn's hand dipped to the holster at her hip, but Rome was already at the Halcyon's open door. Aldo tossed him one of the J20s. Rome aimed it at Jocelyn's gut. Her men drew their weapons, but Jocelyn froze with her hand wrapped around her pistol's grip.

"Here's the deal," Rome said. "Leave me a packet of the gold and one of silver. We keep the food and the guns, too. Everything else, you can have it. But we need you to do this for us. I have to find the guy who's put the mark on us."

Jocelyn chewed her lip. She withdrew her hand. A curt wave

brought her men's weapons down. "Sounds reasonable. Might have been I was too hasty. Let me see what you've got."

Aldo helped Rome remove the money from the bag that he figured they needed. He grabbed the food satchel from Jocelyn's men, glaring as if the guy had stepped on his pet dog—or stomped on Marcy. Rome gave everything else to Jocelyn.

She inspected the coin packets. "That's a heap of change, Jasko. All yours?"

"Every dollar."

"Bounties from a long career."

Jocelyn sneered. "Mine's in here, no doubt."

"You're welcome to look. Meanwhile, you're wasting my time. I have money, you have talent."

She chuckled. "Oh, man, I forgot what a stiff one you were. Maybe that's why I got caught so many times by you and your pale co-pilot, Jasko—you take everything so seriously. You know what though? I like that. I respect that. We can deal. Mount your ride and follow us in. First—you're not being tracked, are you?"

Rome scowled.

"You're right, my bad, that was an insult right there." Jocelyn slapped his shoulder. "Couldn't resist."

"You really gave her all our money?"

Rome scowled, eyes on the dirt track in front of the Halcyon.

"Okay, dumb question," Aldo said. "How much is stashed back on the Condor?"

"Thirty thousand. I gave Jocelyn forty."

Aldo winced. "Sorry. If I had anything not frozen up in my accounts—"

"Don't worry about it. I'm doing what has to be done." Had to keep telling himself, too.

They drove around the back of the houses where Jocelyn's crew hid. A small, lopsided shed with wooden shingles leaned up against the house as if for comfort. Peeling white paint littered the ground. Rome was pretty sure goat dung covered the rest, compliments of the horned critters that roamed the area.

"Getting a power surge," Aldo muttered. "No way those houses are pulling that kind of current. Or even have wires." He shut up when a section of land around the shed lifted up and revealed a paved ramp down into the earth.

Rome drove the steep descent and cringed when the Halcyon's fenders scraped the asphalt. The ramp leveled out into the mouth of a cavern—a great, yawning opening rimmed with white lights.

Jocelyn's shop was in a cave.

Rome stepped out of the car. The musty odor hit him full force and he immediately felt damp all over. He took in the full view of the limestone cavern that stretched a couple hundred feet ahead and out to the sides that same width. The ceiling dripped with stalactites overhead. Rusty supports braced against lumpy walls of chalky, white and gray stone, their orange forms jutting out like discolored bones.

"No wonder we never found all her mod gear." Aldo whistled. The sound echoed forever.

"Setup ain't pretty, but it does its job." Jocelyn whacked her gloves against a pair of bulky, round power cores as big as the Halcyon. They rumbled like the heaviest traffic on the Ninety. "Geothermal fed. Beats payin' for power."

Her boys wheeled the Halcyon into one of several grottos that bulked into the limestone walls on either side of the main cavern. Those appeared to have been carved—laser cut, with smooth edges that gleamed under bright white lights strung at even intervals every four feet.

The driver backed the car in with a half-foot to spare at the rear fender. Not bad, Rome had to admit.

"Look at this stuff." Aldo peered into a rack divided into a dozen shelves. They slumped under the weight of more parts and comp components than Rome had ever seen in one place, even including the repair domes back at FTZ West headquarters. "Tags, holo projectors, code scramblers, comp cloners—wait a second. I want one of those cloners. How'd you get one?"

Jocelyn just grinned.

"C'mon, I promise—zipped lips. You know how much firewall I'd have to punch through if I even wanted to see one that the R&D boys at FTZ have been messing with? You can't possibly have bought one." Aldo raised an eyebrow. "Wait. You stole it."

"No, I made one." Jocelyn pointed beyond the shelves. A fabricator was tucked into one grotto. The machinery was a more streamlined, compact version of the equipment Rome saw at the business center Sara's group used as a temporary base. It was far too high end to just happen to fall into a cave like this. "Where do you think I get all the money for this stuff? Healthy, wealthy sponsor, boys. There's people out there who don't mind ponying up the money for activities such as mine if it means getting humans and not comps behind the driver's wheel."

"I'd lecture you on breaking the law, Jocelyn, but..." Rome shrugged. He waved his hand to indicate their surroundings. "Aldo, put your tongue back in your mouth. We're not shopping."

"Speak for yourself."

"Okay, fellas, keep your hands in your pockets. Get over to Denny. He'll take care of your tags."

Denny was the slim one of the trio who'd met them above ground.

Quiet and focused, he motioned Rome and Aldo to sit in a pair of reclined chairs. Each had peeling chrome and vinyl upholstery, a garish orange covering that appeared to have been gnawed on. It reminded Rome of the dentist's chair, only without the sensors dangling from the ceiling and the hygienist bot's articulated limbs reaching around.

Whatever Denny did to his implant took an hour. The steady ache in Rome's wrist intensified to shooting pains. Aldo, in the next chair, grit his teeth. Sweat dripped down his face.

Denny rolled a chair back and forth between them, wheels clattering on the stone. He didn't speak. If it wasn't for his periodic grunts and the rapid flicking of his fingers on a holo display that beamed from his own wrist, Rome would have guessed him catatonic.

Every so often, Rome got a glimpse of Jocelyn, who wielded a different tool each time. She hurried to the Halcyon's bay or left it with such frequency, Rome wondered if she was the equipment gopher. Only once did he see the work in progress—panels all around the car were tossed aside, leaning against the grotto walls while wires spilled out from exposed spaces. Modules of varying shapes and sizes sat on the floor or on the hood, blinking a rainbow of colors.

"Rome? What're they doing to her?" Aldo's voice was thick with strain.

"Working." Or cannibalizing. If Jocelyn chose to betray them, there'd be nothing he could do to prevent her from stripping the Halcyon for parts and turning them lose in the Appalachian wilds.

"She look okay?"

Jocelyn shook her head. She snatched a part from inside one of the Halcyon's open compartments on the rear flank, thrust it at a woman in gray coveralls, and lit into the gathered workers with orders that hit them harsher than a J20 burst. Her exact words were lost in the clamor of the shop.

"Yep. Fine," Rome said.

"Okay. Yeowch!" Aldo glared at Denny. "Easy! You prod any implant that bad, you could lock out all the primary functions and break the ID pattern."

Denny stared at him, then flicked a long string of data on his displays.

Aldo yelped.

Ten minutes later, they were done. The pain faded as soon as Denny shut down his displays. "Good to go." Those—the only words out of his mouth—rang clear as a proximity chime.

Rome activated his implant. His face appeared, the scruff of beard and a bald head replaced the years-old image that used to live on his ID. This new visage topped part of a very crisp, clean formal shirt and tie. "Donovan Hastent, Department of Defense inspector."

"Don? Nice. I got Malcolm Stewart." Aldo frowned at the brown-haired and beardless tiny representation of himself. "You think I look like a Malcolm?"

"Better get used to it, Inspector Stewart."

"Hey, if we're the same rank, let me be the boss on this one."

Rome rolled his eyes.

The Halcyon was near complete. Jocelyn's people had extruded a brand new windshield. Only a pair of front panels remained on the floor. Its silver sheen was gone, replaced a flat gray of the base model color.

"You're going onto a military base." Jocelyn shook her head. "Always knew you were bonkers, Jasko. Lucky for you, these ugly Halcyons are the number one fleet model used by the United States Armed Forces, in a variety of equally ugly colors."

"Hey! She isn't ugly," Aldo griped.

"Whatever." Jocelyn turned back to her crew. "Marie? Go dirt tan. Code six-five-oh-six-nine."

"Got it." The woman tapped in commands on a bulky comp panel. A long, flat strip of yellow wiring connected it to the Halcyon's dash.

Within seconds, the car's blank gray disappeared, replaced by a flat, monochrome khaki.

"Registration number's gonna take another half hour or so," Jocelyn mused.

"Got to admit, your people are fast. Explains how you got away with so much," Rome said.

"I wouldn't call three arrests getting away, Jasko."

Rome nodded, thinking of the FTZ warrant, of Gabriela's Condor waiting several miles away in a clearing, with Sara safely stowed aboard. "Nobody does forever."

❖ ❖ ❖

They flew north, the setting sun turning the western sky golden outside the cockpit windows. Aldo caught a quick nap, feet tucked under the console, head lolling on his shoulder as he slept in his chair. Gabriela watched the air traffic for the region closely, even with the Condor flying itself. She programmed course corrections around busy areas or known drone flight paths.

Rome found Sara sitting on the hood of the Halcyon. Scratch that—the military colored and coded version of the Halcyon. He slid up next to her. "You wanted to see me?"

She stared at the bulkhead. "What's going to happen to me?"

Rome frowned. He knew this question would come up, but he didn't have clear answers. "Trial. Jail. Your people are tied to a bunch of thefts and assaults, Sara. We can put in a good word for you, since you helped us with the identity of your leader."

"Only if you clear your names."

"One mile at a time."

"I meant what I said." She rubbed at the scar of her implant. "About Reno threatening you. He knew I cared too much. If anything happened to you I'd… it would be the worst thing I could imagine, Rome."

He rested a hand on her leg. "I hadn't thought much about us. Not since you left for the Republic border. Lot of time went by, without a word from you."

"I didn't know what I wanted. As soon as Reno made those threats, I figured it out." Sara smiled at him, but there was something behind the expression—fear, or hesitation, or another unidentifiable emotion. All Rome knew is it wasn't good.

Fair enough. He was fond of Sara—more than that, he couldn't say. Rome didn't break their gaze. "Listen. This is what I know. The only way you have a half chance of avoiding serious criminal penalties is to help us stop Reno and Cuellar. You say you've got feelings for me? Prove it. Work against them, and help me prove my innocence."

Sara's smile stiffened, and collapsed into a thin line. "That's a tight place to put me in, Rome."

"No worse than the one I'm in. Remember whose family has to see my face all over the Net, supposedly aiding killers break free." Rome stood. "We'll be at the base in an hour. Decide by then."

She pursed her lips in apparent thought as he walked back up to the cockpit.

Rome freed the crucifix from under his shirt. What had Andrew said? The truth. The right. They pursued him. He couldn't shake either. Part of him would be perfectly happy to disappear into one of the off-grid sections of America. He'd even consider applying for a visa to the Republic of Texas. Still, he couldn't shake the nag.

He had a job to do.

He had to stop whoever was using Sara and the others to profit.

Nothing would turn him away.

Chapter Fourteen

Bacevich Arsenal had a simple layout: perimeter fence, sentry towers, sensor pickets, and tracked robots on constant patrol. Red lights festooned every location, blinking in time around the entire grounds.

The Halcyon parked before the security booth at the base, engine idling. Sentry bots trundled nearby, ensuring any intruders were within range of their firepower. A lone soldier in fatigues, cap, and boots approached.

Rome smiled for the benefit of the guard and for whoever manned the sensors strung from the post. "Afternoon, Corporal. Donovan Hastent, DOD. My associate, Malcolm Stewart. We're here to conduct a surprise efficiency and regulatory inspection."

"Need your implant, sir." The corporal couldn't be older than 19. There wasn't a single whisker on his face, nor any hair—save for bushy black eyebrows. A finger rested above the trigger on his Omni Combat Weapon—a sleek black rifle in bullpup configuration with a large banana curved magazine at the rear.

"Understood." Rome leaned his wrist through the open window.

The kid extended his own wrist, which bore a band covered in gray and white panels—probably linked to his implant, hidden underneath. Lights flashed as the uplink interrogated Rome's, then Aldo's implants.

Rome held his breath. Time to find out if the alterations worked.

Green lights returned on the wristband. "All right, checks out." The weapon shifted in the soldier's hands. He didn't budge from the side of the car. "Didn't hear about any inspection, sir."

Rome fixed him in his best glare. "Take it you missed the part about surprise, soldier. Are you going to wave us through or should I contact your commanding officer? I'm sure he'd love to be slapped with a perfunctory violation of Code One Twelve, Article Three Three. I've got his signal ready to transmit."

The young corporal's swallowed. "No, sir."

"Good. I'm going to seal this window and signal if we're not through your barricade in the next thirty seconds."

Jocelyn had it right—their Halcyon blended perfectly with the base's motor pool. The falsified DOD registration number passed the scanners unmolested.

"What's our target?" Rome said as they walked a paved pathway to the main admin building.

Aldo shook his wrist implant. A tiny map appeared in 2-D on its face. "Okay, so, if this thing is laid out like all bases constructed in the last twenty years—and it's a Bravo Modular, so it should be—the offline data backups are in this central room."

"Two entrances."

"Yep. One guard at each. A pair of Pikes. They'll be military grade, probably not as dumb as the models we're used to. Don't worry, our implants are good."

"Never said I was worried. You're the one sweating."

Aldo wiped perspiration from his face.

"Stay alert. It's possible FTZ's contacted the base about our warrants."

Aldo frowned. "Not likely. That's outside their jurisdiction."

"I'm not willing to dismiss the possibility."

They entered the building as if they owned it. A female warrant officer even waited at the door, allowing them to go in first. Rome stood in the doorway, blocking the activation sensors so she could enter too.

The base walls were pale gray and white. Brown double lines

demarcated the corridor every 16 feet. Doors were spaced at intervals twice that distance. The entire building certainly hinted its modularity to Rome. He felt if he found the right access panel, he could break apart the entire complex and rearrange it with construction bots at will.

He was also thankful for Aldo's map. After a couple turns he was already disoriented by the sameness of the corridors. It wasn't all clones, however—a scuff mark here, a ding in the wall panel there. Rome catalogued the slight differences as best he could. Like Hansel and Gretel's trail, or like tracking Aldo through a building when he was in snacking mode.

An officer in his thirties came around a bend. He was tall with bulky muscles that pressed against green fatigues that shifted with the light as he strode toward them. His hair was blond, sharp eyes the color of ice chips, and had a long, straight nose. "Can I help you, gentlemen?"

Rome presented his ID. The holo emitted the credentials from his implant in a welcoming splash of color. "DOD Inspector Hastent. We're here to access your security records, per inspection protocol."

The man's nametag read "Bolduc" in stamped white letters, and his rank insignia was a lieutenant's bars. He nodded. "I need to confirm that with my CO."

"Won't be necessary. This is a surprise review, Lieutenant."

Bolduc's face creased with a frown. "We've never undergone one. Sir."

"My department's hardly going to announce something of this nature. Step aside. I don't want to have to write you up in my report."

Two enlisted men walked down the hall behind him. They fixed both the lieutenant and the visitors with a quizzical look. Rome kept his expression neutral, but his pulse quickened. He and Aldo drew too much attention. He could take three men, but not without alerting base security. And in this hall, trying to backtrack to an escape route—

"Have it your way, Lieutenant," Aldo said. "We'll go see your CO if you'll kindly stop interfering with federal business. Your colonel is down this hall. Two rights, is he not?"

Bolduc seemed surprised. "Yes, sir."

"Very well. This way, Inspector Hastent." Aldo crooked his fingers without looking at Rome and walked around Bolduc. He ignored both the lieutenant and the approaching enlisted men, the latter of whom parted so the inspectors could pass. Aldo's curt nod to them drew no further inquiry.

When he and Rome took the next corner, Rome glimpsed them speaking with Bolduc. "Nice work."

"Thanks." Aldo wiped sweat from around his mouth. "Man, I tell you, way easier on a face when a beard isn't mopping up every bit of moisture."

"Don't tell me you're staying baby-faced forever."

"Um, no! First chance I get, I'm growing it down to my chest."

Rome was more concerned about the compact spazzer tucked in a concealed pocket of his jacket. Jocelyn's specially tailored coats had done their job of hiding it from sensors, and it seemed none of the personnel they'd encountered noticed. If Aldo's plan worked, he shouldn't need it at all.

They found one of the two Pike series guardbots standing by a sealed door of black metal. The bot was painted the same tan as the cars and its body was leaner than the ones Rome saw at FTZ West. It had three optic ports on its "head," and the outline of several compartments along its flanks. The door itself bore no numbers or letters to denote its purpose. Only a flat access panel of clear plastic hinted admittance to the room beyond.

[Halt.] The guardbot's tones were hard and deep. It trundled forward. A panel on its right side popped open. Two weapons extended—a spazzer, its muzzle crackling with energy ready to discharge, and a gun whose caliber Rome guessed at .50.

"Nice to see you too," Aldo muttered.

Rome triggered his ID and Aldo did likewise. Instead of scanning them, the guardbot's topmost optic port rotated, presumably focusing on them. [You are not base personnel or members of the United States

Armed Forces. Your presence is not authorized by Colonel Tacazon.]

Colonel Tacazon. Must be the base CO. Something tickled the depths of Rome's memories… "Department of Defense inspectors Hastent and Stewart. Acknowledge our ID."

The guardbot scanned their implants in the same way the bot at FTZ West had. Green lights eased some of Rome's tension, but the robot didn't budge. [Identity confirmed. Anomalies detected in implant programming. Tampering likelihood 15 percent. Do you consent to investigation by base personnel?]

Aldo swiped through screens on his implant with a flurry of fingers.

"We do not consent," Rome said, trying to keep the bot focused on him and not on whatever Aldo was doing. "Our authority overrides any need for investigation. If there are anomalies, I'm sure my partner here can clear them up with our technicians."

[Unacceptable. Access to this room is not granted. Consent to investigation by base personnel required.]

Rome unlatched his jacket and let it fall open. If he were to draw, he'd have a split second to do it before the robot shot him. They couldn't let it contact anyone on base, though Rome was perplexed why it hadn't already.

The guardbot's appendages twitched. Both weapons withdrew into their compartments. The optical ports dimmed one by one, and it sank down onto its base. [Commencing diagnostics.]

The hum of its power core diminished. A couple seconds later, it sat as quiet as a demonstration model at a store.

"That was impressive." Rome let go of his spazzer.

Aldo exhaled. "Thanks. I've got it locked into a diagnostic subroutine. Won't take it forever to figure out the command wasn't from the base's main computer network, though."

"Needs to be long enough to get us in and out." Rome slapped a round, rubbery patch to the access panel. It was transparent, not unlike a jellyfish, though without the wet texture. Amber lights swirled, reminding Rome of leaves on the surface of the Erie canal. The panel emitted a chirp and the black door slid open.

"Nice." Aldo poked the patch. "Where'd you get that?"

"Had it stashed away for a rainy day." Rome dug his fingers under the bottom edge and peeled the patch off the access panel. It shrank down into a slab smaller than his palm and as hard as a plastic comp panel. "I used a similar one a few years back to break the door lock on a mod shop operating out of a town's hydroponics center."

"You're gonna let me take it apart later, right?"

"Put one on your Christmas list."

The room beyond the door was pitch black, except for a glowing blue ring set in the center of the floor. A twin ring shone from the ceiling, which Rome guessed was only a foot overhead. The data terminal was in the middle, lit up in the same pale blue, a thin column with a plastic sheath. Lines of lights trickled down every quarter of the column.

"Wow. Just… wow." Aldo took a lap around the blue circle, stepping as gingerly as when Rome visited an abandoned church one time. His feet didn't make a sound. "That, Rome, is a Maxx Twelve. Computing power makes Marcy seem like a puppy dog more interested in eating its own crap than driving a car."

"Didn't need that visual." Rome approached the column, but took his cue from Aldo and stayed well outside its boundary. "Get on with the next step."

"Yeah, that's the trick."

Aldo rummaged in his jacket pocket. He sprayed a fine mist from a tiny, round bottle. The spray caught blue light and reflected it, revealing the outer shell of the ring. The column was four times as big and extended from the floor to the ceiling.

Rome scowled. He'd thought the rings signified a sensor barrier. Aldo's trick confirmed it. "Don't tell me you're going to try sticking an arm through that thing."

"No way. It's got to be calibrated to detect something—but not particles like these." Aldo wafted his hand through the mist, dissipating the remnants just outside the beams. “See? They go right through. It isn’t any kind of force barrier.”

“Good to know. What next? You have a really long toothpick?”

“Relax.” Aldo grabbed another object from his jacket, this time a brass tube. Its ends were capped in black. It blinked with green lights. “That’s why I borrowed these from Jocelyn.”

Rome’s skin crawled as if the contents of the container had been dumped loose already and were doing who-knew-what to his cellular structure. “You’d better not be thinking about dumping nanites.”

“You know anything smaller?” Aldo triggered the top. It popped open.

Rome pushed the tube away and sealed it. Did anything get out? The lights were still red. “Aldo! We’re desperate, but I’m not that desperate. You could get us all killed! I, for one, don’t want my DNA unraveled until I’m a puddle of biological goop on this base’s floors!”

“Puddle of… oh, come on, Rome!” Aldo hissed the words between his teeth. He whispered like they were in an elder care hostel and the nurses with their bots would sweep in, chastising them for waking the residents. “These aren’t disassemblers. You got any idea how many permits and security protocols I’d need to even get in the same room as those? There’s a reason they only use those on the space habitats, or for building the Mars complex. These are breakers.”

“Not even close to reassuring.”

“It’s just a nickname.” Aldo took the tube back. He opened it again. It took a couple seconds for the lights on top to disappear. The entire cap pulsed red. “They’re specialized for shutting down any security system before it has a chance to realize something’s gone seriously screwy. Limited window of use—you get three and a half minutes, tops.”

Rome tapped his implant.

“What’re you doing?”

“Setting up a timer.”

“Oh. Good idea.”

"Focus. When the blue lights are down—"

"Then I go in." Aldo closed the tube and stuck it back in his jacket. He flexed his implant wrist as if he readied for hand-to-hand sparring.

"What happens after three and a half minutes?"

"The breakers destruct. Fzzzzt. Itty bitty sparks, and then they're gone," Aldo grinned. "No mess for anyone to find."

"You borrowed this from Jocelyn?"

"Maybe."

"How much did it cost me?"

"Not a coin." The blue lights vanished. "Aaand showtime!"

Rome started the timer. Aldo swept his arm in, implant glowing. It exchanged signals with the column, their pulses pinging back and forth with a hypnotic rhythm. Whatever Aldo did while his fingers triggered new command lines, it didn't set of any alarms. Rome kept a hand on the comforting stock of the spazzer inside his jacket.

"Encryption's light," Aldo said. "Not surprising. With the barrier, there's no way a casual interloper could access sensitive data."

"No problems, I take it."

"Nothing I can't handle."

"I'm sure. Have you isolated any information from the truck's theft?" Time was ticking.

"Ah... hang on. This could be something. Nope, never mind. Shipping manifest." Aldo squinted at his display. "Tracking back through the time stamps."

"You could deploy the holo emitter, assuming the data bank has one."

"No such luck. It's meant as a repository. You know, tuck the data here until you need to review it, then you transfer it to a device or network that makes it more user friendly. The way it's packed in here, behind layers of—whoa! Bingo."

"Bingo's good. Get out of there."

"Hold up. I have to transfer the entire packet."

"Hurry, Aldo." Thirty seconds remained. How long would the Pike sentry remain in standby? He had no idea.

"Going, going, going…" Aldo pulled his arm back. "Gone!"

The blue lights on the ceiling and floor flickered, blinked twice, and then sprang to full luminosity. Rome scooted back, even though he was pretty sure he was far enough away from the scanner. His timer flashed.

"That's the whole thing." Aldo ran a hand through his hair. Sweaty as his palms must be, his combed mop was transformed into an unruly tangle.

"Let me see it. And clean up. You don't look like a DOD inspector."

"Huh?" Aldo touched his head gingerly. "Oh, right. Here goes."

A holo vid leapt from Aldo's implant. At first, Rome saw nothing but static, electric snow. For a second, he thought this whole exercise in subterfuge had been futile, but then it cleared. Through the haze, he saw two men in a large room. They were tiny compared with the towering walls and the bulky vehicles that framed them. Rome recognized them as four of the same stealth trucks they'd encountered, minus the docking collar.

One of the men was a short, thickset blond with well-groomed hair. "Robert Brand."

"Who?"

"One of Sara's crew. The one who went face surfing on the road."

Aldo winced. "Nasty. Who's the other guy?"

"Can't see his face. Dark hair. Fatigues. Magnify."

Aldo paused the playback. The image zoomed large enough Rome made out rank insignia. He smiled when he saw the shine of twin silver eagles. "Has to be the CO, Colonel Tacazon."

The miniature men in the image held up their wrists. Rome recognized the gesture. "Transfer of payment."

"Yeah. Bet it's way more high stakes than our blackjack games."

"Can you trace the payments?"

"Not through this."

"No, dumbass, I meant through the colonel's implant."

"Well, yeah. Probably. You gonna get me the implant?"

"If I have to. Come on."

Rome headed for the other door, but before he took a couple steps, light flooded the room from the opposite end.

"Who are you? What are you doing in here?" An officer stood framed in the doorway, hands on his hips. "This room is off-limits to all but senior personnel."

"Malcolm Stewart, DOD Inspector." Aldo flashed his ID far too fast for the human eye to make any sense out of the blur of imagery. "Your security is abysmal, sir, and we're going to have to give you poor marks on that part of our report."

"There's no inspection slated for this month. I've seen the bulletins from Department of Defense." The officer's insignia gleamed in the blue light a second before his face was illuminated. Twin birds.

Colonel Tacazon.

He stared at them, eyebrows knit together. Tacazon's uniform was immaculate—pressed to perfect creases. His hair was shorn around the ears and back of his head to neat black stubble, and where it was longer on top, he'd styled it into an impermeable helmet. His eyes were dark, his skin sallow in the blue light of the column's circular security field. The scowl on his lips, though, was what startled Rome the most.

He'd seen it before.

Before Rome could react to his realization, Tacazon's eyes went wide. "You! It can't be. They were supposed to have you locked up by now!"

His fingers smacked the implant on his left wrist. "Get me an MP! We have intruders in the data archives—fugitives from the Free Travel Zone authorities! Signal to—"

Rome drew his spazzer and sighted, but before he could fire, Aldo threw himself at Tacazon. Rome cursed. Without a clear shot he could stun both men, and dragging Aldo's twitching body out of here would not facilitate escape.

The struggle was short-lived. Aldo swung a wild punch at Tacazon, which the colonel easily blocked. He was a stout man, shorter than Aldo, but the moves he employed emphasized his fitness. He had Aldo in a hold, arm across his neck, with Aldo's implant arm bent at a painful angle behind him.

Aldo was now a human shield.

"If you think I'm coming with you, Jasko, you're crazier than I thought. My men will be here any moment."

"Let him go." If Aldo could get free for even a second—

Tacazon shoved Aldo forward and sprinted through the open door.

Rome fired. The spazzer's flash lit up the room like lightning bolts, blinding him temporarily as his eyes struggled to adjust. Bursts sizzled against the wall.

Alarms blared, like great whooping klaxons. The room was bathed in red.

Aldo groaned from where he lay on the floor. Tacazon had shoved him through the column's barrier.

"Get up!" Rome dragged Aldo to his feet. "Come on!"

They hurried out the door they'd accessed.

"Wait!" Aldo grabbed his arm. "Tacazon went the other way."

The second Pike guardbot rumbled into the room from the same direction. [Halt. Permission to detain is authorized.]

Rome slapped the door panel. Their exit sealed shut. Spazzer bursts echoed inside.

"Oh. Right."

"At least the one you put to sleep is still out." Rome nudged the robot with his shoe. "Got your map?"

"Nope. Implant's still syncing the data from the terminal. It takes up so much memory I can't do anything other than let it compress for a good ten minutes."

Ten minutes and they'd both be locked up.

Or dead.

"Follow me, then."

They hurried down the halls, Rome scanning every wall and floor joint for the marks he'd noted before. There was a dent. A scratch. A stain.

"Main corridor's up ahead." Aldo took the corner faster than Rome.

He stopped.

Lieutenant Bolduc advanced, holding a pistol in a two-handed grip. "Hands up! Get down on the floor, now! Hands behind your head! Do it!"

Aldo dropped. He held up shaking fingers. He scooted back, so Rome could see him.

"Don't move! You will be shot!" The tips of Bolduc's shoes peeked into view.

Rome twisted and fired.

Bolduc swept his gun arm up and jogged Rome's aim off target. The spazzer burst rippled across Bolduc's head.

Rome elbowed into him, slamming the officer against the wall. "Aldo, go!"

Bolduc kneed Rome in the side. Pain lanced through him and he lost his breath. Gasping, Rome brought his arm into Bolduc's face. Bone cracked.

Blood gushed from Bolduc's nose. He twisted a foot behind Rome's ankle. Rome's arm struck the ground when he toppled. His spazzer clattered against the wall.

Aldo punched Bolduc across the back of the head. The officer staggered, braced himself on a door frame—

Rome fired.

The burst rippled across Bolduc's leg, and he collapsed, foot shaking.

Rome upended the spazzer and slammed the stock across his jaw. He knocked the man out cold.

"Geez." Aldo helped Rome to his feet. "You could have just stunned him again."

"Charge was depleted. This thing doesn't carry more than a couple shots."

They ran for the exit, only to find it sealed shut. Aldo used his implant to send a false signal to the access panel, which opened a large enough gap for a few seconds that the two of them squeezed through. Rome didn't like the idea of being stuck between the door's halves when they slid shut again.

Outside, the alarms were even louder. Red lights illuminated the perimeter security bots as two headed Rome's way. Over all the sound, an aircraft engine thundered.

"Peregrine," Aldo said.

The lander was half the size of the Condor, with two turbofans perched on spindly outriggers. It wobbled on rippling waves of exhaust and banked east before dragging in the engines and extending swept wings. It was a tan insect by appearances, and the bubble canopy was polarized, leaving its occupant obscured.

Rome had a good idea who it was. But he had bigger problems.

The security gate was blocked, and human soldiers raced on foot toward them.

"I don't suppose you can shut down all the bots and spring the gate for us."

"Nope." Aldo sounded as miserable as a man finding out he'd eaten his last scraps.

"Okay then. Plan B." Rome took the comp panel from his pocket. He swiped two commands.

The Halcyon's engine rumbled. It bounced over the curb of the parking area, churning up the well-kept grass with its off-road wheels. The two soldiers turned and raised their weapons, but the car was near enough they had to either dive aside or be run over. They chose the first option.

The car's passenger door opened and a blur of distorted light rolled out.

One of the soldiers got up and aimed for the Halcyon, but the blur's vaguely human shape knocked the weapon from his hands. He swung wildly, hitting nothing but air. The blur put him on the ground with a sweep of its legs and a blow to the ribs.

The Halcyon skidded to a halt right in front of them.

"Nice driving." Aldo got in the passenger side.

"Leave room so she can get back in!" Rome queued up the manual drive controls and tore out of the compound. He pulled up the signal on the dash. "Gabriela! We need a lift."

"On my way."

Rome skidded across the grass by the soldiers, slowing long enough for Aldo to open his door and turn his seat aside. The blurred shape, more distinguishable as a person up this close, leapt in.

"Go!" she shouted.

Rome barreled straight for the fence gate.

The Halcyon bashed through it using the inflatable barrier, forming the perfect combination of battering ram and safety feature.

Rome's hands were tight on the steering column. "Thanks, Sara."

"My pleasure." A high-pitched electronic noise whined and the blur resolved into a slender black suit. Sara removed the mask, hair matted to her face. "I've never used the cloak setting on these before."

"Glad to know they work."

Condor 33 hopped over the trees at the edge of base clearing. It dropped from the sky faster than Rome thought should be possible for a vehicle its size, but in a few seconds, it hovered a couple feet off the ground. The left landing ramp extended. Rome hit it going 40 and braked hard enough Aldo's door thumped the interior wall of the bay.

The Condor lunged skyward. Army drones scrambled in pursuit as wind rushed in the bay door.

Gabriela glanced over her shoulder from the cockpit at the bedraggled party of three. "You guys okay?"

"Yeah. Fine. What about our pursuit?" Rome checked the displays.

"I lost them in the clouds. They're drones, Rome—autonomous, yes, but only half a brain." She smiled. "You get what you needed?"

"And more."

"Where to?"

"Did you snag that Peregrine lifting off?"

"Sure did. It's marked on my long-range."

Rome glared at the tiny red mark that dangled on the edge of Gabriela's primary navigational display. "We're going wherever he's going."

Chapter Fifteen

They tracked the Peregrine east across the Lakes and into upstate New York. About ten miles over the Vermont border, it descended into the New England Power Field. Sunrise flooded the array with gold and pink.

"Well, damn," Gabriela shook her head. "He might as well have flown into a forest."

It must be bad if Gabriela even let the mildest profanity pass her lips. Rome couldn't blame her—the Condor's sensors showed mile after mile of churning wind turbines—those familiar, giant egg-beaters with solar strands strung between them like a massive spider's web. They stood 300 feet tall, out here in the middle of the great forested nowhere, and Rome figured Tacazon must be a pilot of Gabriela's caliber if he made it through without crashing.

"All that power generation plays havoc with the sensors," she said. "I can circle, see where he emerges, but we'd have to get very lucky."

Rome patted her shoulder. "Do the best you can. You've got this."

She smiled. "Thanks Rome."

"Well, this is all very heart-warming," came Aldo's muffled voice. "But if you both don't mind moving your feet and shutting up a bit, I'm trying to make sure we don't drop from the sky." He was under the console, head mere inches from Gabriela's knees, with wires and modules swaying by his face. One of the nav backups, half the size of Rome's fist and shaped like a smooth white box, bounced off his chin.

"Ow!"

Rome hunkered down. "Hurts?"

"As in 'ow?' Yes!" Aldo gritted his teeth. Light flickered from a tiny laser torch. "There. Severed that one. Gabby, you getting any override commands from FTZ?"

"They're still coming in but your box in the network seems to be holding them from the nav systems."

"Seems to be?"

"As in, I haven't lost flight control and FTZ isn't steering me to lockdown at their nearest facility, Aldrich."

"Okay, good. Gimme a bit more time and we should be able to block them out completely."

"Be gentle."

"No promises." Aldo winked, even though Rome was the only one who could see it.

Rome straightened and stretched his legs. It was early Friday morning. When was the last time he slept a full night? A few hours here and there weren't cutting it. He could get his body's toxins cleaned out at the end of this mess, but it was anybody's guess whether he'd collapse from fatigue before then.

"Here." Aldo tossed something at him.

Rome caught the object—a dull violet bar wrapped in transparent biodegradable wrap. He smelled the plum. "Fruit bar."

"Enough calories crammed in there to last you until you can eat a real meal. 'Cause I'm pretty sure we ran out of food last night, and I doubt we're stopping at the nearest mart."

"Sharing from your stash?"

Aldo shifted his legs. "My last one."

Rome unwrapped it, and took a bite. He swore he felt energy seep back into his body. "You're a true hero, Mr. Burns."

"Go wrap a car around a tree. And you're welcome."

Sara was buried in holo displays at Aldo's seat. She swiped away images with a frown and pulled up new searches. "I think I've got something on Tacazon."

"He's Reno."

"I know. I found a handful of public statements he'd made as base commander, and cross-referenced those with forums where Reno was prone to comment. He did have a verbal alternator, as we suspected, but a couple of hits matched within 95 percent certainty."

"Rome, the girl's got some skills," Aldo said from under the console. "Give her the bar if you're gonna be ungrateful about it."

"Too late." Rome swallowed the last piece. He was more ravenous than he thought. He brought up the bio from the base's info page. "Colonel Martellan Tacazon, thirty-year veteran, U.S. Army. His background explains an awful lot about his involvement with the thieves. He's served with an R&D branch at Aberdeen. His specialty is advanced battlefield technologies."

"The stealth suits and the truck," Sara murmured. "Both must have been easy for him to access at his base, and with his experience, he'd know the limitations and advantage of the gear."

"There's something else about the dear colonel I realized when we met him face to face. We pissed him off, personally."

"When?" Sara asked.

"When Aldo and I arrested his daughter."

There was a thump from under Gabriela's console. "Ow!" Aldo shimmied out, his face red. "We did what to who?"

Rome dug back through their case files. He transferred the most recent stop from his implant into the console where Sara worked. The centerpiece was a still image of a glaring teen girl with fluorescent hair.

"Oh, yeah. Offender and offensive." Aldo squatted on the deck. "We dropped her off at Rapid City, right?"

"Yeah. Last update I got, she was processed and transferred back to Grand Rapids. Daddy got the bill. And Daddy…" Rome overlaid her detainment record with the files on Colonel Tacazon.

"More than a slight resemblance," Gabriela noted.

"This is why we're the targets," Rome said. "I wondered why

whoever was behind the thefts picked us—sure, I have bad data in my past, but I'm hardly the only pursuit driver drawn from the trouble-making ranks. Tough luck on our part? No. Tacazon had us tagged because we brought in his daughter."

"Okay, makes sense to me. Like you said, man's pissed at us." Aldo replaced a couple panels underneath the console. "Next question is, who leaked him the intel on your background?"

"I've got an angle on the problem. Sara, is there anything else you can tell us about your group that could point us to where they're going next? With the damage we did to the truck's docking collar, Cuellar would have had to find a place to make repairs. A place that didn't ask questions."

Sara nodded. "There's a few locations we knew along the last stretch of the Ninety. They were a last resort—we mostly operated in West and Central."

"Any way you can check for activity?"

"Not with Jorge. But there's a couple people I can ask without alerting him." Sara called up a message input screen. "Gabriela, can I…"

"Got you an outgoing data line," Gabriela interjected. "I'd keep it brief, though, we don't want anyone doubling back on us." She sounded distant.

"Gabriela," Rome said. "We looking okay?"

"Could be nothing. I had a hit on the sensors, but those solar panels down there are creating so many optical decoys," she shrugged, "it made it look like the Peregrine was behind us."

"Keep at it."

"Rome, when we catch up with Tacazon, we've got a problem." Aldo patted his implant. "The money exchange. That's our proof."

"Yeah, I know."

"Every transaction he's made has been deleted from his implant by now. We can't trace it unless we know the financial institution, or the receiver." Sara's face was pinched with emotion. "And none of us three had implants."

Rome had thought about seeing what was recovered from Robert Brand's dead body on the highway by checking his contact at FTZ, but she was right. No implant, no data. He drummed his fingers on his leg. "Then we're stuck, unless Tacazon confesses."

"Not necessarily," Aldo said. "You can delete files from your implant, remove apps, even wipe the entire operating system for resale or trade-in, but not all implants kiss their data good-bye. The feds, for example—every FBI agent's implant provided by the department is federal property. So they got a ghosted backup to keep track of everything going into or out of the implant. "

"You can retrieve deleted data?"

"Possibly. Maybe. Look, I've never seen it done, or even seen somebody who has one, but I heard it third-hand."

"If you think we can trust your source."

"My last source got us into a U.S. Army base."

"Fair enough. If we get ahold of Tacazon—"

"It may have the same kind of cache. I'm betting on yes, seeing as how he's a senior officer."

"We don't need him, Rome," Sara insisted. "We just need the implant."

Aldo winced.

Rome also remembered her former interactions with implants. "You volunteering? We'll need it to be quick."

"I'd be happy to."

"Good." Rome's implant buzzed, sending a tremor through his wrist. Could be a sensory mirage—why would anyone contact him? But it was a real message, text only.

Freddie.

<Six minute window. It's the best I could do.>

Rome smiled. "I'll be right back."

He headed for the Halcyon's bay. Once there, he projected a keypad from the holo emitter of his implant onto his arm. <Good news, I

hope.>

<Not really. They managed to get your tags reactivated.>

Fear jolted Rome. For the first time since the warrants were executed and Gabriela came after them with Thad on their tail, he was frozen. <How long do we have?>

<I don't know. The information's compartmentalized. Only Cho has the details. But there's a half dozen Condors already in the air, for the last 24 hours.>

This whole time they were being hunted, even with Gabriela shielding them. <I need you to do me a favor.>

<Seems to be my specialty these days.>

<We have a target. Colonel Martellan Tacazon. See if any signals have come into FTZ West from Michigan on military channels.>

Tense seconds passed before Freddie responded.

<Military? What are you mixed up in?>

<Come on, Freddie.>

<I'll see what I can find. Meanwhile, you'd better land and scatter.>

Rome scowled. How did she know they were in the air?

Gabriela.

The Condor's nav system.

FTZ must have figured out what was going on before Aldo could cut them from the sensor net. <Hurry.>

<You too. Be careful, Rome.>

<Rarely am. Thanks anyway.>

"Rome! Rome, get your ass up here!"

He got to Aldo's side as two bright red pips flashed on the main navigational display. "Bogeys."

"Yeah. Pair of Condors, FTZ Central." Aldo jerked a thumb at Gabriela, who had a headset in place and one hand pressed to her ear. "She's on the signal with them."

"Shhhh!" Gabriela glared at him. "Condor Four Seven, this is Condor Three Three. Please send again. Signal is weak and variable."

"Three Three, we detect no loss of signal on our end." The voice was female and stern as an irked Jocelyn. "Your ship has been implicated in abetting fugitives from FTZ custody. You will land your aircraft, shut down all power, and submit yourselves to custody."

Aldo pulled Rome aside. "Man, you have got to see this."

"Yeah, I saw—two Condors, coming up fast on our six."

"No, no, no. This."

Aldo's implant shone a holo in his face. Rome grimaced and moved his nose out of the light stream. The pattern of the display looked familiar. "Hang on. Is that…?"

"Yeah. The hijack signal Sara's thief team used to override the nav systems in any vehicle around them. You know what that means."

"Jorge's striking again."

"Maybe with Tacazon."

Rome glanced over his shoulder. Gabriela argued with the voice on the other end of the signal, faking her way through a malfunction. He touched her shoulder.

She covered the microphone. "I can't stall forever. We're coming up on populated areas of Massachusetts. I have to land."

"I know. But I've got a place for you to land."

Aldo twisted his wrist so she could see the hologram.

Gabriela's eyes widened. She let her hand drop away from the microphone. "Standby, Four Seven. I am preparing to land."

"I'm sorry, Gabby." Aldo patted her arm awkwardly as if he would break her.

"I know." Her smile was winsome. "But you three had better go strap into the Halcyon."

Aldo paled. "Aw, man. Not again."

Rome couldn't see anything except the drab bulkhead through the windshield of the Halcyon. It didn't stop him from experiencing the twists and turns of Gabriela's evasion. Everything lurched. Rome's inner ear protested, as did his stomach. For a second, he had no idea if he was level or if the Condor was inverted.

Aldo stared directly into the displays that emanated from his comm panel. "Okay. Okay, we're good."

"I know."

"Not talking to you."

Rome's stomach felt like it dropped out from inside him. Sara yelped from her seat behind Rome and Aldo. She was secured in a web of straps—as were they—with her eyes squeezed shut.

Gabriela's voiced buzzed from the dash. "I've got a nice place to set you down that ought to provide decent cover. I'll find a way to get to you guys, either when I lose these rookies or by hiking on foot. Godspeed."

"You're the best, Gabriela."

The floor underneath the Halcyon rumbled open. Sunlight poured in. Rome glimpsed treetops at an alarming proximity to the underside of the Condor.

A strip of paving flew into view.

The grapples overhead released. For a moment, Rome and his passengers were suspended in midair. Blue skies and white clouds were on the horizon until legions of pines crowded their field of vision. Condor 33 shot ahead and banked crazily up into a pair of thick white clouds. Two more Condors, identical save for the large "47" and "46" painted on their tails, stayed in pursuit, though with movements far less graceful and speeds that slowed too much as they tried to match Gabriela's maneuvering.

The Halcyon was below the tree line. Rome slapped the controls to modulate the inflation of all four tires. They hit the road with such a blow he was convinced they tore the chassis apart, but he kept his grip on the steering controls and fought against the car's swerving as the back end skidded. The tires squealed.

Finally, their path straightened out. The speedometer clocked them at 75 miles per hour.

Rome sagged in his seat. "Piece of cake."

"Incoming!" Aldo pointed.

Four cars raced toward them from the wrong direction, filling both lines of traffic on what Rome noticed was a narrow road.

Gabriela dropped them on a one-way street? In the middle of a forest?

He had no more time to contemplate the screw-up.

He loosened his grip on the steering column. If they were going to survive the next few seconds, he had to take it on some faith.

Rome dodged left, letting a bright red car as sleek as a fighter plane rush by. An immediate jog right breezed past a yellow truck more suited to hauling cargo. He didn't bother checking the clearance Aldo's comp panel flashed—he didn't want know if the distance was measured in feet or was better noted in inches.

Two more vehicles. One was a Halcyon painted hideous neon green with bold pink stripes. The other was a 40-year-old Andromeda, a discontinued model from the defunct Nissan motor company. Rome cataloged, even as both cars raced up at top speed.

He eyeballed the distance between them. Wide enough? "Aldo, cut the safeties on the coolant."

"What? Why?"

"Do it!"

Aldo flicked the proper command. Red lights outlined the windshield.

"Rome!" Sara cried.

Rome toggled the left side pressure until the little bar displayed on the dash pulsed white at a towering column of scarlet.

They were so close to the onrushing cars Rome saw panicked expressions on the faces of both drivers… and one of them looked like a skinnier version of Roman Jasko.

A sound like a thunderclap boomed from the left side of the Halcyon. Rome hung onto the controls as the car jerked up, left wheels leaving the road. They bounced the top of the pink-striped Halcyon, squealing along the roof.

The whole car slammed back down onto the road as it left the makeshift ramp. White gases sprayed all along Rome's side of the car, lapping onto the windshield. He put the Halcyon into a sharp left turn, skidding across the lane and onto the shoulder of the road. The off-road tires engaged, stopping them near enough to a line of trees that Rome swore he heard the fenders scrape bark.

All four cars braked ahead.

"Man-o-man!" Aldo whooped. He pounded both hands on the dash and then punched Rome in the shoulder. He grinned like a maniac. "That was insane! Nobody, not even Thad is going to believe it!"

"You almost got us killed!" Sara struggled free of her straps. "What did you do to the car?"

"Over-pressured one of our two coolant lines." The white gases petered out into a tepid wisp. "It's fixable—probably even while we drive—if the self-sealant wasn't damaged. But I knew it would give us enough lift."

The silver and green Andromeda pulled near to them—driving backwards. Not too shabby.

The driver, though, was more shocking than the maneuvering. "Dad?"

"Jake?" Rome rubbed his face. Thick whiskers scratched his hand. "What on earth are you doing here?"

"Me? Doing here?" Jake Jasko was the same height as his father, though all gangly limbs and ropy muscle. His hair was the same black as Rome's was before he'd shaved it, and worn far longer with intricate designs cut into the sides. Hazel eyes were wide with astonishment. "Dad, you're on our track."

"You're not making sense."

"Ah, Rome…" Aldo enlarged his holo display. "Found us."

Rome stared at the interweaved loops of roads covering eight miles between the tiny hamlets of Windsor and Peru in western Massachusetts. Gabriela had dumped them on the Mass Hike—

Atlantic Driver Course Experience, one of a handful of sanctioned motor parks where civilians could gain temporary registration. You paid a fee, and drove for minutes, hours, or days. The pass was good only for the property. Once you left the boundaries, driving was illegal.

Five more cars shot by in a blur of riotous color. Rome saw why it was popular. But as to why his son was here… "I thought you were in trouble for your lame-brained graffiti stunt."

"Nice to see you too." Jake rolled his eyes. "But, wheels out! That move you did, Dad! Totally hands-on!"

"Yeah, it was."

"You're all over the Net. You didn't do any of that crap, did you?"

Rome spotted a bruise under his right eye. "What do you think?"

Jake must have noticed his stare, because he probed the discolored flesh. "Got this telling one of the guys the Net's full of sh—junk."

Aldo cleared this throat. He pointed at a different part of the state's geography with a certain flashing red marker.

"Jake, we've got to go."

"Right. I got to go log out, anyway. The concert's tonight…" Jake trailed off. He waved his hands. "Do you, I don't know, need some help or something?"

From his teenage son? The same kid with such poor impulse control he couldn't keep steady employment, not even with Massachusetts's Infrastructure Rebuild Corps? "You'd better apply again with IRC. Roads and bridges won't fix themselves."

Jake snorted. "Okay, sure, Dad. Whatever." He walked back to his car.

The Andromeda. "Hey, Jake."

His son turned.

"Nice ride." Rome couldn't hide the smile. "And nice moves."

Jake shrugged, but there was a ghost of smile in return. "You too."

Rome stuck with the next pack of cars that came along, driving them all the way back to the Mass Hike's entrance. Dozens of garages and workshops were crammed together on a huge lot, domes and hexagons packed in like a kid's toy blocks. A pair of glassed in restaurants, observation stands, and rows of stores were perched above the mad array.

He had to admit, he thoroughly enjoyed powering past the teenagers in their modded rides that tended to herk and jerk around corners. Breezing aside the guys—and some girls—who were old enough to be Rome's parents was fun too. But there were a few men, whom Rome guessed were in their late 70s, who gave him a run for his money.

All in all, it made for an excellent cover. Even in the chaos of the workshops, Aldo found them a maintenance exit that bypassed the main security gates.

It only fooled the authorities for 20 minutes.

"Local LEOs," Aldo said. "A pair of black and whites. Not even pursuit drivers."

"You still got a fix on Cuellar's signal?"

"Yeah. Westfield."

"Westfield? Are you sure?"

Aldo gave him a withering glare.

"Right, you're sure."

"What's wrong with Westfield?"

"Nothing." Rome didn't want to say anything. He had a ridiculous feeling that if he spoke his premonition aloud, it would come true.

He drove the entire the distance once they got onto the Ninety. So many warning notices and safety violations lit up the dashboard he wondered if the optics would stay permanently red. Aldo disabled them all, routing the alerts into the comp panel's memory without having them first appear on the dash.

"Jorge's not going to run," Sara said. "He isn't that kind. He'd prefer to stay and fight."

"Thanks for the intel."

"I want you to be prepared." She checked the magazine of one of the J20s. "Because he will be."

"Cheery thought," Aldo muttered.

They followed the signal from the stealth truck off the highway. Just as Aldo intercepted an alert from FTZ, one of their vehicles had tagged the Halcyon.

"FTZ East has Security on us," he said. "I'd expect a herd of their interceptors any moment now, so whatever we're planning for Tacazon and his buddy, we'd better be fast."

"Get me close enough, and it will be," Sara said.

Rome was too disturbed to contribute to the conversation. There was something about the tree line, the streets, the buildings... He knew them. A few businesses had changed and the road was repaved. There were added traffic sensor posts, standing like slender silver sentinels. But it was all familiar enough.

The school's appearance around a bend hit him worse than a physical blow. It was a cylinder, two stories tall, with one sixth removed as if someone took a slice out of a giant cake made of blue glass and beige concrete. Cars filled a parking area nearby. They were packed impossibly close for anyone to access. Even as he watched, two rows rearranged with a tight precision to allow a Famtrac to park.

More cars lined both sides of the street, exactly a half-meter apart under rows of juvenile maples.

One of them was the stealth truck.

"I've got a pair of Condors incoming," Aldo said. "Probably fifteen miles out. We'd better move our asses."

Rome was already out the door. Sara passed him a J20. Aldo took one, too.

The school's door slid open.

"No." Rome halted, halfway across the street.

The cars coming down both lanes braked. Passengers inside waved at him, trying to get him to move, but the automated navigation refused to budge. So did he.

Colonel Tacazon and Jorge Cuellar came out the front door, pulling a woman and a child by their arms.

"Oh, great," Aldo said.

"They've got hostages." Sara held her gun at the ready. "We can still disable the truck..."

"No, we can't." Rome's legs wouldn't work.

"Why?"

"Because that's my daughter, and her mother."

Chapter Sixteen

Tacazon tugged Vivian toward the stealth truck, but stopped at the curb when he spotted the trio that stood in the middle of the street. "Jasko," he spat. "You're insane. The authorities will be here any moment. Get out of our way, and nobody will come to harm."

Rome's grip tightened on the J20, as if he squeezed the metal flat. He imagined it as Tacazon's face.

"Let them be, Reno." Sara raised her rifle. "You know why we're here."

"If you think you're getting a confession out of me, you're crazier than he is."

Aldo walked slowly to the side, but before he got any closer on his arc toward the truck, Jorge Cuellar came around the opposite end.

He had Kelsey pulled in close, with a Hunsaker .45 caliber tucked against her ribs. "Stay put, or the chica gets her innards painted on the road."

A roar grew on the horizon. Rome recognized it—Condor engines. More than one set. "Tacazon, leave them alone. You and I need to deal with this. It has nothing to do with my family."

"You see, it actually does have to do with both our families, Jasko. Dragging my daughter off like some common criminal. Does that make you feel better? Somehow make your life more worthwhile, that she gets tagged with a record?"

"She was breaking the law. I'm paid to catch people like her." Rome heard more engines of a different sort. One was a Panther. If he could delay Tacazon long enough... "That why you boys picked me as the one to take the fall?"

"I couldn't ask for a civilian more perfect," Tacazon said. "My partner agreed. We were making so much money it was worth the risk. Now you're going to let me drive away to enjoy that money, and by the time I get over the borders, it won't matter whether people believe you or not."

The stealth truck lurched from its spot, bashing the tail end of a blue Famtrac. It ripped the fender off, shoved it out into traffic, and trundled toward Rome and Sara.

Cars all around them backed up, driving down both lanes in a close herd, like sheep huddling for safety. Rome targeted the truck's wheels as it rumbled toward them. Probably a smart move on the nav's part.

Someone yelped. Out of the corner of his eye, he saw Kelsey break away from Cuellar. As he drew back his foot, she pummeled him with blows, screaming, seemingly oblivious to the gun he still held.

Aldo rushed in, slamming his J20 into Cuellar's gut. The two went down in a tangle of limbs and weapons.

The truck was only a couple car lengths away. "It's projectile resistant!" Sara warned.

"Aim for the front left." He opened fire.

Sara joined him. The tracker bullets struck the front fender, the armored body, and then found their intended target—the left wheel. By Rome's count, more than two-dozen shots hit the tire before they penetrated its surface. It didn't even blow. All it did was sag in rather anticlimactic fashion.

The AI in charge corrected and sent it skidding toward Rome.

Sara shoved him aside hard enough he lost his balance. He tumbled into the next lane.

The truck's AI must have had some of its safety protocols still in place because it braked hard, swerving to avoid Sara.

Then the back end exploded.

The sound was deafening. Rome's ears rang. Heat washed over him like an ocean's wave, drowning him. Flame was everywhere, racing up the truck's body.

Sara. Where was she?

Black smoke obscured his view.

He glimpsed her arm, fingers still clutching the J20's grip.

A rush of wind cleared the smoke, accompanied by the sound of a Condor's engines. Rome saw the aircraft hovering over the school. He smiled…

And then he froze.

It wasn't Condor 33. The tailfin showed a 47.

Tires spun. A long, gray Ford Altair took off in the opposite direction, breaking five traffic laws. Famtracs and passenger cars got out of the way of the wide vehicle, its exterior covered with huge curved windows.

Driving.

It could be Cuellar, though from what Rome had seen of the Peregrine's escape from the base, he had no doubt Tacazon was skilled at the controls.

Ignoring the hovering Condor, Rome used his jacket as a shield from the flames. He got Sara's arm looped over his shoulder. Together they staggered away from the wreckage.

Sara coughed, her face going red. She hung onto him.

"Thanks for keeping me unsinged." Rome sat her on the hood of the Halcyon.

She coughed again, but nodded through the spasms.

"Roman Jasko." The voice boomed from the heavens. Not godlike, unless the Creator was a stern lady pilot. "You will stand fast and submit to detainment. You and your accomplices are in violation of—"

The message broke off in a sharp screech. Signal jammed?

Aldo jogged over. "They got away, man. I'm sorry."

"Don't be. Get in." Rome helped Sara into the car. "Nice work blocking the obnoxious transmission."

The Condor flew in a slow, wide circle around the street and the surrounding buildings. Rome swore the pilot was trying to set up a decent shot with its EMP, but for whatever reason, she couldn't depress the nose or the wings low enough for the right angle.

"Um, you're welcome, but it isn't me." Aldo glanced down the road. "Great. More trouble? Really?"

Rome didn't have to wait at all to find out what the "really" was. A Halcyon, similar model to his, was marked up with the FTZ Security logo. FTZ East.

But that wasn't the engine noise he found familiar. The purr was far too smooth, far too even to be a Halcyon. No, it had to belong to something more high performance.

"What're we gonna do?"

"Can't sit here on our butts." Rome started up the engine. "If we cut over a few blocks, we might beat Tacazon to the Ninety."

The front end of the Security Halcyon crackled with pent-up energy discharge. EMP.

Rome smacked the controls. With the truck blocking the lane and the automated traffic bottlenecked as their nav systems tried to get everyone out of danger in orderly fashion, he didn't have a chance to get clear of the blast. EMP resistant or not, it would render his car as inert as a stone.

Fine then.

Rome secured his straps. "Everyone hold onto something."

Aldo moaned. "I hate it when he says that."

"Why?" Sara braced herself on the sides of the car.

Rome held the Halcyon in Park, revving the motor until the speedometer numbers jumped wildly. The car trembled, begging to leap.

He reached for reverse.

A Rishi Panther—metallic blue with a broad, gold and black, checkered pattern along the running boards—bumped aside a pair of Famtracs. It filled the space directly behind the Security Halcyon. Rome noticed the same sparks from its front end.

The EMP blast was bright as a bolt of lightning, and the crack it made in close quarters was as sharp as a snapping whip. There was no way for the Security car to avoid it. By the time the last bolt played over its body, the Halcyon veered off the left side of the road, crossing the wrong lane. Inertia carried it into the side of a passenger car.

The Panther interposed itself between the dead Security vehicle and Rome's Halcyon. He saw his expression—jaw slack and eyes wide—in the dark windows. The window rolled down, revealing a dour face.

"'Sup, Enrique!" Aldo waved cheerily.

Enrique flipped him off.

"Such rudeness." Thad was out his window, arm draped atop the roof. His grin was as brilliant as the EMP burst. "For all this mess, Roman, I should have held out for better pay."

"They'd drop your contract for this."

"Somehow I suspect that is the least of our worries. And no appreciation on Enrique's finest endeavor." Thad waved a hand at Condor 47. The aircraft continued its bizarre loops. "Is what Gabriela says true? This colonel, he has set up you and Aldo? Just as you said?"

"Every word."

The FTZ Security men got out of their car—two tall, burly guys with the pale skin of indoor types. "Nobody moves! Stand down and…"

Thad spazzed them both.

"Help me get this wreck out of the way," Rome ordered.

Thad slipped back into his car. Together, the Panther and Halcyon shoved against the wrecked stealth truck. Rome knew his car was fire resistant. He hoped Thad's was. It helped that a pair of fire drones appeared overhead, red lights flashing against scarlet bodies the size of old oil barrels. Their trio of turbofans blew smoke away as they draped the truck in white foam. It was pushed aside, clearing enough of a lane for Rome to drive around, followed by the Panther.

Thad's voice carried through the car's communications. "*Madre*

Dios. These thieves, they play rough."

"Thad, they've got my family, too."

The Panther's speed surged. "Let us repay the *pendejos*. I will follow your tracks."

Rome kept his glare fixed on the road and punched the accelerator.

Enrique's handiwork kept Condor 47 in a helpless spin, but by now, every FTZ East branch—not to mention every law enforcement agency within fifty miles—was alerted to the presence of the two rogue pursuit cars.

Upside—Aldo tracked the Ford Altair easily. "Not so easy when you can't play ghost," he muttered.

"Casper." Rome's knuckles were white. He swept them along a row of four freighters. Everyone one of them shot off a distance warning, which Aldo's comp panel digested.

"Casper what?"

"The ghost. He was friendly. It was a kid's show."

"When, in ancient Rome?"

"Hysterical. My grandfather watched it."

"This is how you're doing stress?"

"Better than shooting holes through traffic with the J20 until I hit our target."

"Ah. Good point."

Sara leaned from the back seat. "Get me in close enough and I can get aboard."

"Get aboard?" Aldo laughed a manic, desperate sound. "This isn't a cruise hydrofoil. You'll go splat on the road!"

Sara slapped the back of his head. "You know how many times I jumped between moving vehicles while I was running with them?"

"No. And, ow."

"I do. Get us close."

"That could be a problem." Rome indicated the rear view.

Thad tailed them, one lane to the left and a car's length back. Beyond him, three FTZ East Security cars approached, lights flashing. One was a Halcyon, and two were big CM Obsidians—six-passenger vehicles, with six wheels apiece. They were surprisingly nimble to the average passenger. Each wheel operated independent of the other, allowing the Obsidians to change lanes with speed and precision even Rome was hard-pressed to match. By the way they caught up, Rome knew someone drove each one, albeit with AI assistance.

"I explained as best I could the reason they all should steer clear of this pursuit," Thad said through the signal. "They did not agree."

"I can see that. You have any ideas?"

"Drive faster."

"Already doing it. I was thinking something more inconvenient to them."

Thad laughed. "I may have a handful of such inconveniences aboard. Allow Enrique a moment to prepare them."

Aldo kept the Altair bracketed in the car's sensors. It stayed a red outline, visible through a dozen cars in front of them. Traffic unzipped, peeling off onto shoulders and medians. Automatons didn't bother to put them back on the road, leaving Rome a clear route to the Altair.

"You sure you're up for this?" Rome asked.

"I'm sure," Sara said. "I owe Reno for the mess he's made. I owe everyone else the same."

"There he goes!" Aldo flipped his palm through his holo displays.

Thad's Panther braked hard, allowing the FTZ Security vehicles to race by. Projectiles shot out from the front as tiny gray spheres. Rome didn't see where they hit until one of the Obsidians braked and accelerated again and again. It shook so hard he thought it would lose a wheel, three of which tried to go in three different directions at once. Finally, it steered into the dip of the grassy green median. Men poured out of two side hatches.

Thad got behind the FTZ Halcyon, but its driver was skilled enough to avoid being tailed. The two vehicles traded lanes. Each jockeyed for a clean shot with EMPs, even as they avoided other cars and the automated traffic cleared out the lanes.

"I'm lined up for a burst," Aldo said. "EMP is charged to 90 percent."

"No. Shut it down," Rome said.

"What? Hey, it's the only way we'll get it to slow down."

"The Altair could be hardened against it."

"And if it isn't, we can stop them right now!"

Rome swerved around a pair of freighters stuck in the center lane. Apparently their comps had decided the safest action was to huddle in the middle of the chaos at a plodding pace. "Dammit, Aldo, I'm not taking a potshot at the car containing my family!"

Aldo stared through his holos. "Well, fine! So what's your genius plan?"

"Make sure they're targeted, and transfer the triggers to my control."

Aldo muttered under his breath. His fingers stabbed through the displays as he set up the commands.

"What is it?" Sara said. "Without the EMP, there's no way to shut them down."

"There is a way to reel them in," Rome said. "Are we ready?"

"Grapples are up!" Aldo crowed. "Whenever you're in range."

Green numbers popped up in the left corner of Rome's windshield. They dwindled with each passing second.

Meanwhile, a flash from behind broke his concentration. The Halcyon was wreathed in sparks. It spun down a steep embankment on the right side off the Ninety, its front end crunched between a pair of tree trunks.

"Nice shooting, Thad."

"De nada. The last Obsidian's proving more a nuisance. He's coming up on your six. I'm too far back to catch him and… I have more pressing problems."

Proximity alerts chimed. "Condor's back, and she brought her buddy!" Aldo announced.

Condors 46 and 47 roared in from the southwest, bracketing the road with a pair of EMP flashes. They washed over the Panther like a wave, dousing Thad's car completely. Rome saw the skid and its indicators died completely from Aldo's displays. He heard the signal break off in static. The Panther shone iridescent blue under the pulses before it stuttered to a dead stop, smack in the middle of the Ninety.

"Pretty decent of him to take one for us," Aldo murmured.

"Only if we catch our target," Rome said. "Range to target, 300 yards."

They both moved so fast they caught up with the swarm of traffic ahead. It was everything Rome hated about driving—the herd of Famtracs, the long lines of freighters, the individual passenger cars grouped in threes and fours by comps seeking to conserve fuel with ground effect assist, all packed together by programmed intelligences seeking maximum efficiency and safety.

It meant five miles of nearly wall-to-wall vehicles with nowhere to go when two human driven wild cards entered the mix.

Suddenly the Halcyon swerved hard right. Rome corrected its course. His heart jumped. "Aldo, tell me I just felt a really big gust of wind."

"Sorry, no." Aldo scowled through the displays. "Our buddies up in the Obsidian? They're good. One of them's good."

The Halcyon swerved again. Rome was ready, though this time the steering fought with him for a few seconds before it came back under his control. Not good.

"Yeah, they're trying to override our nav."

"You want to stop them?"

"Okay, what do you think I've been doing?" Aldo stabbed through a command line and swiped it over to a stream of data on the opposite side of his display.

"It all looks like playing with light and air to me." A third attack. This one turned into an all-out struggle. Rome strained against the steering column. He stomped on the accelerator, pushing the Halcyon as fast ahead as he could, which was hard to do when the car skittered and jumped like a rabbit on the run, straddling two lanes at a time. "Get in there and shut them down!"

"Working on it!"

Fasteners clacked. Wind rushed into the car. Sara's window was open. She had a J20 propped out the window. "I've got them."

"Put it away!" Rome snapped. "You'll get everyone killed."

"The safeties should automatically engage and force them off the road."

"That's great. Experiment with the possibility when my family's not stuck inside their ride."

"Ha! Got 'em!" Aldo double-punched through the holo.

"You locked them out?" Rome grimaced as the steering column wrenched hard left. A Famtrac brushed by them near enough to set off a proximity warning. "Why the hell am I still having a wrestling match with controls?"

"Still trying to get past their blocks. That's not what I meant," Aldo gestured forward.

A string of six freighters ran in a single line in the right most lane. One by one they peeled off, starting with the front vehicle until they spread across both lanes. The next thing Rome knew, there was a wall of freighters three vehicles wide, running down two lanes. He didn't think too much about how near they were to each other or how close their tires spun to the edge of the pavement.

"Get through those," Aldo muttered.

The Altair braked no more than two feet from the fender of the closest freighter. Whatever Tacazon and Cuellar had planned, it wasn't coming to them fast.

Rome still fought for control of his car.

The range for the magnetic grapples dwindled. If he could get a good, solid hit…

"Coming up behind us!" Sara called.

The other Obsidian was only a handful of car lengths back. It passed a Famtrac, then pushed up behind a solo freighter until the larger vehicle obediently moved aside.

Ten feet from the Altair.

EMP discharge rippled across the front of the Obsidian.

"I've got a clean shot!" Sara was half out the window, her shouted words were torn to wisps by the wind that rushed by. "I can get them off the road."

"I can't get past the blocks," Aldo said. "They've got me locked out of their nav system."

Rome's steering controls stopped fighting. The whole setup went slack in his hands. The column shuddered, then started to sink into the dash.

"They're putting us on full auto!"

Range…? The readouts were dead. Solid black.

Rome slapped the grapple trigger.

The projectiles shot out.

For an instant, Rome imagined they scraped pavement, falling short of their target.

One did, and was torn free of its cable. The other slammed against the back of the Altair and stuck fast—the cable taut as a guitar string.

The steering column disappeared completely under the dash. The accelerator and decelerators retreated with the gearshift. The Halcyon—fully controlled by Cuellar and Tacazon—altered its course toward the side of the road. Except now, it was latched to the rear of the Altair.

"Reel them in," Rome snapped.

Aldo grinned and flicked a command.

The cable shivered. Somewhere under the front of the Halcyon the winch whirred, shaking the whole car.

Shots exploded.

Sara.

She fired on the Obsidian, but whoever the driver was had enough skill to maneuver in a fashion that caused even the tracker bullets a severe headache. The Obsidian closed its distance.

The Halcyon pulled on the grapple. Since its navigation was no longer under Rome's guidance, he couldn't make it bring the Altair closer, but Cuellar and Tacazon had already taken care of the problem—they dragged themselves off the road. The Halcyon went sidelong, skidding and pulling on the Altair. Meanwhile, the distance closed to just a few feet.

"I'm out." Rome slipped his restraints and opened the window. Hot air blasted around him.

"Rome! Don't get killed!" Aldo gave him the spazzer and a thumbs-up.

Rome squirmed out of the car. Sara was already crouched on the roof, J20 slung over her back. "If we're going to do this..."

Rome launched into a run down the windshield and over the hood of the Halcyon. He lost his footing at the edge, but managed to push off as hard as he could. For a split second, he was in the air. He knew what Gabriela must love about piloting. Him... well, he'd be happy with a private Condor right then.

Rome banged onto the top of the Altair. His hands scrabbled for purchase on the slick sides. He plucked his knife from his pants, swung it up, and jabbed it into a slender seam were the windows began their curve. The blade held.

The sudden stop sent a lightning bolt of pain through his right arm. He slapped his left atop the Altair.

A thump.

Sara was on the vehicle with him. She lay flat and grabbed his left wrist. With her grunts, pulls, and his pushes with both feet, they got on the roof without either slipping off or smearing the pavement.

The Altair skidded madly to the left, pulling so hard the Halcyon's cable twanged.

The Obsidian was two car lengths back.

"What happens to us up here when the EMP goes off?" Rome yelled.

"I'm not waiting up here to find out!" Sara swung her feet over the left side with the grace of a gymnast. Both boots bashed through the window.

The panel was made of a composite material that crumpled out of the way, rather than shattering shards everywhere. Rome was torn between elation at Sara having made it inside and fury at her endangerment of his family.

Suddenly, the freighter accelerated, moving out of the phalanx Aldo had formed. True to safety protocols, their comps strung them to the left and the Altair went right, getting around them. The Halcyon's back end bounced half on the road and half on the shoulder.

The Obsidian fired.

"No!" Rome scrambled for the broken window.

The pulse flashed short of the Altair. It hit the last of those six freighters and its systems died. There was nothing to stop it from colliding with the freighter ahead, which tried to break and steer sideways. The comp on the second freighter recognized that the Altair, the Halcyon, and Obsidian were all laden with human passengers. The calculation was simple. The sacrifice was easy.

The second freighter banged against the dead one. They crunched hard, veering down the median into the slope. The collision took a third freighter… and a fourth, leaving the other two to rapidly change course. They surged ahead, running at full speed for the only gap in traffic available.

When Rome caught his breath, he dove into the car in the same manner Sara had. The problem was his lack of agility. He banged the back of his neck on the open window frame, but the good part was he landed on something soft.

A lap.

"Rome!" Kelsey stared at him, face upside down, eyes red from crying. She looked as astonished and angry as Rome ever remembered seeing her.

All he could do was lean up and kiss her.

"Need some backup!" Sara was between the middle pair of seats. She grappled with Cuellar, who's knife was poised over her neck. She had a grip on both his wrists, but Cuellar's greater weight pushed her down between the seats.

Rome was in the back row—a bench huddled against the broad cargo portion of the Altair's rear section. Kelsey was on the left side, Vivian on the right.

"Daddy! Daddy, help us!"

That alone jolted Rome from his haze of pain.

He got off Kelsey, pushed off the bench, and put his shoulder into Cuellar's middle. The blow broke Sara's grip on his wrists, splitting the pair apart. The knife was Rome's problem now.

Cuellar punched him in the low back near his kidneys. The strike stabbed through Rome's abdomen. A second punched lanced across his face, stunning him. He gritted his teeth.

Fine.

Rome brought a knee around and was satisfied by the snap of a rib or two. Cuellar yelped and slashed with the knife. The blade caught Rome's left shoulder, tearing the cloth and cutting a line of fire across his skin.

"Jorge! Hold him back!" Tacazon was the driver. The scenery outside the Altair's windshield—tilted on its side due to Rome's vantage—jerked back and forth. He felt the car's floor shift underneath. "Their car isn't responding to your override! Whoever's in there has control back."

Rome grinned. Blood dripped onto his teeth. Atta boy, Aldo.

Sara's arms slithered around Cuellar's neck. His face turned crimson. He swung the blade without care or aim. It made a wet, meaty sound where it found Sara's side.

Rome punched Cuellar square in the face. A tooth broke and skittered across the carpet.

Vivian screamed.

Sara sagged back, clutching her side. A bloody blade stained the floor. Red ran between her fingers, soaking her clothes.

Rome grabbed Cuellar by the collar with both hands and slammed him against a support by the door-frame. The man's head rattled like a loose gearshift.

Rome hit him as hard as he could in the stomach, a blow channeling all the fury for everything taken from him.

Air rushed out in a great whoosh. He slammed Cuellar's head against the support, again. His eyes rolled into the back of his head. He dropped, out cold.

Rome lurched to the front of the car. Somewhere in his belt… there it was. The compact spazzer he'd used at Bacevich Arsenal. He jabbed Tacazon in the back of the head. "Pull over."

Tacazon did.

They let the Halcyon reel them to the side of the road. Outside was a swarm of activity—FTZ Security men and women shouting orders, the pair of Condors roaring overhead, the rest of the traffic at a standstill. Rome wondered if they'd shut down the entire Ninety.

Kelsey was out of her restraints. She had a First Aid kit open and applied a thick set of wound sealant to Sara's stab wound. "The bleeding's stopping," Kelsey said. "She'll be okay. Still needs a hospital."

Rome reached for Sara's hand. Her grip was still strong. "Hang in there. Kelsey, are you hurt?"

Kelsey shook her head. She hugged Rome with one arm. "Thanks for coming after us."

"You know I wouldn't ever do anything else."

He hugged Vivian tight. His daughter cried until Rome whispered a song into her ear and rocked her from side to side.

"Don't kill me, please." Tacazon held the back of his head. "I'll give you whatever you want."

FTZ Security showed up at the window, spazzers in their hands. "Sir, open the door! Put the weapon down and disembark!"

Not yet.

Rome let go of Vivian and maneuvered to Tacazon. He glared

into the man's face. Some officer. He bet Aldo knew a dozen people in uniform with more honor.

"Only one thing I need." Rome pried open his knife. He grabbed Tacazon's wrist. "Hold still."

Tacazon screamed as Rome dug his implant from his wrist.

Chapter Seventeen

Aldo was right. Colonel Tacazon had erased his implant's memory, but it contained a deep backup. FTZ Security held him and Cuellar in custody until military police could access the implant.

It told them everything they needed to know.

"Man," Aldo said. "I still don't believe it."

Rome's jaw clenched. "I do. Let's go."

"Go? You're bleeding."

It didn't matter. He had to find Gabriela.

She'd landed twenty miles away, her Condor locked down by FTZ Security officers. But in the aftermath of the chase, she and the officers made a quick flight to the side of the Ninety, joining the rest of the crowd.

Once Rome showed her the data, her cheeks went red. "Who can we alert?"

"FBI. DOT. But only after we get back to Seattle."

Gabriela speared the young FTZ woman in charge of the East detachment with an accusatory glare. "Am I clear for takeoff now?"

"Yes, ma'am. We'll load up our team."

Rome stabbed a finger at her. "You keep Tacazon and Cuellar in custody. I don't care how many people you have to put around Cuellar's hospital room. Make sure his implant's killed."

"Yes, sir."

Gabriela was already back in the cockpit. The Condor's engines rumbled.

"We gonna load her up?" Aldo jerked a thumb at the Halcyon.

The body was dented in several places. Black marks marred the sides of the under carriage. Two tires were flat and the front end was mangled where the magnetic grapple cable had torqued it with far too much strain, looking as if someone took taffy and twisted it.

Rome cringed. "No. Leave her here. We'll come back."

"Okay. Yeah. Let me get my stuff." Aldo went back for his tools.

Amidst the crowd of Security cars, the three landed Condors, and the horde of emergency vehicles, Kelsey and Vivian sat on an extendable ramp in the rear of an aerial ambulance. The vehicle had a smooth, rounded shape, a tubby version of the military Peregrine. A dark-skinned man shaved bald and wearing a red jumpsuit checked their vitals with a handheld scanner.

"How're you holding up?" Rome knelt by Kelsey.

"Okay. Shaken, obviously. They didn't hurt us."

The bruise on Kelsey's upper arm said otherwise. But Rome didn't push it.

"Daddy, the concert's tonight." Vivian's eyes welled with tears. "Are we gonna miss it?"

"No, pumpkin, you'll be on time."

"Are you coming?"

He leaned in and kissed her forehead. "I have to take care of something, first. But I'll be there."

Gabriela pushed the engines so they could get to Seattle in a few hours. It was a far more crowded ride than she usually hauled, what with a dozen FTZ East Security types aboard.

Rome checked his implant. Sara had sent an image of herself, bruised, but smiling in a hospital bed. A med-drone hovered at the edge of the picture—a fist-sized ball floating on four ducted fans. <No worse for wear. Go get him, for us.>

Rome nodded.

"Hey, got word from FBI field office in Seattle," Aldo said. "They've got agents coming over to West headquarters."

"Good. We have to make this quick and quiet."

"Supposedly they're coming in their civvies, no lights, unmarked cars."

"That could still make him run."

"Yeah, well, it's the best we got."

Rome's implant buzzed him again. This time it was from Freddie. His eyes widened. "Aldo, I've got a data packet I need you to open and process."

"Really, Rome? What'd you do, forget how to open one?"

"It's a monster."

"No duh. Gonna take me a while to pull apart something that big."

"How long?"

Aldo smirked. "Maybe four minutes."

"Smart ass."

The file was accompanied by text. <It's the most I could scrounge up on such short notice, but if you read what I did, you'll be too busy scratching your head to care.>

Rome typed the response onto his sleeve. <You are the best. No matter what anyone says about your age.>

<Get over yourself, rookie.>

"Hey. Rome? How's Sara?"

Rome looked up. "Herself."

"Oh, good. Hey, do me a favor, will you?"

"What?"

"When we take this guy down, try not to pound hm too much."

Rome didn't make any promises.

Aldo took two and a half minutes to decrypt the packet. Rome knew he was finished when he stopped chewing on a granola stick and spat a couple raisins through the holo display.

"Aldrich! If you get any of your crumbs in my plane's hardware, I will flip this thing right over and dump you in the Mississippi!" Gabriela harped.

"Sorry. My bad. But… but…" He snapped his fingers, gesturing at the information streaming across.

Rome read it. "Freddie wasn't kidding."

"Right? The money flows right to Colonel Tacazon."

"And in from the sales of the stolen money, plus the implants."

"But check out the money going out."

"Mod shops," Rome murmured. "That's where Jocelyn got her high-end machinery."

"Not just her. There's listings for at least a dozen more, all with their coordinates scrambled."

"You can break those down, right?"

Aldo raised an eyebrow.

"Forgive my doubt." He glanced back at Gabriela. "How long 'til Seattle?"

"Another hour." She reached for a control. "You need me to go faster?"

"If there's any way—"

The roar of the Condor's engines drowned him out momentarily. Aldo yelped as his butt slid out of the seat. Only a last-minute slap at his restraint trigger secured him in place. Rome had to content himself with gripping the back of Aldo's seat until the acceleration eased.

"Yes," Gabriela declared.

There was a rare break in the brooding cloud front that rung Seattle by the time they arrived. Gabriela swept down, wings brushing along the white and gray wisps. She slapped at a control. The overlapping flight coordinator message went mute.

"Show's all yours, boys," Gabriela said.

The Condor dropped like a stone to the landing pads at FTZ West headquarters. Rome led Aldo and the East Security personnel out the hatch, jumping the last foot.

"Hold up!" Aldo huffed as he jogged. "Man, I wish the car wasn't broken."

Rome did too, but he didn't want to wait.

A handful of men and women waited in the lobby. They wore plain, businesslike civilian attire, but Rome tagged them as FBI the moment he realized they'd disabled the Pike security robots. Two stood quivering, wheels trying in vain to engage, lights flashing with the irregularity of a lightning storm. Black boxes were fixed to their sides.

"Special Agent in Charge, Dana Scarlett." The woman was blonde and in her forties. Her eyes were dark brown and cold. "You're making a devil of an accusation, Pursuit Specialist. Especially considering if I acted on the outstanding FTZ warrant, I'd be slapping you in restraints right now."

"Understood. My tech has all the data you'll need."

"Sakai, get it." Scarlett flicked her fingers at Aldo. A short man of Japanese descent moved in, his implant bared. "No one's left the premises. I have Security in building advised. He's up in his office."

"Let's go, then."

"Hold here. This is a federal matter."

"Fine by me if you tag along." Rome made for the nearest elevator.

"Uh, Rome?" Aldo stayed by his side. "Those were the feds."

Scarlett barged into the elevator, accompanied by Sakai. "You've got nerve, Jasko."

"So I've been told."

The hall outside the office was abandoned, save for the two guards. Both men froze at the size of the quartet moving down the hall.

"FBI." Scarlett and Sakai's wrists flashed holographic renderings of their badges, bobbing in the air was they strode toward the doors.

"Stand aside."

The guards stepped away without protest.

Rome passed the secretary's desk, not sparing a glance at Mrs. Liu. She worked at her displays as if armed federal agents and a pair of surly contract pursuit specialists barged into her boss's domain every day.

The last door slid and their target smiled. "Ah, Roman Jasko. Can't say I'm surprised to see you here. Though, a little forewarning from my Security staff would have been nice. I imagine your friends have something to do with that."

"Director Marcus Cho, this man has serious accusations against you," Scarlett said.

"I'll be he does. Did you consider that he's an unhinged guy?"

"Unhinged?" Rome flexed his fingers. He daydreamed Cho's neck between them. "You set me up. Set us both up."

"Sounds like a great tale. You're lacking proof."

"We have Sara, Colonel Tacazon, and Jorge Cuellar. They're all the proof we need."

"I have no idea what you're talking about. Who are those people? Well, two I recognize as your colleagues in crime. Agent, I suggest you arrest this man and his partner for the death of my Security people. The two men who left their families fatherless, remember?"

"Okay, Rome," Aldo growled. "Forget about the part where I said not to beat him up."

"Easy. I know the whole deal, Cho—how you hired Colonel Tacazon, how he lined up Sara and her group, how you took your cut of their robberies, how you keep mod shops supplied."

"Why on Earth would I do any of that? I've got a comfortable job. Make a decent salary, allowing me to live among the more well-to-do set in Seattle."

"Greed. Simple as that. You make money as head of FTZ, then turn around and make money on the criminal aspects FTZ hires contractors like me to combat. You're playing both sides."

"Again, you tell a great tale," Cho said. "But I doubt the FBI's going to go along with the word of a disgraced Driver. I admit to nothing."

"You don't have to. The data doesn't lie."

Agent Scarlett played back some of the data Aldo had transferred to Sakai. Rome caught a glimpse of the tiny video of Tacazon and Brand dealing for the delivery of the truck. More data—Aldo's list of mod shops, complete with coordinates and, to Rome's surprise, bank account numbers.

Cho's smile froze in place. The man was good. He never let the congenial attitude slip.

"What was that about… nothing?" Aldo sneered at him.

"I need my attorney."

"I'll bet you do," Agent Scarlett said. "Director Marcus Cho, you are under arrest for conspiracy, robbery, racketeering…"

Rome tuned out the complete list of charges, which Scarlett made last longer than a prayer. He felt suddenly fatigued, realizing their job was finally done. Rome waited until the two federal agents left with Cho in magcuffs, then sagged into a chair—the same chair in which he'd been given the contract to take down the highway robbers.

"I guess this means I can go home for the day." Mrs. Liu stood in the doorway, her arms folded.

"Sorry about all this, Ma'am." Aldo fidgeted with his hands. Rome thought he might salute. "We, uh, maybe Security can help you from the building? I could walk you down, if you like, ma'am."

Rome snorted and laughed. It felt good to laugh.

The woman joined him, her voice bright and brassy like a bell.

Aldo glared at them. "What's so funny?"

"Don't pick on him, Freddie," Rome said. "He's still green."

"I'll say." Freddie patted his shoulder with a display of motherly affection. "You were never like that—not after a good five years, at least."

"Fair point."

Aldo just stared. "Freddie? The Freddie?"

"The. Rome tells me you're the best passenger tech out there."

Freddie squinted at him. "Don't prove him wrong."

"No way, Freddie. I mean, Ma'am. I mean…"

"Easy, Aldo. Sit down, until the Feds come back up for us."

Aldo flopped into a seat. He wiped sweat off his forehead. "Rome," he said. "I'm starved."

Crowds spilled out of Vivian's school like a wave. The night air was cool and moist. Streetlights embedded in the pavement gave off enough illumination for pedestrian navigation, and cut enough light pollution that a smattering of stars shined. Overlapping conversations took on the sound of an avalanche. Parents extolled their child's performance, neighbors and acquaintances greeted each other, and kids teased and challenged.

Rome let it all decline into background noise as he replayed the best tunes of the concert in his head.

"What'd you think, Daddy?" Vivian swung around, her skirt spinning like a wheel.

"Beautiful, Pumpkin. You and the music."

"Did you really like it?"

"Loved every minute." Rome smiled at Kelsey, who walked beside him. "Nice company, too."

She laughed. "Aldo, is he still like this around women?"

"What women?" Aldo guzzled a cup of lemonade. "Oh, you mean the Halcyon. Yeah, he talks way more smoothly to anything with four wheels than anyone in a skirt."

"Shut up."

"No, wait, I gotta hear." Jake came up from behind Vivian and tickled her. She squealed, and, when she swatted at Jake, he swept her up onto his shoulders. "Dad's got a lot of stories to tell."

"Maybe when present company is older." Rome draped an arm over Kelsey's shoulders. "Your mother's pretty young."

She elbowed him, but laughed again.

"But you're going back out, right?" Jake asked. "On the Ninety."

Rome nodded. "We got our portion of the contract. So did Thad, and he earned it as far as I'm concerned. FTZ tacked on an extra 30 percent for our trouble."

"You know, the manhunt," Aldo muttered. "And the paying Jocelyn for—"

Rome's glare cut him off faster than a tech's override signal. "The feds were kind enough to put in a good word for us, too. I understand the news Net is full of stuff about our innocence right about now."

"Yeah, I saw it!" Jake's arm pulsed with moving text and images. He slid a sleeve down over it.

"But we're not going anywhere for a while. I'm here to spend time with all of you." Rome arched an eyebrow. "As long as that's all right with you, Kelsey."

"I think I'll adjust. How's your friend?"

"Sara?" Rome frowned. "Recovering. There's a chance she'll be pardoned from some of her time, but I doubt she'll escape spending work hours with IRC in Washington or Oregon, maybe elsewhere in the Ninety FTZ West's jurisdiction."

"She did good at the end," Aldo said. "Glad she wasn't beating on me, anyway. Oh, and speaking of beatings—I got to catch up with Gabriela. There's a crumb-crusted console with my name on it. Her words."

"You'd better do it. Don't forget to extend our offer. I'll catch up with her later."

Aldo tossed them all a mock salute. "You got it. We'll be back in a couple days."

"Wait, where are you two going? I thought you were overseeing the repairs of the Halcyon."

"Um, duh. Marcy? I'm going to dig her out from under the rock and try for a reboot. Not sure if she'll survive it, brains and all, but it's worth a shot." Aldo hustled off to a waiting FTZ East Security Halcyon.

The sight of the car made Rome queasy. He needed his ride back.

All this standing around, not driving, was enough to make a man sick for lack of motion.

"What offer?" Kelsey asked.

"Of employment. I'm expanding Resolve Interception. Could take on a new driver, if he's interested in the work—and if he's willing to play by my rules. If that's the case, I'll need a decent pilot with a plane of her own."

"It'll be difficult stealing her from FTZ. I thought the Condor was their property."

"It is," Rome smiled. "Not the only bird available, though. In the meantime, Jake…"

"Listening, Dad."

"Keen on a trip back to the Mass Hike?"

"Yeah! I'm driving."

"Only once we get there." Rome kissed Kelsey on the cheek and lifted Vivian down off her brother's shoulders. "I'll bring him back late."

"Be careful."

Rome ran a hand over the smooth curve of the Andromeda. "Always am."

Epilogue
Three Months Later

The windows of the Halcyon were darkened against the midday summer sun. Rome couldn't see a cloud anywhere in the turquoise sky. Famtracs poured by in a steady stream, heading west toward Devil's Tower and Yellowstone. He knew because Aldo had destination coordinates marked for all surrounding vehicles that advertised their destinations on the Net.

"Three of a kind, deuce." Aldo flicked the holographic set of cards so they spun—diamond, spade, and club.

Rome nodded. "Not bad. But not a straight." He flipped over his virtual hand.

Aldo moaned and rolled his eyes like some zombie out of the old vids popular a half century ago. "And just like that, I'm down forty bucks. Again."

"Quit griping. I buy dinner every other week. You get your money back in food most Fridays."

"True," he scowled. "Marcy? Financial. Aldrich Burns."

[Confirmed. Transfer to Roman Jasko in the amount of forty dollars complete.]

Rome burst out laughing.

"What? Hey! Marcy, I did not authorize!"

[I have programmed in the amount in the event Driver Jasko wins. Given the statistical probability of said event, I deduced it would be more efficient to streamline the process and make the transfer automatic in the event of his win.]

"Can't argue with the comp's logic," Rome chided. "Well done, Marcy."

[Thank you, sir.]

Aldo mouthed the same words with a sour expression on his face.

An alert chirped across his holo displays. Aldo swiped away the cards, making them ball up and decrease in magnification until they disappeared. A map took their place, complete with flashing red lights. "Traffic disturbance up ahead," Aldo announced. "Both lanes are braking."

Rome swiveled his seat to face front. The cars lost speed. A trio of freighters switched lanes to the right, leaving a gap for the Halcyon. Marcy slid them into the space, not slowing like the rest, per her programming. "Marcy, get me a signal to Kestrel Six-Oh."

[Affirmative.]

Did her tone have a more chipper lilt to it? Rome knew Marcy was a simple navigation and safety comp, but it sure seemed to him her attitude was improved after having been forcibly removed from the Halcyon.

"Pursuit One Twelve, this is Kestrel Six-Oh." Gabriela, however, was her usual brisk, businesslike self. "You've got a glitcher five-point-five miles ahead, right lane. Unsafe lane switching, high rate of speed. Nav's malfunctioning. It won't respond to FTZ attempts at override."

"Copy, Kestrel Six-Oh. We're seeing signs of the disturbance down here."

"I'm sending the coordinates your way. Aldrich, do you have them?

"Yes, dear," Aldo muttered. "Data's complete. Plotting the intercept. I've got a program that ought to do just the trick."

"Glad to hear it, boys. FTZ West has the bounty pending."

"What, just us? Thad isn't going to horn in?" Rome said.

"I've got him off chasing down a freighter-jacking. He says you shouldn't worry yourself."

Rome rolled his eyes. Sounded about right. "Remind me why I

paid so much to steal him away from Del Norte."

"Because he's an awesome Driver. Arrogant, obnoxious, yes, but awesome." Aldo flipped over a holo and widened the view. "Got the target."

"Let's do it." Rome put his right palm on the dash, once more. His pulse pounded the steady rhythm, increasing with his pre-chase anticipation. "Confirm authorization, Marcy."

There was his certification, its seals and date of renewal updated. The USDOT logo burned brightly.

[Certification confirmed. You are authorized to conduct pursuit.]

"Love it when she says that." Aldo dug a fruit stick out of his pocket and bit the end off.

"Log the time and heading. Prep occupants."

Restraints wrapped around them and controls snapped into position. Rome grasped the steering surface.

[Current velocity 88 miles per hour. Safety systems of the surrounding traffic have been notified.]

Rome put the accelerator to the floor.

Made in the USA
Middletown, DE
05 June 2022